HAVE YOURSELF A
Legendary
CHRISTMAS

J.P. STERLING

TIMELESS
CHRISTMAS
TALES

Contents

Blurb

Warning: Contains one crumbling hotel, one handsome handyman, and one very charming dog.

When I roll into town to sell an old hotel, I'm expecting peeling paint and dark hallways. That's quite alright.

What I didn't count on?

Finding Pinsch Charming.

Yes, that is *Pinsch* as in Doberman pincher.

He's not royalty, but he's adorable. I'm not so much of a dog mom, but he instantly claims me as his person.

Oh yeah, I also meet a local handyman, Logan Legend, who fixes things. He's quite impressive too. As you might have guessed he's the hero of this story. Between Logan's easy nature and Pinsch Charming's assertive presence, my plan to leave begins to wobble as the three of us start to feel suspiciously like a family.

Still, I have a plan.

Sell this hotel and move on.

Fate takes another giant hammer swing to my plan when Logan and I accidentally uncover a hidden love story within the hotel's walls. Love notes from decades past reveal a woman who once sacrificed everything for the man she loved. I can't help wondering if the past is trying to tell me something.

I came here to sell a building. I might leave with a love story of my own.

Love wasn't on the schedule. Oops.

Have yourself a Legendary Christmas is an old-school love meets modern rom-com mayhem. It's perfect for fans of Hallmark Christmas romance.

One

Penelope Lane

It's the Januariest January that ever Januaried. *Oh wait...* My head startles back as my brain finally shifts into gear. I remember, it's not January! It's only November. With squinting eyes, I attempt to scan the blinding white-blanketed yard. How did winter get this miserable so fast? There's no doubt about it, my frozen shoulder and stiff neck steadily remind me I'm smack in the middle of what I call the wintertime freeze.

Yes, it's as miserable as it sounds.

With the spike of my three-inch leather boot anchored into the snow, I trudge through shin-deep drifts outside the Chateau de Mare. Appropriately named because it used to be a Victorian mansion owned by one of the town's founding families. It's placed right on the edge of the water with its own impressive beach. As the town grew, it was expanded and restored to become the most luxurious hotel in this part of Eastern Long Island.

Today, it's my headache.

The last owner had attempted to rebrand with little success and was unable to stay afloat in this economy. He hoped for a fast sale, but nobody bit before he had to shut the doors to the business.

How is that my problem?

I'm not a fan of the place or even the little town, as I try to stay within the five New York City boroughs. My boss insisted I fight for this listing, citing it "a find-of-a lifetime." I dug my heels in. He ended up giving me a promise—acquire this listing, sell it, and I'll be given a promotion. I wasn't going to turn that deal down. I quickly snagged the listing without any problems.

Surprise—no surprise—no one has called about it. In a last-ditch effort to get the buzz going about this place, I'm hosting an open house, praying for a buyer to crawl out of the decrepit woodwork.

Oh, speaking of my boss, my phone buzzes. Since my phone has basically become an extension of my hand, I'm already holding it, and answer it after the first vibration. "Vernon."

"Morning, I'm in your office waiting for you. I have news. Where are you?"

"I'm sorry, Vernon. I'm not actually in the city right now." I hold my voice even while I explain to my boss I'm out of the city. "Remember, I'm outside the Hamptons for that hotel open house."

He isn't a bad boss.

It's the nature of the job.

Work/life boundaries don't exist at any real estate company. For the most part that's okay. My job as a real estate agent is helping me to achieve financial independence with ample room for upward growth. Even though I'm pretty much married to this job as I run around New York City, trying to make my mark, it's slowly paying off. I finally have a career that seems to sync with my stubborn personality. Once I set my mind to it, no hoops or roadblock can hold me back.

"Oh, I'm so sorry," he gushes, his New Jersey accent coming in strong. "I totally forgot. That's too bad. The Myers called about their penthouse listing, but if your unavailable, I can certainly meet with them."

Wait. What?

My eyebrows arch to the heavens as my heart collides against my chest. I met these potential clients years ago while I was working as a waitress. We've been friends for a while. They'd always said when they were ready to sell, they'd hire me. This will be my first listing with eight beautiful zeros all lined up in the neatest more bountiful row. I can't rescind fast enough. "I can come back first thing tomorrow morning."

"Perfect." His smile is audible. "I'll set up an appointment."

"Thanks." Nerves bubble in my gut, seeming to whisper a reminder this penthouse listing is a dream listing. It couldn't have come at a better time. I've been working sixty-hour weeks for years as I wait patiently for the break I deserve.

"Call me as soon as you are in town." Vernon's voice sounds as if he's not speaking directly in the phone anymore, a clue he's likely already distracted.

"I will." I end the call and my mind goes blank. I tap my finger to my chin and think. My brain is so maxed out lately with work, it's hard to remember what day it is.

Oh. My sign!

Where is it?

It's not where I put it in front of the building when I listed it all those months ago. I was in an awful big hurry that day as I barely did a walk-through and put up my marketing. I distinctly remember placing it here. I tap my foot, marking my territory as I scan the vast snow-covered garden until I spot the For Sale sign half buried under the fresh powder.

That's not even the worst part!

My breath hitches in my throat.

Lovely.

Someone had drawn a mustache on my face.

I trudge off the walkway to even deeper snow drifts, the snow almost up to my knees. Glad to be wearing tall boots,

I can't imagine how soaked I'll be after this. There's no way I can leave that damaging photo laying around. Without proper winter gloves, I quickly reach over, plucking the sign from the pile, all the while pretending my hands aren't already frozen. My knuckles buckle together, matching the frozen kink in my neck.

At least I'm matching.

I eye my photo and contact information on the sign.

Even lovelier.

I'd been given a nickname.

Penny Pees

A wordplay on my actual name, Penelope.

I've heard it before. My middle school experience has left me with a slew of jarring memories. "Moving on…" I murmur, and I brush the snow off the sign, tuck it under my arm, and stare back at the hotel.

A cold shiver trickles up my spine. It really is an impressive feat of architecture standing near the ocean. This poor place shuttered just before last Christmas. Each window is still adorned with an evergreen wreath—now brown and withered. There must be a hundred of them. But even those fluffed red velvet bows do nothing to hide how run-down the place is, with shutters nearly falling off the hinges. Peeling paint, hanging fascia, and an actual hole in the front door that I can see through are a few more of its lesser qualities.

Sighing, I resist giving up. People don't have as much use for these big, old hotels. Sure, it has a beach, but travelers want more amenities than only that. They want modern pools, en suite kitchens, and air-conditioning—all the things this place doesn't have. All the things that will cost a fortune to add. It's likely a lost cause.

But I said I'd try to sell it, and that's what I'm here for.

I plow forward, ready to get this open house over with. I adjust the sign as it rests in the nook of my arm that's now frozen into a bicep curl. At least I can count this as my work-out for the day. I dig through my purse for the master key while grumbling, "Why haven't we swapped to a keypad for this one." I fumble with fingers that hate me because the air is too frigid for easy movement. After a failed first attempt to insert the key, I finally angle the key just so, and it slides into the keyhole. I click it once before it releases. I let out a giant sigh as I'm able to push my way inside. We won't talk about the totally creepy creak in the hinges announcing my presence and echoing into the foyer.

Stepping inside, I first note it's not any warmer. With the boiler turned off, my breath puffs out in little clouds as I stomp the snow off my boots. Cold shivers run all along my spine. I drop my sign near the door and tuck my arms across my chest as I scan the high ceilings. My heartbeat revs, the open supporting beams are bowing along the ceiling.

Bowing isn't healthy for beams!

Am I safe here?

My lips roll in as I force myself to look elsewhere. To the walls! This time my heart stops. Littered with so many cracks, the once white plaster walls have stained into a buttercream color—yum, speaking of butter cream, I could certainly go for something sweet. My stomach literally grumbles, yearning for a little sustenance. It brings a whimsical sigh to my lips because I have no time to eat.

I turn my attention back to the buttercream walls as I'm terrified to look anywhere else. With every glance, my chances of selling this place seem to plummet even lower than before. How is this place not condemned? Cracks typically indicate bigger issues. I can only hope they are superficial—cosmetic—and not foundational.

With squinted, cautious eyes, I glare at the grand chandelier dangling above my head; its teardrop-shaped crystals dull from a layer of dust that promptly triggers my nose to itch. I flex my face to keep my sneeze inside, because once I start, it never ends. I'm a chain sneezer.

Along with dirt, something flowery and ghostly hangs in the air—like expensive vintage perfume. That smell is actually rather intriguing, reminding me of historical romance novels I've read. Like if *Gone with the Wind* had a scent, it would be this.

A lump forms in my throat, and a mellow sadness washes through my extremities, causing me to backstep and stare.

Everything was left exactly as if it's waiting to be reopened in only a few minutes. It's heartbreaking, really. The once-executive front desk still has a tarnished silver bell and a placard that says *Ring for Service* in cursive. Behind the desk, an old-school key rack lines the wall, each hook fitted with a key. It's like someone forgot to live their life today to open this place up, and now the place waits.

A long Queen Anne sofa flanks a coffee table with advertising brochures spread out, as if it too is waiting for its friends to return. Everything in this room was once expensive, but the most impressive is the massive stone fireplace. I'm compelled to slow my steps to marvel at the intricate rose and vines carved in the weathered stone. If this fireplace is original to the hotel—which I assume it must be—this would have all been carved by hand and taken hours. Maybe it's my imagination, but a faint smell of woodsmoke lingers around the fireplace, pricking my nose again. It's not annoying but brings in a more masculine-smoky note to the *Gone with the Wind* scent. A very nice complement to the buffet of smells going on in this place.

I run my hand along the pale stone mantel. Not surprisingly, my finger collects a layer of dust, and it places a niggling in my gut that wasn't there a moment ago. It's the one that comes when I am unsettled.

It's too bad this place had to fall so hard.

A chill ripples up my spine, urging my fingers to grapple for my belt and tug, pulling my wool peacoat tightly closed as my phone vibrates in my pocket. As if on autopilot, I retrieve it, not even checking who it is as I already know. "Hey, Vernon."

"I got a request for a private tour of the penthouse. Is there *any* way you can be here tonight to show it?"

Pressure floods to the front of my brain. I thought I had already put out this fire. "How did they hear about it? I thought I was going to list it when I got back. It shouldn't be public now."

"Word gets around fast. You are my best employee, but if you aren't here to take this tour, I'll have to do it. Then it makes sense for me to take the listing. Who knows when an opportunity will come like this again. It's fine though, really. You can always keep selling our micro-units in Brooklyn."

I sputter out a half laugh, assuming his dig about the micro-units is his attempt at a motivational speech. "It's at least a three-hour drive, and my open house is at one." My head spins. I'm running off coffee and not a morsel of food as I rushed to get down here today, leaving before the sun was up. I hate being hasty, but he's right. Opportunities don't come around all the time. I add the hours in my head while I draw in a long breath. "Can you schedule the tour at eight."

"I'll see what they think." His quip is filled with urgency, and I mirror his tone.

"All right," I rush out, as I pace through the foyer, speeding down the hall. I wish I had time to tidy the place a little. I prefer to put my special staging touches on my listings, making sure everything is perfect. It's not going to happen this time. "Talk later." I end the call in a hurry, this time stowing my phone in my pocket.

I let out an even breath, and I say a prayer. *Please let this place attract a buyer.* I can certainly use the paycheck, even though it's a long shot. At this point it feels like a hundred-year-old roadblock.

A quiet niggling creeps into my head. It was Vernon who insisted I needed this listing. Something in my gut whispered the listing wasn't what he was telling me. Now a looming foreclosure is about to stain my résumé. It doesn't make that much sense, because he's exceptional at what he does.

How had he not seen all the problems with this place? Or maybe he did.

Would he have pushed it off to me on purpose?

Everyone knows it's my listing.

Shaking my head, I push all those thoughts away. I didn't get where I am today by dwelling on my potential failures. I'll give it a good push. It will be wonderful if someone local buys it and gives it the time and attention it needs. As of right now, I haven't the faintest clue who that could be.

I sure hope he or she is out there.

Squeak. Squeak.

My ear attunes to the tiniest noise. I arch my gaze out the window, surveying the empty street. I quickly determine the noise is not outside. I step toward the desk, my eyes scanning around for an open window or something that would catch in the wind. With no electricity in the entire place, nothing is moving—as it should be.

Squeak.

My ear follows the sound *down*. For my life I can't place where it's coming from. I turn around. Unease settles into my gut. An awful lot of horror movies begin like this. To settle my nerves, I retrieve my phone and turn on the flashlight, shining it forward.

Nothing.

Squeak.

The sound is so soft, yet as a New Yorker, I've heard that sound before.

Now on a mission, I frantically scan all the corners, looking for a hole, or at the very least the recognizable droppings. Sure enough, behind the desk, there's a perfect little round hole. With floor-to-ceiling curtains drawn halfway, a sliver of light creates the creepiest shadow, but I don't miss the flicker of movement that darts behind the long velvet curtain. My hand flies to my mouth as I suppress a scream.

"It's a mouse," I hiss out and hop back, my blood pressure racing. I don't startle easily, and I hesitate on my toes as squeaks seem to come from *multiple* places. There's no way that one little mouse could make all that noise.

My gaze runs the floorboards. Just as I thought—droppings litter all along the wall. A lot of droppings. Way too many for one tiny mouse passing through.

Squeak.

My breath hitches in my throat as I'm still holding back my scream. My eyes swell as a gray dart of fuzz scurries out from behind a sheet of peeling wallpaper, crossing right in front of me, disappearing behind the curtain.

This is a problem.

A huge problem.

I spin on my heel and rush toward the exit. There's no way I'm hanging out here a minute longer. I'm calling for help!

Two

Logan Legend

"I knew you had a screw loose." Dad's raspy voice hangs in the chilly air. I'm able to resist a groan as Dad may be pushing sixty but has the hearing to rival any Labrador. I was hoping to have a peaceful morning, maybe catch a bass or two off my little private dock. I love my dad dearly, but we work together Monday through Friday. I look forward to Saturday mornings to refuel, and to put it bluntly—get a break from his overbearing ways. I flick my gaze over my shoulder. Sure enough, he's trudging through my backyard snowdrifts while favoring his good knee. Seemingly unashamed, he has never had qualms about barging in.

"Be careful who you call crazy." My lips slide over my teeth in playful warning. "It seems to run in bloodlines."

"What are you doing back here?" He huffs between broken words as he plods forward. He thinks he's masking his pain, but there are always signs. I can imagine all the ways his knee is firing off sirens, begging for the replacement the doctor ordered months ago. Dad's so stubborn—not to mention nosy. He doesn't slow until he's right next to me, peering off the side of the dock at my ice hole as if he's some inspector. His bottom lip rolls into the only expression of humility he's capable of—if you can even call it that—and he grunts, "Nice hole, but it's so cold. If I join you, I'll have to grab my chisel to get my coat off later."

"You're right. It is a nice hole, and it is cold." I cut my gaze back into my ice hole. The water is unbothered with no light reflection as the sky is clouded over. With the exception of the two false alarm tugs I had earlier, the water has been without activity. "Fish still need to eat, even when it's cold."

His leathered skin creases in the corners of his eyes as the mischievous gleam he's never without sparkles cyan from the center of his light-gray eyes. "Where's my pole?"

"Right next to the ice auger." I nod to the small plastic sled I packed full of tools and tackle and drug out onto the frozen lake below me. "You're digging your own hole."

"Aren't we all," he mutters, braiding a metaphorical tone into his words. He shimmies forward, lowering first to his bottom, and then hangs his legs over the dock to drop onto the ice. As he heads over to the sled, he barks more commands, "And coffee—"

"In the thermos," I cut him off as I lift my pole out of my hole, making sure my bait is still there. It's been a while since I've had any movement. "If you join me, that makes you the one with a screw loose."

"Always have been certifiably insane." Snatching his pole, he inspects the fishing line, rethreading the bobber *his way*. "Oh, before I forget." He pauses to set his pole aside and retrieves the auger. "Your mother is planning a surprise birthday dinner for me."

"So much for the surprise." I drop my line back into the hole, not the least bit shocked he knows about his surprise party before I do.

"Now, I don't want you making a big deal about it. You don't need to buy me any gifts." His breath puffs out heavily as he steadies the auger above the ice, drilling a perfect hole for himself in a mere few seconds.

"Got it." My gaze lingers on him as he's limping more than normal. I know better than to say anything about it though. His ego will never handle me offering to help him. "No presents."

"Although...I could use a new socket set." His face is straight at my level, causing me to quirk a brow. He needs another socket set as badly as the Sahara Desert needs more sand. He's been collecting tools for forty years. Limping back to the sled, he swaps the auger for his pole, and then he tacks on, "Or a new drill."

A chuckle sputters out of my mouth. Deep down, he's a giant kid who can never get enough of his toys. "I'll keep that in mind."

It's quiet for a beat as he drops his line into his hole and stares at the bobber. I inhale, taking the break in conversation as my time to scan the lake. This really is a dream location, living right next to the best bass fishing lake in Long Island. I've worked my whole life saving money to buy this plot of land, and then I built this little house. There's nowhere else I'd rather be on Saturday mornings. Fishing in my backyard is a dream come true, even when it's not as quiet as I prefer.

"What do you have going on after this?" Dad's never been good with silence, and he speaks after only a few moments of peace.

"Well." I open my mouth and then shut it. I know exactly what I'm doing. The problem is, I'm not sure I need Dad to know. It's crazy how a thirty-year-old man still worries about his dad's opinion. However, when it can potentially affect my livelihood and the business we've run together for over a decade, I need to tread safely. "I, ah, I actually took on an extra project from the local history museum." I reach behind the back of my head, pretend to scratch it, and then hook my hand on my neck and hold it there. It feels nice to hold on to something steady.

"What kind of project?" Dad's gruff voice already grumbles with disapproval. He's never been about a change in routine.

"Uh, it's not much." I wave my hand in a dismissive manner, even though my chest tightens, hurting I'm acting this flippant about something I'm passionate about. It's best I mask my excitement, at least for now. "Just something they called me about, and I thought it seemed interesting. You know I've been experimenting with old book restoration, and digitizing things into a blog..." I drop my voice into a mumble, downplaying how large of a commitment this is for me.

"Digitalize?" His half snort forewarns his opinion.

"Right." I'm quick to agree because I don't need a full lecture today. He told me when I was in grade school not to waste time learning to type, because computers "were only a phase." Any technology beyond a standard calculator is lost on him. He values working with his hands, not sharing the same vision I have for our business. He's always concentrated on the heavy construction side of preservation, but there's another whole side of preservation that we've never even explored. "Oh." Changing the subject, I pull my pole up, the bobber and bare hook swing from side to side. "Look at that. I think it's time for new bait."

His gaze follows me as I drop down to the ice, slide my feet over to the sled, and rummage through my tackle until something catches my eye. Settling on a wax worm, I pull off one glove for better dexterity while I rig up my line again.

"If you talk to your mom." Dad's voice is softer now, hinting that he knows he's upset me. "I don't really need a cake. It's not a big deal—"

"Got it," I cut him off, a smirk already brewing in the corners of my lips, as I know what's coming next.

"But, if she insists, it's been a while since I had a good red velvet cake. You know the one she makes when her sister comes to visit."

I hold my gaze steadily on my line. "I know the one."

"I don't know why Bridget always gets one. I've been married to your mom for almost forty years, and I've never had one."

"Doesn't she make you the cookies and cream one you like?" I give him a side eye, not feeling the least bit sorry for him. He's plenty spoiled.

He throws out a hand in gesture, playing up this innocent act. "I'm saying, red velvet would be nice, but I don't want anyone to make a big deal out of it."

I walk back to my hole and lower my line again. The breeze has picked up, wafting the scent of pine from the unsettled forest across the lake. The temperatures are set to drop as the day goes on, and as long as Dad's out here flapping his jaw, ruining my serenity, I doubt I'll catch anything. "What do you think?" I sigh, giving up. "Another fifteen minutes, and if we don't catch anything, we can run over to the hardware store to pick up stuff for Monday's job? Might as well get an early start."

"Hardware store?" One of his unruly eyebrows hikes above the other. "That sounds like a Monday thing."

I blank as I know he didn't come all the way over to my place to fish. He hates fishing. "Well, what else do you want to do then?"

"Nothing." He shakes his head as he stares into his hole. "I just came over here to talk about my party."

"The party you didn't want me to make a big deal about." I glare at him as if I'm daring him to make eye contact with me.

"Yeah, that's the one." He doesn't even try to hide the smirk growing on the corners of his mouth.

"Okay." I'm slow to speak now that I've caught on, and I throw out a joke. "Did you want me to take notes?"

"That's a great idea." He moves to the side, taking his pole with him. "Why don't we go inside?"

Rolling my bottom lip under my teeth, I resist the urge to shake my head. Dad always knows how to get exactly what he wants. "All right, Dad." I yank my pole up too and drop it in the sled before I level my gaze back at his. "Let's go plan a party."

Dad retrieves his phone, as if he's getting ready to take notes, and his brows lower. "I have a missed call from an unknown number." He scrolls up a bit until he taps on the phone again. "Looks like they left a message."

He's quiet as he listens. I pack up my sled and tug it toward my house, drifting my gaze back to him right as he lowers his phone. "Ah, sounds like there's a potential problem at that old hotel downtown. Something about holes in the wall. The realtor is hoping we can take a look at it." He cuts another quick glance to his phone again. "It's not even noon. What do you think, we run over there, and I'll treat you to lunch downtown."

I want to remind him it's Saturday, but Dad's forever a workaholic with a big heart, who can never say no to anyone who needs help.

So much for a peaceful Saturday. Someday, I'll be able to flat-out tell my dad no, and then go back to fishing while he runs over to look at this job, because it's my day off. I blow out an even breath, because that someday is not today. "Why not?"

Three

Penelope

Just like that, I'm quarantined in my rental Honda, sitting cross-legged in the driver's seat with my quivering palms steady on the dash. If I'd known this was how I'd spend my morning, I'd have packed chocolate. And perhaps, a little chamomile tea or something else to calm my nerves. What I did was nothing less than a complete mental breakdown.

Tears. Screaming. And a good amount of foot stomping back to my car. And now I'm itchy. I'm not even allergic to mice or really anything, but the thought of them scurrying all around has me scratching my arms like I've been wrestling with poison ivy all morning.

Maybe it's nearing that time of the month, or this is what happens when you finally reach your maximum stress level.

I don't have time for rodent infestations!

Yes, crying about it isn't going to help, but it's one thing I can do to stop my life from flashing before my eyes. The years of struggling in New York, trying to pay rent. The miles and miles of pavement I've stomped out in toe-torturing heels as I ran all over the city to kiss up to every possible client. I can't forget about the three months I lived on Cup of Noodles soup as I scraped up every penny I could, because I had no idea when I was getting a paycheck.

No, sir.

I can't think about any of that.

I'm selling this hotel *today.*

Rodents or no rodents.

Preferably without rodents.

I tilt my head to the side, weighing my options.

I can't quit now.

I'm committed.

Maybe the rodents aren't as bad as I'm thinking?

It's highly possible there's only the two *giant* ones I saw.

My gaze drops to the side as I war with my own mind.

Maybe not highly possible.

Plausible? Yes.

Desperate for help, I called Legend Builders.

They weren't my first pick, as I need an exterminator, but that went to voicemail. I called people until I found one who called me back. I have never heard of this business before, but Google says they're highly rated handymen. In a desperate need to fidget, I scroll back through the website and eye their credentials: Jerry and Logan Legend.

Jerry Legend: Owner/General Project Manager

Logan Legend: Historic Preservationist. *That sounds fancy.* Architect. *Even fancier.*

And they were right here as fast as they said they'd be.

Their little Ford pickup rolled up under the covered entry-way about an hour ago.

They waved. I cringed as I'm *not* going back inside that building until the mice are gone, and I haven't heard a peep from them since.

Oh, am I indebted to their kindness. If they can evacuate those mice, I can get on with my day, and things can only go up from here. Leaning to the left, I hope for a glimpse inside the huge hotel front windows. With the sun hitting the glass with a glare, all I see is the reflection of my car in front of it.

What is going on in there?

Tapping my fingers, I stare at my phone clock. My open house is supposed to start in less than twenty minutes. I toss a glance over my shoulder. No rows of cars lining up to break down the door. I wasn't expecting a huge rush of people, but I had remained optimistic that I'd find that one perfect buyer.

The arched front door swings open with zest. Like so much more zest than I've had all morning that it fuels me with excitement. I yank on my door and eagerly slide off my seat, shutting the door with a swift motion.

It has to be good news!

My gaze latches to the father/son duo walking out. They are definitely father and son, with the same square jaw and matching heights. The dad wears a baseball hat that says Legend Builders. It's the same dark crimson as his jacket.

The son doesn't look at all like what I had assumed he would, based off the credentials I had read online. I always thought architects were lanky with square glasses and wore the kind of shirts that worked well with pocket protectors. He is wearing nice trousers and a dark flannel shirt. He has thick dark hair, cut a little longer on top, leaving enough length to ruffle in the light wind. When his gaze lands on me, his serious cobalt eyes lock in. He removes the dust mask from his mouth and calls forward, "You must be Penelope."

"I am." I blow out an uneven breath as I step forward until we are a few feet from each other, and we create a little circle in the parking lot.

"Nice to meet you. I'm Logan." His voice is a blur of masculine inflection. He adds an efficient nod my way and then looks at his dad. This gives me a front-row seat to his side profile, and his dark stubble framing his jaw with a rugged yet refined edge. It is neatly trimmed, but it's long enough to hint there might be rebellion there. Pursing my lips, I can't help but admire him. I've never been one to swoon over facial hair, but with him standing out here in a fully loaded leather tool belt, he's like walking click bait. "This is my dad, Jerry. Or as I like to introduce him to everyone, The Legend*Jerry* Builder himself—"

"Nice to meet you, too," Jerry cuts off his son. His voice sounds similar to Logan's, but Jerry adds in more friendly inflections. He extends his hand to me. As I take it, he says, "We've got bad news, good news, bad news and more bad news."

My brain immediately starts to swell with stress, and I barely murmur, "With that much bad news, let's start with the bad."

"Well, you have a huge rodent infestation under the wood floors. It doesn't appear to take up the entire first floor but does include the main gathering rooms. The guest rooms are likely fine." He lifts one broad shoulder, and tacks on, "We won't know until someone actually gets in there to remove them."

"Okay." I shift my weight from one leg to the other. I had already expected that much, and it wasn't too bad to hear it. "How about some good news?"

"We found the food source." Logan picks up the conversation. "It's a layer of cockroaches that cohabitates down there."

A shiver stitches up my spine as cockroaches are one nasty bug I can't handle. "Oh, lovely." Sarcasm seeps into my tone, and I blink back that visual. "I bet it's crowded."

"They are definitely enjoying having the place to themselves," Jerry says as he passes a genuine smile to me. His eyes are kind, and a wave of welcome washes over me. It gives me the sense I can trust this assessment.

"How is that good news?" I force an upbeat tone in my voice.

"I called my buddy who runs an extermination business," Logan offers. "He can treat the place for both roaches and mice at once. Since we know where the food source is, we shouldn't have to look any further. Sometimes, if it's not clear where the food is, and if you treat the mice, they can come back because you didn't get the food source."

"Great, a two-for-one deal." I'm sarcastic as I run a hand through my hair, tucking the loose strands behind my ear. I let my hand linger on the back of my shoulder as tension builds. I'll have to explain all this to Jin Park, the owner—he's not going to be happy.

Logan's gaze steadies on me. It feels heavy, and I have a hard time looking directly at him when he continues, "Do you want some more bad news or good news?"

I shake my head back, unable to imagine what else they found. "I give up. Just let me hear it all."

His gaze wafts back to his dad, and they share a look before Logan reports as if he's reading off a checklist. "Good news regarding the infestation, there's really only one guy in town who can treat this. I messaged him, calling in a favor, and he'll be able to look at it tonight. I can't say for sure, but the best-case scenario would be the mice are gone in a week. Worse case, it could be months. If you want, I'm happy to forward his contact information to you."

"That is good news?" One of my eyebrows perks above the other, as I'm not feeling the least bit better. "Sure, send me his information. Clearly, I need all the help I can get."

"More bad news about the infestation is that it's so populated, we don't recommend anyone going in there. Even if they don't see anything, the mouse droppings alone pose a health hazard for disease."

"Got it." I nod again, this time with urgency. I have zero desire to go back inside that building until I've been reassured many times that the mice are gone forever. "I'll stay away."

"And for more bad news, the building has a lot of rotted wood. If it were a random beam, you might be able to get by, but from what we can tell from the quick assessment, it's structural. It needs to be repaired as soon as possible. If you want me to talk to your client, I'm happy to explain all of this to him, but I wouldn't advise selling the building in this condition."

"Oh, wow," I breathe out, tension rising from my shoulders through my neck and filling in the back of my head. This isn't how my morning was supposed to go. "So, no open house today," I murmur, willing my brain to recalibrate everything that needs to be done now that my plans have been throttled. "So, the rot, is that something you can help out with?"

"Absolutely." Jerry's friendly tone does nothing to calm the ever-rising pressure in my brain, but it does make me offer him a weak smile.

"Timeline?" I squeak out. I had lost track of how much bad news and good news were left. In the theme of the morning, I'm assuming the timeline is bad news.

Jerry scratches his chin, looking back at Logan, and they pause, seeming to know some secret code in each other's gazes. Logan cuts a glance back at me first. "Best-case scenario would be this Christmas. Worst case would be next Christmas."

"Christmas?" A sharp click of my tongue flicks off the roof of my mouth, and I sputter out, laughing, "Let's plan on *this* one."

"It's a big project, even if everything goes perfectly, which when you're dealing with buildings this old, nothing ever does." Logan's voice is even like it's a speech he's rehearsed every day for years. "You have nothing to worry about. It will be good as new when we're done, and hopefully it will bring the buyers begging."

I remind myself of the amount of experience these two have.

It will work out.

It has to.

I stare back at Logan, noting again how strikingly handsome he is. Even if this building crumbles to the ground, at least I'll have someone gorgeous to look at. A ripple of wry relief drips into my gut, and in a strange way I trust him. It might be that half crooked smile he's flashing this way.

The thing is, even if I didn't trust him, I don't have a choice. We can't sell the place like this. "Is it too late to ask for a bid?" It's half a joke as they are the only game in town qualified. Of course it's going to be a fortune.

Logan's heavy gaze is unwavering. "Certainly, we can pull something together, and as I said before, I'm happy to talk to your client and walk him through everything."

"Right." My hand finds the back of my shoulder again, this news sinking in with layers. I had planned on getting paid this month. I didn't plan on hearing it might be almost a whole year. "I'll make some calls, and I'll be in touch." I have no idea how I manage to offer a glimmer of a professional smile. Maybe it's the ease in Logan's expression that pulls it out of me as we exchange handshakes. Logan and Jerry walk away, leaving me to stare back at the hotel in front of me.

Is this even going to be worth all that work? The location is perfect, next to the beach, but at what point do you just level the thing and start over?

Or easier yet, let the bank have it.

The tension in my head pools in the front of my brain now, throbbing out a pulse. I don't have time to think about this right now, as I have a penthouse in New York I need to get back to. Since the hotel isn't selling for a while, I need that sale. It could be my last paycheck until the hotel is ready. It's actually quite amazing how that penthouse fell into my lap the exact moment I didn't even know I needed it. Selling that will give me the time I need to get this place ready. Everything always comes together.

Not willing to waste another minute here, I march forward to lock up and get on the road.

Hopefully the next open house goes better than this one.

Parking in Manhattan is a nightmare, even when money isn't an issue. I returned my rental car as soon as I arrived in the city. I'll always rely on the subway and a decent pair of shoes. Since I'm fighting against the clock, I dig out my emergency fifty, the one I always have neatly tucked in the side pocket of my wallet, and I hail a cab. "Park Avenue" I breathe out as soon as one leg slides onto the back seat. "Building 432. You can drop me off right on the corner of 57th Street."

One of the many things I love about taking a cab is they always pull forward with urgency, and I'm instantly pushed back into my seat as the cab driver peels out.

Cabbies speak my language.

Time is money.

I have a few moments to rummage through my purse for my baked foundation and brush. Thankfully my compact has a little mirror, but the sun has long gone down. I do my best to refresh myself with only the New York City night lights in the backdrop and random reflections of traffic lights that seem to bring more glare than clarity.

My stomach grumbles as we pull up to the curb. I force myself to forget I still haven't had a proper meal today. I'd survived off a protein bar I grabbed from the gas station. That, combined with many sticks of peppermint gum.

At least my breath is fresh.

When the cab stops, I bustle out, checking the time on my phone, and then my watch to make sure I'm not late. It's three minutes before eight.

Right on time.

Actually, to a New Yorker, that's early. Charging toward the front door, I steel my shoulders back and will my mind to focus on only positivity when I nearly bump into Vernon coming out of the building.

I startle, doing a double take.

Yeah, it's Vernon's black leather coat and neatly trimmed gray beard. His never-quite- smiling-business-neutral expression pins on me. "I'm so sorry, Penelope."

"Sorry about what?" My breath is even as I run my hands down my coat, making sure it's smooth and professional.

"The client was in a hurry, and I was available."

"Wait a minute." My throat cinches tight as if a string is gathering it together in one slow tug. My gaze flashes to the doorman, who moves in front of the door. I cut a glance back at Vernon. "You gave a tour of it?"

"I know the sellers requested you, but the buyers had a red-eye flight to catch back to Dubai. I wanted to give it to you, but I couldn't risk losing the sale. Our company needed it."

Is he saying what I think he is saying? His voice disappears, and my doubts and anxiety take over. His chapped lips move, but I don't hear any of the words. They are drowned out by the traffic behind me—horns beeping, and people bustling all around me. The background noise ticks up so many notches in volume, my brain pulses from the sensory overload.

Not that long ago, I was winning at life.

Sure, I dropped out of college a year before graduation, but I had people skills I was sure would be more useful than any paper certification. I worked at a high-end restaurant with the goal of putting myself in close proximity to all the people with a better life. I'm stubborn, and it didn't take long. I seemed to impress some of the right people, landing this job.

Everything was lining up perfectly.

Until today.

It's like I woke up in an alternate universe.

One where I can only find disappointment.

Vernon's words cut back in, and I finally make sense of them, hearing the last part, "How did the open house go?"

What open house?

I struggle not to bite back, as my head throbs with all the stress from that colossal failure. Thankfully, I manage to keep my ramblings from bubbling out. "It was postponed after I discovered some rodents, but I'll talk to the owner about it."

"That's disappointing. I was hopeful you'd sell that." Vernon has a tinge of a smile on his face. I guess it's impossible to hide your joy when you signed a contract for the millions he did. "I know it's late, and you've had a long day." His gaze slides above my head as if he can't stand to give me direct eye contact. "I'll let you get on with your evening. We'll chat in the office tomorrow about the hotel." He stuffs one hand into his coat pocket and gives me a new smile. One I hadn't seen before. It's gross. Like he knew he screwed me over. "It's probably best if we let it go back to the bank anyway. It was never going to sell for market value."

"Sure thing." I adjust my purse strap higher on my shoulder. I'm surprised it's possible to make out any words with the amount of pressure swelling in my head. My gaze has morphed into a tunnel vision that lasers in on his chapped lips and gross smile. I can only think of one thing.

This wasn't an accident.

Vernon wanted that listing for himself, and he made sure I didn't get it by sending me to that hotel this morning. My eyes narrow on his back as his scrawny shoulders get smaller as he walks farther away from me.

I got played.

Now the question is . . . what am I going to do about it?

Four

Logan

Dad whistles while he works like he's one of those Disney dwarfs. I've mostly gotten used to it, but it's fairly rough the first few minutes in the morning before the coffee kicks in.

"It looks like they did a nice job cleaning up the place." Dad's whistling lessens as he ambles behind the front desk, inspecting everything that had been done in the last week. The floor, which had been previously covered in droppings and bits of either peeled off or chewed wallpaper, is now swept clean. The wood, though not shiny, teases the smoothness of its earlier time when it was new and well cared for.

"It certainly looks a lot better." I stuff my hands in my jacket pockets and look up, surveying the open beams above us. Those are what worry me. The original architects went with an open concept, leaving the high ceiling A-framed in the lobby with wood beams exposed throughout the main gathering space. Though meant to be functional, the beams would have been gorgeous in the early days. Now they are cracked and deeply bowed in the middle, sagging as if the weight of holding up these walls all the years has taken its toll. They are struggling with their last breath before they give up and fold.

Pulling out my tape measure, I don't waste time as I start on my list of beams to order from the lumberyard. They are always stocked, but these are special sizes, and I expect the turnaround time to be longer than usual. We already lost a week with the rodents, and I can't imagine the owners are happy sitting around waiting for this place to be repaired.

I stride to the load-bearing beam above the front entrance, as it's the most frightening one. It hangs at a precarious incline, like it's already slipping. I'll feel a lot better once that one alone is replaced.

"So, my party is this weekend already." Dad hangs on my heels as I measure and jot my findings down in the little notepad I always carry in my front pocket.

"Already? Wow." Pretending to be shocked, a chuckle slips out as this is really the only thing he's talked about.

"Yeah, I found out your mother invited over fifty people." He takes a sip from his open coffee cup. Call me a tad anxious, but I will never understand people who walk around with coffee cups that don't have lids—and in construction zones on top of it. It's a level of danger I will never attempt.

"I thought it was going to be small." Letting go of my tape measure, it snaps back into place. I take a few steps to the side as I eye the next beam over. "Maybe it's a setup?" I fold my arms in front of me and stare back at him. "Maybe she knows you've been spying on her this whole time, and she's setting you up to teach you not to snoop."

"Oh no." He wags his head back and forth while taking another slow sip from his piping ceramic cup. "I already confirmed the reservations. She knew I didn't want her to make a big deal out of it, but you know she's getting—" His voice drops off as our gazes are pulled to the front entrance door whipping open. We aren't expecting anyone, as the place is still wrapped in exterminator caution tape and looks as if it's condemned. "Did you order lunch?" I joke right as my breath hitches in my throat, and my words are swiftly whisked away.

Standing tall on stilettos and promptly at two o'clock, a woman I've met briefly but haven't forgotten has manifested right before my eyes. "Penelope Lane." Her name on my lips sends a weird smack right to my chest, and I blink as if I'm not sure I'm really seeing her here.

"Good morning, boys." She steps forward, the sole of her shoes reverberating on the wood floor, echoing in a way that makes me want to stay silent until she's done all her stepping.

"I wasn't expecting you here." I return my tape measure to my tool belt. My gaze magnetically hooks on her as she passes in front of me, her scent wafting over with such ease it permeates my air space in no time. Against my better judgment, I take it in and hold it. Soft at first like rose petals. The white ones that are powdery. After only a moment, the spicy amber undertones hit me, I find myself pushing the pads of my fingers together and doing a finger flex.

"I came as soon as I heard the rodent guys had cleared the place for humans again." Words are flowing out of her mouth, but between her sweet, infused voice and her long, silky mahogany hair flowing down her back, I enter a bit of a brain fog, where oddly all I can do is stare.

She's clearly not my type.

The clicking of her shoes as she waltzes over the floor, inserting herself. It's highly annoying.

Those high cheekbones, framing her face so perfectly. They are stunning but she's on another level. She could be one of those big city models. She's certainly not going to hang out in a small town spending lazy Saturdays on the lake.

And her eyes swirl with so many hues of blue, they look like kaleidoscopes when the light hits them just right.

She's exquisite.

But again, not my type.

Nope. I prefer a woman who's softer with a warm smile. Penelope's lips are pinned in a straight line forlornly when she says with sternness, "I can't waste another day getting this place ready for sale."

My brows bend, tensing in the middle as I recall the day I met her, and the few times we've spoken on the phone since. She only ever reported herself to be the real estate agent. "Pardon me for sounding confused, but I'm a little perplexed." Jabbing my hand through the front of my hair, I remind myself I haven't put my hard hat on yet. "We walked in the door fifteen minutes ago. We haven't even started construction. We are far from even close to being ready to sell..." I watch her face for signs of recognition that we're somewhere on the same page. I understood from the contract we signed, Dad and I are completing a structural and column replacement that could take *months*, which means she doesn't need to show up in her clicky heels and silky hair for at least that long.

"Right." Her palm slides to her hip as she squares her stance with me even more. "I know what the plan is. I'm here to push it along faster."

"Excuse me?" My eyebrow quirks, and the hair on the back of my neck prickles. "Faster? It's day one. Literally hour one."

"Obviously, I know that." She waves her hand dismissively before motioning down the hall with her gaze. "I can't afford a bad open house. I'm going through every room in this place, inch by inch, making sure everything is perfect."

"This is an active construction zone." I shift my weight from one foot to the next. "It's unsafe for you to be traipsing all over while we work."

"Relax. You won't notice me at all." She pins her pointed expression on me, displaying she's clearly not even close to relaxed. If anything, she's uptight and a complete control freak. In my years of work, I've never had anyone babysit me doing my job. Clearly the woman has trust issues. She hired professionals not babies.

Again, I struggle not to ask her what she thinks her job title is. Supervising a remodel job is beyond the scope of practice for a real estate agent. Somehow, I manage to trap my jaw shut and shift my gaze back to Dad. Maybe he's dealt with crazies like this before and knows what to do?

Dad's wide eyes peek out from behind his coffee mug as he takes a slow sip. His perfectly timed sipping fills the room with silence. It's evident this is his sign that he's not getting involved. "What is it that you're going to do?" My voice is low, gravelly.

"Oh, you know." Her breath comes out light, as if this is a routine day at the office. "I'll pitch in where I'm needed. Actually"—she tilts her head farther as she gazes all the way down the long hall— "I might start by painting that wall by the kitchen. It seems to have a lot more dings in it than it should."

"You're going to paint..." I lose control of my mouth and blubber out, "wearing that?"

Her eyes narrow as her gaze appears to scan around my face before she replies in an assertive tone, "I'll be fine, thank you." Without waiting for approval, she spins on her heel, marching straight down the hall, her heels clicking the whole way.

My gaze cuts to my dad and I mouth, "Control freak with trust issues."

"I like her." He lifts his mug to his lips, sealing away his expression behind his mug, his perfect prop to assert he's not saying another word.

"Yeah, isn't she just lovely," I mumble as I retrieve my measuring tape and refocus my attention back to the support beams. "If she's worried about the project staying on deadline," I murmur to myself as I cross the room to get the measurements of the back wall. "She needs to stay away from me. She's wasting my time."

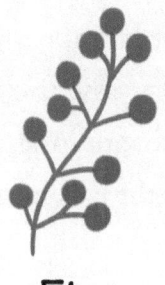

Five

Penelope

Drawing in a long breath, I hold it in and appreciate the way my lungs stretch as I stare down the long hotel hallway, eyeing every scratch, stain, and ding. It's going to take a miracle to get this place ready. Jin wasn't happy to hear about the infestations, but he also didn't seem to have a sense of urgency to get the sale back on track. If I didn't know better, I would suspect he wants this place to go back to the bank.

With no other prospects for a paycheck anytime soon, I'm not ready to give up yet.

As much as I didn't want this listing, it might have been a blessing in disguise. As I've finally seen the light of day of Vernon's true character, I get a sinking feeling in my gut whenever I think about continuing to work for him. Yes, he gave me a job when I needed one, but I put my entire heart into this job, and he did me dirty.

I don't want to work for him. My blood actually boils when I simply think about it. My left eye twitches, and I let out a strangled sigh before I mutter, "I can't ever trust him. Nope. Not ever again."

Good thing I have a plan. I rub my hands together in anticipation as I go over the plan in my head *again.*

This hotel has the potential to pay out hugely if given the proper care and attention. I'd have more than enough money to live on for a couple of months, maybe even a year if I cut my coupons right. I can focus on getting my broker's license and starting my own firm. Sure, it sounds extreme. Yes, I could quit and look for another job with other agencies, but I work too hard to risk having my listing stolen from me again.

Nope. I will not be a victim ever again.

First comes the hard part—clean up this dump. I suck back a deep breath and hold it for a long pause. Then I push the air out of my cheeks and deflate my lungs while murmuring, "Calling this place a dump is an insult to dumps."

I take slow steps forward, allowing myself time to memorize the color of wood stain on the trim that matches the wood floors. Since that's a theme throughout the building, we won't be changing that, but I definitely need fresh paint on most of the walls, and there's no reason we couldn't do something other than the dull eggshell white that's on there now.

A vintage olive yellow, perhaps?

I tip my head to the side and mull it over. It might warm the space up, while still staying mostly neutral.

Tipping my head to the other side, I give myself a truthful rebuttal—it might also make it look stuck in the 1960s, and that's not what I'm going for. Pushing my finger pads together, I flex my hands as I ponder.

A shade of blue?

Blue always has a way of muting the energy in a room, making it more relaxing, and being so close to the water, it might be perfect. It doesn't feel right. Maybe not special enough?

When I make it to the end of the hall, I round the corner to find a wide door I hadn't noticed before. It's about double the width of all the other doors with extra length on top. Arching my head back, I follow the door almost all the way to the cathedral ceiling. *What on earth is this for?*

Oddly, it has the only mismatched doorknob I've seen so far. Instead of the normal large brass globe, it has a tiny little knob like one you would see on a kitchen cupboard.

Tilting my head to the side, I study it.

A huge door like that would normally lead to a ballroom or gathering space, but it's right next to the exterior wall, and there's definitely not enough area for a large room. It could possibly be a luggage closet. I've heard some people used to build these into homes for extra storage, but without a proper doorknob, there's no way to lock it. Who would store anything in a public closet?

I lean forward and place my palm on the door. The wood finish is scratched and marked in so many directions, it appears as if an animal has attacked it. I run my hand down until my fingers brush against the little knob, and I twist it slowly, pulling it open. There's not so much as a creak in the hinges, and it opens smoothly, revealing a dark room. With no windows, the only light visible is the stream from the hallway, and that's not enough for me to make anything out. I quickly take out my cell phone and turn on my flashlight. My jaw drops.

Inside is a massive evergreen tree with gold candleholders strapped down right on top of the branches. My head tips to the side even more. I've never seen a Christmas tree with actual candles on it. My fingers brush against the pine needles, confirming the tree is artificial, but I'd never be able to tell that from looking at it alone. I move closer, tipping my head into the nearest candleholder. A small plastic red tealight rests inside the stained glass. Again, I wouldn't know it wasn't a real candle unless I was this close. I tip my head back, taking in the tree. It's a full Christmas tree in all its splendor, with glass Christmas ornaments strung from every bough and crystal beads wrapped, dangling with the most perfect pattern. A thick velvet ribbon spirals from the bottom of the tree all the way to the top, where it's crowned in a Christmas star the size of a TV.

I marvel at the genius of it all. It's a Christmas tree room.

It must save hours every year, as there's no setting anything up or storing all the ornaments in little boxes. You wheel it down the hall and close the door until it's time to bring it back out. Hmm, who would have thought? I shake my head and with new inspiration, I turn back to my dull wall. A vision pops into my head of people strolling down this hall, all dressed in their finest holiday attire, and I instantly make up my mind.

Evergreen.

Like the most vibrant Christmas celebration.

That's the color I need.

I'll paint this hall the color of Christmas. It will give it enough character to make it stand out. Since this hotel has always been known as the place to have Christmas weddings, it makes sense I lean into that. Why change what has always worked?

I tap my chin and scan the length of the wall, measuring with my eyes. I should be able to get by with one can of paint. It's an expense I'll have to foot, but it should be worth it.

"Coming through." Jerry's voice reaches me first. A moment later, he strides through the wall with a cheery smile on his face. "Don't mind me. I'm running out to the truck for the ladder, and I parked in the back alley today."

"No bother." An idea sparks in my head, and I immediately rush out, "Say, I bet you never saw a Christmas tree room before."

There isn't even a single pinched line of stress on his face when he pivots to give me his full attention. "Are you talking about that one right there?"

"Did you know about that?" I pause for a beat before I say, "I couldn't fathom what was behind this massive door, and I'm still a little stunned."

"It's one of the touches that makes this place so special." He nods with full assurance. "Most of the townsfolk have attended events here at some point. You must not be from around here."

"No, I'm not. I'm mostly located in the city." Since we're going to be seeing a lot of each other over the next few weeks, I smile and decide we might as well get to know each other a little. "Sorry if it feels like I'm intruding. I'm seriously not trying to encroach on your space, but I really need to make this place look amazing in the shortest amount of time possible."

"No worries." His gaze looks past me as he studies the wall behind me. "Is this the wall you're painting?"

"Yeah." I follow his gaze back to the dull wall with so many scratches, it almost looks as if it has an Art Nouveau texture on it. "Any tips before I start?"

"For painting?" He doesn't hesitate to reply, as he leisurely crosses his arms over his chest. "I'll give you a few tips. You need to wash this wall well. A lot of people think that dullness is the paint, but it's actually filth. You never want to paint over that. Get lots of soapy water. Keep changing the water and keep washing until it's clean. If you get a nice clean wall as your base, you'll be set for the next step."

"For sure." I nod. "I will scrub it."

"After you're done washing it, come get me, and I'll inspect the wall to make sure there's no signs of mold or deep cracks. I'm here, and you might as well use me."

"Well, that's awfully nice of you." I tilt my head toward him, feeling so much better about this project. I was overwhelmed with all the tasks that need to be done, but this may go smoother than I thought. "Thank you. I will ask."

"No problem at all. I already have all the paint you need ordered already. It should be ready for pickup this afternoon."

"Oh, I was going to try to give it a pop of color."

"Color?"

"I was thinking about painting it like a Christmas green, since this hotel is well known for its Christmas weddings."

"No." His lips thin into a line. "I wouldn't advise that. With this being a building of historical importance, I don't recommend changing it or adding extra decorations to it that aren't original. People are going to want to experience it as it always has been. This wall has never been green. You have no historical reason to make it that color. I would refresh the color that's on it, leaving it true to its beginnings."

I'm not stupid.

I understand the importance of historical buildings, but I'm not selling this as a museum. I open my mouth to speak but close it when his eyes narrow on me. "Okay, I'll think about that, but I'm pretty sure it needs to be evergreen," is all I manage. I flash a look up the hall, where I know there's a small janitor's closet, still stocked with the basic cleaning tools. "And I'll start scrubbing."

"Very well." He steps to the side, walking around me. I let out a heavy breath while I trudge my feet back to the closet. Just as I thought, a mop bucket is right where it logically would be in a hotel like this, and there's a full stack of rags. I push the bucket over to the water faucet and turn the knob. There's a hearty squeak that comes from the metal rubbing on the metal, but that's all the action I get. It's a humbling reminder the water is off.

I'll have to haul water from somewhere.

Not sure where, but there has to be a neighboring business that won't care. Standing up straight, I pull my shoulders back and stare out down the hall. This is beginning to be way more hassle than I had dreamed of, but I won't entertain a negative thought. Nope. Only positive vibes are allowed. So what if I have to haul water from somewhere else. I'm making this place immaculate and selling it for a million bucks. I might as well grab some lunch or something while I'm out, and hopefully the restaurant won't be too bothered if I order a gallon of tap water.

It's definitely an odd request.

But at this point, I have no shame.

An hour later, I burst through the back door of the hotel, lugging a three-gallon bucket of water with me. Lunch was a great idea. Now I'm refueled and ready to get to work. Upon further inspection, it appears I've beat the Legend men back from break.

Even better.

I have a plan.

One that involves Harry Connick Jr., a ladder, and the rest of my day. It's going to be worth it. My hair is up, my earrings are tossed back in my purse, and my shoulders are back. Well, I make a slow neck roll, circling my head, and it most definitely feels like I'm still rocking a frozen shoulder, but I'm going to pretend I'm healed.

I pour a good amount of water into the mop bucket and proceed to push the bucket with my foot as I make my way back down the long hall. Not wanting to come up short, I had grabbed several rags, and I dumped all but one into the water. Holding on to the last one, I dunk it and then wring it out with both of my hands. Water droplets sprinkle out, some trickling on my shoes. In hindsight they are not right for this job. They are a horrible choice, but it was an automatic selection when I packed. I don't let it slow me down.

I kick off my heels, scurrying up the ladder with bare feet. It's so much more comfortable this way. Not to mention safer, as I don't have to struggle to balance. A muscle pulls in my shoulder as I stretch to the side, reaching as far as I can to the corner as I need to do this in an orderly manner. I smile to myself because it reminds me of the name my favorite foster mom had given me when I was nine: Miss Organized. What can I say, I like things to be neat.

Especially back then when everything I owned could fit in one suitcase, and I was forced to pack it every few months, but I digress...

For the most part, I'm able to wipe away the dullness. A layer of grime around the doorframe is the most stubborn. I assume it's from people's hands always brushing over the door. Whatever the reason, it's there. I scrub, leaning my weight into the wall, and a bead of sweat buds on my forehead.

Phew, it's warm up here on a ladder, even with no real source of heat in the building.

I stand up straight, wipe my forehead, and take a little breather as I stare down the hall, getting a daunting reminder that I still have a long way to go. With another deep breath, I step up to the last rung. The one that you're not supposed to stand on, but I need to reach the top corner, as these ceilings are super high. I balance on one foot and lean as far as I can. My bare foot slips forward, and my breath hitches in my throat as I tilt, but I'm able to grab the wall and steady myself.

"Calm down," I whisper, as my breath slowly releases. I don't have much to go, and then I can move down another rung. Tightening my grip on the rag, I stretch to the corner, the metal ladder whimpering as I shift my weight. My heart rate ticks up a notch. Without any issues, I'm able to wipe the cobwebs from the corner, and I place my hand on the wall to steady myself and descend a rung.

This isn't so bad.

I'm about to sing along to the playlist blasting on my phone when the door swings open. Apparently, I didn't place the ladder in the *best place*, leaving plenty of overlap for the door to whack my ladder. Like an ax to a tree, my ladder goes timbering over in one direction.

My heart feels the slip first, crawling up in my throat as if desperate to protect itself. I'm propelled in the opposite direction of the ladder, and my body positions to land flat on my back. I gasp but can't call out for help as my breath is already stolen from my lungs.

It all happens so fast, and I cringe as I wait to feel the impact.

An impact that never happens.

What is happening?

There's a thump.

Somehow, I'm not splat on the ground. My limbs aren't crushed, and I wave them around to prove the point. I've endured a much softer landing than I anticipated.

It's more like cradling.

My brows dip down as I inspect my exact location.

I'm sprawled out in a set of arms!

One burly arm is bracing my body tucked under my knees, and the super-impressively strong arm is supporting my back. With panic still hammering in my chest, I whip my head around to see who's holding me.

My face is just inches from Logan's!

His gaze levels with mine with such intensity, a trail of goosebumps spirals up my spine. In the best way, it reminds me I'm not paralyzed from falling.

Nope.

That didn't happen.

I'm instead being cradled by the most masculine man I've seen all year, and if I don't move soon, I'll be intoxicated by his smoldering-of-something-swoony scent.

"Easy there," Logan's gentle rasp breaks the silence. Musk and cedar waft off him, further pulling me into his aura, and I'm about to get dizzy. There's a humorous glint sparking out of the corner of his eyes now, but he makes no movement to let me go.

Blinking several times, I fight wooziness. I'm not sure if I'm lightheaded from falling or from this sudden touching situation. My heart slams against my chest wall as I watch him watch me. It might be the most entertaining thing I've seen—*ever*.

His eyes are the kind that can tell whole stories in a single sweep. So many colors and emotions whirling within. You'd never know it by the solemn expression he carries around, but when I'm this close to his face, there's no denying it. It's almost like he knows what I'm thinking, because he casts his gaze down, giving me enough emotional clearance to finally speak.

"Thank you," I breathe out with a weakened breath, and I reach forward, unsure of what to do with my hands. On one side of me is Logan's nice-looking chest, adorned in cozy flannel. I certainly don't want to confuse the situation by touching him. On the other side of me is the air, which I haven't exactly had the most success navigating today. I leave my hands floundering in front of me as I feel the need to brace myself.

Logan's one step ahead of me, seeming to understand my quiet struggle. With a smooth motion, he lowers me until my feet touch the ground. I'm quick to stand. Maybe a little too quick? Once again, I'm lightheaded as a rush of heat spreads across my face. A nervous chuckle sputters out of my lips as I'm all too aware of the warmth from his touch lingering on my skin, even though he's no longer touching me. "Thank goodness you have fast reflexes."

His gaze softens, layering with something more underneath it. "It comes from years of working in active construction sites. You never know what's going to come flying at you, and it's exactly why I warned you. It's not safe for you to be here." Logan's expression is neutral, but his tone is not condescending. It's more like a kind warning. "And not to mention, it's not smart to put a ladder in front of a door."

Truthfully, I had forgotten about the ladder. With his gaze boring into mine like that, all I can think about is how my skin is tingling. It's been years since I've been held by a man, and even though I didn't seek this out, it feels invigorating. "I'll, ah, try to be more careful." I run my tongue over my lip, alleviating some of the dryness. "Thank you again."

His lips part, as though he wants to add something, but he quickly closes his mouth, and then opens it to quip, "No problem." He turns away, scanning down the hall, and says, "I'll let you get back to work." His voice is smooth, like silk brushing over my skin.

He doesn't move an inch.

My body is still tingling from where he touched me.

I wonder if he has tingles too?

I eye his chest again. He has a nice build, but it doesn't seem to be tingling. Not that I know what that looks like.

Silence expounds, and we both stare at each other again. In a way, I feel compelled to ask him a question, something to get him to stay, but I have no idea what. His gaze lingers for a beat longer than what would be normal before he pivots and quietly strides down the hall.

I blink out of my trance. I've never lost my ability to speak before. He must think I'm an absolute lunatic from the way I fell and then stared at him. Swiping my hand through my hair, I smooth it down.

What just came over me?

My cheeks are still warm with a glowy feeling I don't fully understand. My gaze is magnetically pulled to follow Logan all the way down the hall until he's gone.

Breathing a sigh of relief, I turn to the wall. My brows bend down as I study my feelings. It's odd because I'm not as embarrassed as I would think. I'm flushed, but it's different than humiliation. It's accompanied by a light fluttering in my gut. If anything, I'd say it's a curiosity.

And pure attraction.

So. Much. Attraction.

Six

Logan

By the time five o'clock rolls around, I remove my tool belt and set it against the wall, leaving everything else out so I can pick up where I left off tomorrow. It's been a long day, longer than most since I felt like I had to constantly keep one eye on Penelope to make sure she wasn't breaking any bones.

It's a totally different vibe working with a woman walking around here. I don't think I'll ever get used to it. Especially one who is such a distraction, for the lack of a better way of putting it. Why are women so stubborn?

I had clearly warned her about the dangers of hanging around a construction zone, but she didn't listen. She's lucky she's not laid up in the hospital right now, as I've seen plenty of men break their backs from falling off a ladder. It's no laughing matter.

"You go ahead. I'm finishing up this little bit of trim I have left." Dad breaks my concentration. "I'll lock up."

My gaze cuts to the wall he's working on, still half finished. I'd been so zoned out: I didn't realize he still had an entire wall left. Normally, we work the same hours and help each other until the day's job is complete. It's rare we don't walk out together, but I have a pile of old books sitting at home, and he still doesn't know about it. It's hard for me to explain I can't always work later anymore. Things are changing, as I need them to. Nobody warns you about the pain you feel when the changes you need to make to be happy are more than likely to break your dad's heart. "Aw, I didn't realize you weren't done. I can hang out."

"No, that's nonsense." Dad waves a dismissive hand in my direction. "This will only take me another fifteen minutes or so. I got it. Plus"—he tips his head to the side like he's arguing with himself— "I accidentally found out that your mother's sister is flying into town for my party, and she's needing to be picked up from the airport right about now. If I make it home before your mother leaves, she'll lie to me about where she was, and well, I will hate for her to have to lie."

"Wait a second." Dad's been talking nonstop about this party. He's shared many random details that have all jumbled up into a big knot in my brain. One thing that doesn't make sense is why my mother's sister would fly all the way up here from Florida for a little birthday party. "She's coming for *your* party? Isn't that a little far to travel?"

Dad raises his broad shoulders, only offering a smug and a silent smirk. Even though he insisted this whole time that nobody fuss over him, he sure likes the attention.

I can't ever remember him having a party all to himself either. He's one of those working dads who always made everything about me and my sisters. The years ticked by like a thief. I still can't believe my dad is going to be sixty. Sure, his hair has thinned, but he hides it well by always wearing a cap. Since we've always worked physical jobs, he's stayed trimmer than most men half of his age. I barely notice how his skin has leathered. When I look at him, all I see is his eyes that match mine, and the best friend he's always been to me. I didn't realize at the time I heard about this party, but I'm glad my mom has gone out of her way to do this for dad. It's almost like he needed a little recognition.

"Well," I raise my tone to add an air of teasing, "maybe she heard about that red velvet cake Mom was making for you. You know that's the cake she always gets."

"She's not getting my cake." Dad wags his head with serious flecks sparking out of the corners of his eyes. "I'll let her have a piece, but I'm getting all the leftovers. Do you know how long I've been waiting to have one of your mom's red velvet cakes all to myself?"

"I'm guessing sixty years?" I chuckle, as one would think he's joking, but Dad is serious about his cake. There isn't anyone I've ever met who can make a cake like my mom. Nothing she can say or do makes you feel more special than when she makes you a birthday cake. Everyone who knows my mom knows that about her too. She bakes magic into her cakes.

"Darn right," he asserts, mocking a tough guy tone.

"It's going to be worth it." A lighthearted chuckle bleeps out of my chest before I blank for a moment. Then I suddenly recall, although his party is tomorrow, and it's all I've been hearing about this week, I haven't gotten him a gift yet. I certainly won't leave him hanging like that. My gaze floats to the front window, confirming the sun has long set for the day. These winter days are so short, and I hate to duck out on him, but if I must stop by the hardware store on the way home, I would like to leave on time tonight. "Since you said you don't mind me leaving, I'll go ahead and take off."

"I'll see you tomorrow." His gaze is fixed on the trim as he marks his measure on it with a lead pencil. "Oh, by the way, Home Hardware has their cordless drills twenty percent off this week."

I give him a side-eye. His gaze is still locked on the trim, his lips pinned in a straight line. "Ah, sure, whatever, Dad." I laugh through my words, all the while I'm thinking that sounds like the perfect idea for his gift. "See you tomorrow."

Seven

Penelope

I tug at my hair and scream for forgetting to pack conditioner. I've been using the freebies at the dive motel, but it only succeeds in weighing my hair down. Feeling gross, like a layer of film covers my once-shiny hair, I throw it all back into a messy bun.

I grasp on the kitchen doorknob and turn as my stomach churns. The churning started this morning, manifesting my nerves about this project. Later it morphed into more of a hungry rumbling sensation. I should call it a night and head out for dinner, but the more I clean, the more I realize this place is disgusting. No respectable buyer is going to pay the kind of money I'm asking. I can't believe I didn't see it when

I listed it. Maybe it was the months of sitting on the market, but I can't turn a blind eye. I push the kitchen door open, and my jaw drops. The kitchen floor concrete has erupted from the center, swelling into a mound with cracks spiraling out of it like little rivers tasked with the job of covering the entire floor.

How is that even possible?

This place is crumbling from the ground up.

Even footsteps pad from behind me, and I toss a look over my shoulder, finding Jerry beaming his friendly smile. "Are you heading out too?"

I blow out a breath, hoping I don't look too disgruntled. "Nah, I'm going to be here for a while. I don't have anything else to do since I'm staying at a dive hotel with no one to talk to. Plus, every time I think I've made progress, I open another door, where I'm met with a mess bigger than the last one. Look at that floor." I motion forward. "I'm getting ill just looking at it."

"Well, don't do that." Jerry chuckles as if he doesn't have a care in the world. "Trust me, life's too short to get sick over material things, especially an old hotel like this one."

When I don't join in his laughter, his brow bends down and he tacks on, "Hey, I've done hundreds of these projects. Some even worse than this. I know what I'm doing, and I'll get everything repaired so it looks new again. Better than new, because it will maintain its original character."

"I hope so." I'm still clenching the doorknob, and my fingers nervously fidget with it. I've felt instantly comfortable around Jerry, so it's not his presence that makes me anxious. It's everything else. If anything, knowing he's on board with this project is the one thing that keeps me sane. I look past him, seeing the light on the other end of the hall has already darkened. "Did your partner in crime head home already?"

"Logan?" Jerry props one shoulder against the wall as if he's preparing himself to stay and chat for a while. "Yeah, he had to head out. It's my sixtieth birthday tomorrow, and I suspect he still needs to get me a birthday present." He snickers kindly, the lines in the corners of his eyes defining more.

"Ah, happy early birthday," I coo and then go blank. I'm not normally anti-social, as I got where I am with this job by having excellent customer service and taking the time to get to know people. Ever since the penthouse swindle, I feel closed off and desperate to recover. Other than the business negotiations, I haven't said more than a few words to these guys. That's not like me. I appreciate their help. I offer a genuine smile. "That's exciting. Do you have any big plans for the special day?"

"Yes, actually I do." His smile takes an impish slant. "My wife and son are throwing me a surprise party, but I've already uncovered all the details. It's going to be a lot of fun. I haven't had a birthday party since I was a boy."

"That sounds wonderful." My mind plays a movie, flashing forward to tomorrow and showing Jerry at a party with lots of loved ones. There's a lot of laughter in the background, and everyone is celebrating. It's the kind of scene my memory is void of. Being bounced from foster home to foster home, I never grew up with a family or the typical memories. It doesn't make me sad to think about it though. Even though I never experienced it, I don't feel the loss of what I'm missing out on, but those tend to be my favorite scenes in movies.

"Hey, you should come." His voice ticks up a notch and a mischievous glint sparks out of the corners of his eyes. "We'll have plenty of food and *cake*." He wags his eyebrows at me, tacking on. "Homemade red velvet."

His antics are endearing, but as much as I fantasize about those cozy, big family events, it's not a place I'll ever feel comfortable. It feels more like fiction than ever being able to be a reality. "That's so sweet of you to invite me, but I'm sure you'll have plenty of company, and I don't know anyone."

"Sure, you know someone. You know Logan, and he's always boring with no one to talk to."

A snort chuckle leaks out, as that's an odd thing to say about your son. Logan didn't strike me as someone who is boring. My cheeks heat as I think about him and how he caught me earlier. My memory instantly draws back to his musky smell, and I warm even more. "Ah, I, ah, am sure Logan has plenty of people to talk to," I murmur quickly as I race to get my mind off Logan and back to something else. "I wish you a happy birthday. You're going to have a wonderful day."

"He's not so bad. Maybe a tad too serious." Jerry's eyes don't waver, staying locked on me, but they seem to cloud over as he takes on a distant expression. "Once you get to know him though, you learn he's the most unserious-serious person. With him—" Jerry lets out a heavy sigh, as if he's reviewing a long list of memories before he continues, "He's never met a stranger. He's one of the most big-hearted people you'll meet, but sometimes he's slow to reveal that." He pauses to tilt his head to the side before adding on, "Well, that and his last girlfriend really did a number on him."

My eyebrows bunch together as it feels a little invasive having Logan's dad just spew personal information about him, but my curiosity piques. Since he's offering, I ask, "What happened?"

"It's been nearly three years. I think she was using him until someone better came along, but he was willing to give her the world." He shifts his weight from one leg to the other as his expression stays neutral. "He's no saint, but he's a good guy. Sometimes I wish he'd learn to be more extroverted, but then again, that's sort of his thing to be quiet. Or maybe he's afraid to open up, because he doesn't want to get hurt again. He's fiercely loyal. He's been the best friend and business partner

I've ever had. Either way, he's coming to my party tomorrow, and I would also love to see you stop by."

My heart pitters against my chest wall from the feeling of being put on the spot. How do I say no to such a sweet man? "I'll see what I can do."

The tips of Jerry's lips twitch, teasing a smile. "Noon. At the Broken Ribs Steakhouse."

"I'll try to make it. Thank you for the invite, but for now I better get back to work." I pivot, pulling my gaze back to the kitchen. "These grimy walls aren't going to clean themselves."

Jerry eyes brim with something that feels like pride. "See you tomorrow."

"I'll *try.*" I hang on to the word, drawing out the last two syllables. He turns on his heel, heading out the back door. I return my attention to the kitchen, crossing the room while slugging my mop bucket behind me. I'm not sure about going to his party. That's clearly a pity invite if I ever heard one. That's going to be awkward as I don't know anyone—except Logan.

And I don't really know Logan.

I doubt he cares to even talk to me.

He's always seemed too standoffish, but maybe what his dad said is true.

Maybe he's just quiet?

Silent type.

My cheeks heat as I'm back to thinking about how random that was to be in his arms. Warm. Safe.

Stop it!

It's absurd to think about. I need to keep cleaning so I can get paid.

He didn't mean to hold me. I literally fell into his arms.

His nice, strong, manly arms...

Eight

Logan

It's Saturday, and I'm up earlier than my usual work time, as I'm anxious to look at these books before the big dinner. It feels like I'm waking up out of a long haze, as I've been unhappy working construction for a long time. I didn't know how to use the skills I had to pivot, and I still don't know how to tell Dad, but thankfully I have time for that part.

After I make a full pot of coffee, I head to the back of my little house to settle in. Last summer, I converted the back bedroom into a small study. It should have been an easy decision. I dragged my feet for three years for the sole reason that when I moved in, I had planned this room as a child's room. I was dating a gal, and I thought everything was going well. We talked about marriage. Though neither one of us seemed to have a sense of urgency to get married, I thought that's where we were headed. Maybe I freaked her out, but she ended up breaking it off not much later when she found someone better. Perhaps I'm too sentimental, but there was an odd finality in hanging bookshelves along all the walls and bringing in a workbench. Sure, I can certainly remove the shelves if I ever do need this room for something else. Seeing that I've been on only a handful of first dates since then, it appears I'll have a cozy little study for a while.

With a full window above my desk that lets in the morning sun, it's the perfect place to do my work. I'd never had an actual office before. Being excited, and not really knowing what to do with it, I recruited a fair number of plants. It started with one my mom gave me, but it turns out I enjoy the way they greet me each morning. Now I have several spider plants on my bookshelves and a cactus on my desk. It makes it homey. Who would have thought I'd be starting a new business venture at this age? That seems to be the theme of my life. Things don't usually go the way I planned, but I keep going.

I pull out my desk chair, plop down, and slide my laptop in front of me. Today's project is to write a blog post for my website on the project to give it a little publicity. Oddly, I don't see it as a chore. My heart ticks up a notch at the prospect of this new beginning. I always loved books, but I had a ready-made path set for me to work side by side with my dad, and I never questioned it. I love my dad, but I never loved the work the way he did.

I tilt my head to the side as I war with myself. I'm grateful for the income, and so many opportunities this business has brought me, but I'm learning it's okay to want something different.

I open a Word doc and stare at the stark white screen. Tabbing over until I get to the center. I type the title I spent an hour coming up with yesterday, "Guardians of the Pages." I can't resist a smile as I love giving a nod to construction and to my love of fantasy stories. I chuckle lightheartedly to myself as I move my cursor down.

Buzz.

My cell phone vibrates in my front shirt pocket, and I slip it out. An eyebrow quirks when I see it's not my dad. It's my mom. More than likely, she's calling to confirm that I'm coming for lunch. Shaking my head, I smirk. Of course, I wouldn't hear the end of it if I missed it. "Morning, Mom." I lean back into my padded desk chair, giving my back a nice stretch.

"Your father threw out his back," her voice rushes out. Despite the grim news, her tone is rather calm. "I need help getting him to the doctor. He's stuck on the floor." A muffled moaning emits from the background on her side of the phone, assuring me this is no hoax.

"I'm on my way." Jolting, I'm already en route down the hall, headed to the door. This isn't the first time this has happened. It's never a full-out emergency, as he seems to go back to normal after a few days of rest and some prescription anti-inflammatory drugs. However, thinking of my spry old man lying on the floor makes my heart pound against my chest. "What happened?"

"Nothing out of the ordinary. He was sitting in his recliner this morning, watching a little TV. When he went to get up, he made his usual groan, but it was followed by a thud. I looked back, and he was on the ground."

I swipe my keys off the hook on the wall and fly out the door. "I'm on my way," I assert again right as I reach my truck. "Give me five minutes."

"We aren't going anywhere."

Dropping my phone onto the passenger seat, I start my truck, shift into gear, and press the gas down a little lower than usual. Dad's tough. He'll bounce right back, but it stinks that had to happen on his birthday. I take a couple of turns extra sharp, round the final bend in the road, pull into his driveway, and stomp on the brake.

Mom's already peeping her head out the side door, her muted blonde curls pinned up like they are when she gets her hair done at the salon. My heart sinks. She's been working so hard to make this day special. Talk about a huge disappointment. Sliding out of my seat, I slam the truck door before I jog up the walkway. "How's he doing?"

"Fine, except for the fact he's stuck."

I take the screen door handle from her, pulling it open more so I can squeeze in. My gaze immediately zeros in on my dad, keeled over on his side in front of his favorite recliner, exactly how I had pictured him.

"It's no time for napping, Dad," I risk a joke as I stride forward.

"Ha ha," Dad mumbles, his voice a tad nasally. "You didn't need to run all the way over here. I just need a minute to rest."

My lips smash together as I hold all my words back. Dad's never going to agree he's in bad shape. I lean over him, reaching a hand down. "Grab on, and I'll pull you up."

Dad latches his hand into mine and puts his other hand on the ground to help push off. As soon as he rises off the floor a little, I take my free hand and wrap it around his shoulder to boost him. Dad's not an overly big guy for working construction all his life. He is compact, and he lifts fairly easily. When he tries to straighten up, his hand flies to his lower back, and he winces and remains hunched.

Mom comes in on the opposite side, sliding an arm around his waist as she gently nudges him toward the door. Dad's brows bunch together and he groans out, "Valeri, you're blocking my chair."

"You're not getting back in your chair," she asserts as her gaze pins on me as if she's asking for help. "You need to go to the clinic first."

"That oughta be a treat," Dad says with another grumble.

"If you start moving your feet in the correct position, it won't take long," she encourages him as she moves another step. "You need to start taking it easy. No more working so late."

Allowing her to help guide him forward, Dad finally takes her hand, and together we shimmy toward the door. "Enough about last night. I didn't want Penelope working all by herself."

I jolt as my ear attunes to what he's saying. "I thought you were about ready to leave after me. How late did you stay last night?"

Mom playfully glares at me over Dad's hunched back. "Midnight. I was about ready to start planning my funeral clothes."

"Ha!" Dad snort-laughs. "You're not getting rid of me that easily."

We're at the door now, and I pivot until I'm in front of Dad, pulling him forward. Mom holds him up from behind. Dad grows a twinkle in his eye as he calls back to Mom, "Don't you be checking me out. Logan's going to see it."

Mom's laugh is a pitch higher than normal, adding in more feminine inflections. My lips roll in as I resist an eye roll. After forty years of marriage, the banter between these two never stops.

I shuffle my feet backward, leading him slowly down the walk. "Dad, you're going to have to start easing up a little. You aren't twenty anymore."

"Right, I'm sixty," Dad asserts with cheery dominance. "Hurry up, so we can get this over with. I have a party to get to."

Chuckling, Mom cuts her gaze at me and then back to him. "That's supposed to be a surprise. How do you know about your party?"

Dad's quiet as we take a couple more steps forward, and I study Mom's face. She's smiling, not showing even an ounce of disappointment. If anything, she looks amused.

"Call me Sherlock," Dad eventually says, his words a little broken like he's struggling to move while also holding back laughter. It's good he's laughing about something, considering his back is in a table position with his head aimed directly at his feet. This is going to be a long day, and we need to keep our spirits up.

"So, Sherlock," I say as I grab the passenger door handle with my free hand and pull it open. "Are you ready to investigate the inside of my truck?"

"Sure," Dad says. He turns his head to the side as he steels his gaze on my mom. "But only if my lady comes too."

Mom's already opening the back door with a quiet smile on her lips. "Of course I'm coming."

I tighten my grip around Dad's back as he lifts one foot into the truck, a little groan slips through his lips. I'm swift as I lift him the rest of the way and make sure his feet are tucked inside the door. I'm about to shut the door, but he looks at me with his crooked gaze from being hunched over, and says, ""Logan, did you see that? You'll know when you find your woman. She doesn't only stay by your side when you're successful, but she fights to stay by your side when you're down." He points to me, before tacking on, "Remember that."

"Got it, Dad." I shut the door with a sense of urgency. It seems like he's getting a little loopy. Maybe he hit his head when he went down to the floor? I hurry to the driver's seat, get in, and quickly reverse the truck.

"I'm texting everyone on the guest list to let them know the birthday lunch is postponed," Mom reports with a serious tone from the back.

"Are you *sure* we need to do that?" Knowing how excited Dad was and how hard Mom worked, my heart sinks to a new level of low.

"Hey, I'm fine with that," Dad's voice shoots out of him with full alertness. "I get the cake all to myself."

After a beat of silence, Mom replies, "I guess you do."

"Then it's worth it," Dad's reply is quick, drenched in a mischievous chuckle.

"Of course it is." I join in his chuckle. "There isn't anything better than Mom's cake."

Nine

Penelope

This might be the dumbest thing I've ever done, but Jerry is one of those sweet older men, who I couldn't say no to. It would be one thing if I never had to see him again, but how do I blow off his personal invitation to his birthday party and then show up Monday to work next to him, especially since he knows I'm sitting alone in a hotel with nothing else to do.

I'm good at being social, even though a lot of the time it feels like I'm faking it. I pretend to love all the rubbing elbows and small talk. I hardly get nervous anymore, especially since I've done so many big events in the city. This little party is nothing. I dress down, in jeans and a sweater, doing my best to pull off the French front tuck. Since it's Saturday, I don't even glance at my heels. It's ballet flats all the way. I'm only going to stay a few minutes. Enough to say hi to Jerry and do my due diligence.

Arriving a few minutes fashionably late, the restaurant hostess greets me and points to the backroom that has a chalkboard beside the door with the words "Legend Party" written next to the room number. With a birthday present in hand, I scan the place. It's noon on Saturday, and laughter and chatter surround me. As I step closer to the reserved party room, my heart sinks.

The room is eerily quiet. The lights are on, and the tables have matching blue-and-black tablecloths. A Happy Birthday Jerry sign hangs over the back wall, but not a single person is in sight.

There's no way I beat everyone.

Did I get the time wrong?

Pulling out my phone, I check my messages. Nothing from Jerry or Logan. *This is awkward.* I clench the small birthday package to my chest, as there isn't even an established place for the gifts.

Now what do I do?

Drop the gift and leave.

The dull buzz of the fluorescent lights hums above me—almost as if they are reminding me I'm a geek who shows up way too early. Maybe I completely got the time wrong?

Well, I tried. Lifting a shoulder to no one, I turn on my heel to head out, right as the floor creaks behind me. Logan looks through the door. "Penelope." His gaze connects with mine. "Are you lost?"

"Not lost." I reposition the present in the center of my chest like it's a shield. "Your dad invited me, but I must have gotten the time wrong. I see I beat everyone."

His lips pull into a half-smile that doesn't match the reflections in his eyes. "Dad invited you. When?" His voice grates with an unusual edge.

"Last night when we were both working late. It's weird because I don't know anyone, but I couldn't say no, not when he was so sweet to stay with me last night." I look back at the empty tables. "Can I help set up?"

"Nah." He steps forward, scanning the room. "The party was canceled. Dad threw out his back. My mom texted all the guests, but I guess she didn't know you were invited, or I would have called—"

"Oh," I interrupt, "I'm sorry about your dad. How is he?"

"He's fine. Mostly an ego thing. It happens every few years."

"His ego happens every few years, or his back goes out?"

Logan's smirk widens, showing his perfectly even teeth, and it does something to me. He's one of those men who can't help but be handsome. "Maybe both."

My shoulders fall, releasing some of the tension of the day as I realize I'm off the hook and free to go home. "That's terrible, tell him I'm sorry that happened but happy birthday from me." I extend the box to him, and add, "This is from me."

He stares at the box for a moment before taking it. "You didn't have to get him a gift."

"It's nothing, really." I shrug, downplaying it. He doesn't need to know I spent an hour at the drugstore this morning looking for the perfect mug. "I noticed he never has a lid on his coffee when he drinks it. It sort of makes me nervous, so I got him a travel mug."

Logan's body leans away, and he tips his chin up as if he's studying me. "That's awfully sweet of you. And very observant."

"I'm a pretty observant person." I narrow my eyes playfully. "So, if there's no party, what are you doing here?"

"Oh." He half grunts as he drags his hand through the front of his hair, leaving a long wispy strand to dangle. "I stopped by to pay for our room. They had a no cancellation policy this close to the party, so I owe them money."

"That completely stinks but makes sense." My lips bunch to one side, as I again start toward the exit. "Well, I'm sorry about your dad. I guess I'll see you Monday."

A male server, in a pristine white uniform, bounds through the open door, carrying a massive tray laden with a giant mound of salad, another mound of spaghetti, an expertly stacked pile of breadsticks, and an impressive-sized bowl of mixed fruit. He strides with precision until he gets to the buffet table at the back of the room and sets the tray down, plucking each separate dish off the table to fill the buffet. "Oh," Logan calls out to him, taking a step in his direction. "There won't be a need for food anymore. The party is canceled."

Spinning on his heel to face us, the waiter says, "It's part of the 'no cancelation' policy. The food was already being prepared, and it's on your bill. You might as well eat." He walks away before Logan says another word.

"This is absurd, they didn't cancel the food." Logan's jaw drops as he steps closer. "All of this food is going to go to waste."

Logan is quiet as he stares at the food, and I say, "You might need to ask for a doggy bag."

He smirks at me, a little smug. "You have to help me eat this."

Despite my churning stomach, I lift my shoulder, tipping my lips in a smile. "I'll help you box it all up to take to your dad. They won't have to cook for a week."

"No." He holds up his palm in a stop motion. It takes me all of two seconds to find myself gazing at it for an embarrassingly long amount of time. A broad palm, he has exactly the kind you'd think would build a house. The pads are calloused yet clean. Long fingers, square at the ends, and everything about his hands looks masculine. Like he could hurl two-by-fours around all day and never tire. They are very nice hands . . . Blinking, I realize he's still talking, "You came all the way here, and you brought a gift. The least you can do is grab a bite before you leave. It won't even make a dent in this."

"Ha!" I force out a devious noise. "You haven't seen me eat, have you?"

A hungry gleam in his eye stares back at me. "That sounds like a yes."

"It's a 'why not.'" I step forward, unable to resist the scents wafting over me any longer. Logan has a standard white buffet plate ready for me as soon as I step next to him. I take it and say, "Thank you."

He grabs another plate for himself and starts heaping loads of spaghetti onto his plate. "Oh, my dad is going to die when he sees what he's missing out on."

I grab the spoon to the fruit, taking a reasonable-sized portion. "I feel terrible. Is there anything I can do to help?"

"Now that the food prep is done for the next week, not really." He slides over in front of the breadsticks and piles several onto his plate until he can't balance another one. "It's one of those things that sounds worse than it is. He'll be off work for a few days. A week tops. He's too stubborn to stay down any longer."

I take the spaghetti scoop and pop some onto my plate.
The oregano instantly fills my lungs, and I'm glad I stayed for
lunch. Replacing my scoop back in the bowl, I pivot to find
a table, and Logan gestures forward. "After you."

We each take a side of the long table directly in front of the
buffet. I eagerly retrieve a fork and aim it at my pasta but pause
to peer at Logan—he's already digging in. His gaze catches
mine. "Something wrong?"

"I feel weird. I've never had a whole buffet to myself."

"It's not to yourself. I'm here."

"I wasn't even supposed to be here." I'm not sure why I feel
the need to half-whisper over my plate. "Your dad pity invited
me."

"Nonsense." One side of his lips tips into a smirk. "I fully
invite you, so dig in." He gestures with his fork back at my
plate. More silence, but it doesn't bother me. With his hair
falling in front of his forehead when he hovers over his plate
and his muscular forearms resting on the edge of the table, he
certainly is a fine-looking dinner companion.

Twisting my fork in the pasta to wrap the noodles, I can't
help but try to make small talk. "I have to say how much
I appreciate your dad and you fitting this project in at the
last minute. I don't know what I would have done if you
wouldn't have stepped up."

"I'm happy to help." His tone lowers, emphasizing sincer-
ity. "It's actually my favorite building in town. I would have

been sad to see anyone else try to salvage it, because I don't think they would be able to do what we do."

Leaning over my plate to slurp up my first taste of noodles, my shoulders relax at the zesty sting of the garlic. I fight to eat in my most ladylike manner. "I didn't realize you had a favorite." Skepticism leaks in my voice as I tease, "Isn't that bad for architects to play favorites?"

"Maybe," he says, raising his eyebrows at me. "But I can't help how I feel. I grew up here. Many of my Christmas memories are traced back to that hotel. They always had concerts and Christmas brunch, not to mention it was the starting location of the town Christmas parade and yearly charity ball. They always hosted hot chocolate and cookies. A lot of history is there, and that offers more than the leveled parking lot that will happen if it falls into the wrong hands."

"Right." Because he's sharing a little of his personal life, I feel free to ask questions. "So, you're from here, then. What was it like growing up here?"

His brawny shoulders rise and lower. "I suppose like anywhere, except, you know, this is where my people lived." He points his empty fork at me before he stabs his pasta again. "And did you grow up in the city?"

"No." I drop my gaze to my plate as I hate when the conversation turns to my past. I don't have a problem talking about it, but it always seems people have a hard time hearing it. I've learned to change the subject. "So, I bet you enjoy the beaches, then?"

He's chewing, but it slows, and he tilts his head a measure closer until he finally swallows. "I like the beaches fine. That was a diversion, huh? You don't want to talk about where you grew up?"

I blink. Most people let me get away with that. "Ah, it's fine. I grew up in a few places. Long Island. Vermont for a while. Jersey."

"You moved around a lot?"

"Yeah."

"Army brat?"

"No, maybe just a brat." I slurp another noodle, the echoes of my flat joke hanging in the air.

He doesn't even twitch into a tiny smile. "How come you moved so much?"

"I was a foster kid," I rush out as I stab my fork in my spaghetti. "But, yeah, I've been in the city for a while now, and I work in real estate." I'm rambling nonsense now. He clearly knows I work in real estate.

"Got ya." His gaze shifts downward as if he's catching on to my insecurities, and he blows out an even breath and then says, "So, Jets or Giants?"

"Jets," I'm quick to reply. "But not much of a fan of football. What about you?"

"Giants." His answer doesn't surprise me at all. He scrapes off the rest of his pasta and looks at me. "Are you ready for seconds?"

I check my pile, and it's gone down, but I'm nowhere near done. "Not yet."

"Don't you like it?"

"I feel weird eating your dad's birthday meal when he's not even here, but it's delicious. Especially since I didn't have a proper meal all week. I don't think I would have been able to resist if you hadn't insisted."

Logan quirks an eyebrow, making his forehead ripple into lines. "Ah, gee, I thought you were here because you couldn't pass up the company."

Picking up on his playfulness, I smirk. "That's not bad either."

He stands with his plate in hand. "My company isn't bad either."

A flirty laugh slips out of my lips, and it freezes me.

Where did that come from?

I don't do flirty laughs. Sassy, yes, but never flirty. "Well," I start slowly, concealing any lingering inflections of flirty. "I usually eat alone, as you can probably tell from how much I work."

"There's always a first time for everything." He flashes me a smirk that's a tad higher on one side, as if he's hinting at something else.

Now rushing to scrape off the last of my food, as I don't want to take up any more of his time when his dad is laid up at home. I take my napkin and wipe my mouth. Marking my meal complete, I set my napkin on the plate and then pick it up while I stand. "If you need any help boxing up the food, I'm happy to help."

His gaze moves over my face. "Nah, that's fine. I'm going to eat a few more rounds while it's still warm, and then I'll take care of it."

"Okay then. Thank you for dinner. It was lovely." I raise the pitch in my voice, suddenly aware of how close we are standing, and I take a small step to the side. "Enjoy the rest of your food. Remember to tell your dad happy birthday."

"Maybe next time we can talk about your trust issues." His voice is deep, as he shovels more pasta into his mouth.

"What?" Blindsided, I blink, and stare at him. "I don't have trust issues, and what would it matter to you?"

"The fact you've been hovering over every little thing I do at that hotel, instead of letting Dad and I handle it..." He chuckles as he gleefully adds more pasta to his mouth and shakes his head. "Don't worry about it. I'm messing with you."

"Sure..." Tossing my hand up in a silent wave, I add, "See you Monday."

Inside, my heart is hammering against my chest as it hadn't really occurred to me before that I would have offended Logan or his dad by being there. I was anxious to get things moving. I mean . . . I may be a workaholic, but I don't have trust issues.

Do I?

Ten

Logan

When I return to my parents' house, it's already afternoon.
I burst through the front door with my stuffed to-go bags
dangling from my arms. My brow lowers to find all the lights
in the house have been dimmed and the window curtains
drawn tight. Across the room, Dad's in his chair, one hand
on the TV remote and the other resting behind his head as he
stares at the TV.

"Hey," I ease into the conversation as I hesitate to even
enter the room. It's like he's in mourning with the way he's
darkened the whole house.

"Hey," his mumble is barely audible, like even his throat is
too stiff to talk.

Sliding my foot forward, I risk conversation. "Are you drinking water?"

"I'm old, Son, not senile," he grunts as he attempts to lean forward, but grimaces and retreats into his chair. With a huff, he adds, "I thought I had time. You know, I literally was getting off this chair, and I threw out my back, and now I'm stuck."

"Ah, it's a small setback." Starting to feel the weight of the bags, I cross the tiny room to the counter and drop them. It's quiet with only the chatter of Dad's TV show in the background. I open the fridge and start rearranging the many condiments they have stacked. Dad's a condiment guy. He can never have only one barbecue sauce open. He's got a different one for every day of the week. "I brought a present from the party and the leftovers from the restaurant," I call out with my head still in the fridge. "Can I fix you a plate?"

"Nah, your mother made me eat so I could take my muscle relaxers. I had cake."

"Cake?" I pop my head out from behind the fridge. "Just cake? It's almost two o'clock?"

"It's my birthday, and I hurt my back. If I want to eat cake for lunch, let me."

"Got it." I stack the to-go boxes in the fridge as neatly as I can. "You and Mom will have dinner in here. And lunch to-morrow." I take another stack of boxes and try to scooch them into the packed fridge. "And probably dinner tomorrow, and lunch the next day..."

When I close the fridge, I focus on Dad, whose eyes are closed as if he's resting. I pivot, ready to see myself out, but he breaks the silence with a heavy sigh and then mumbles, "Work's been, ah, a lot lately. I've been thinking... I should maybe, I should, start cutting back. I've got things to do here. You know, before we know it'll be spring, and I have all this yard work I never get caught up on. Those bushes behind the house need a good trim. Every time I've hired someone to do it, they don't cut them straight. It's always a mess, and I don't trust anyone to do it."

My breath catches in the back of my throat. I can hear clearly. It's the inaudible part braided into his words that makes me stare with wide eyes. He's pausing, rambling, and taking deep breaths, almost as if his words are making him lost. Still, his eyes remain clenched, which is the most telling.

It's rare Dad's ever this vulnerable. Maybe once in a while with Mom, and I hear it secondhand but never with me. He's always been the pillar of strength. Ever since I was a little boy, he had me believe he was invincible. A weight moves over my chest, looming like a dark cloud that pulls the breath out of my lungs. I move forward until I am standing in front of the couch, only an armrest from Dad's chair, and I sit. I wasn't planning on staying. I already spent so much time at the clinic today, and more time at the restaurant. I've got mountains of work to do back at the house, but I smile softly at Dad, even though his eyes are closed. "Whatever you need to do, Dad."

Time ticks by for a beat of silence, and I stare at my hands, lining up the pads of my fingers, and flexing them together. Unsure of what cutting back means for Dad, I know better than to ask. He'll let me know when he's ready. The TV program switches to a mop commercial, raising the volume a little, but I don't miss Dad's question.

"Did you say you brought me a present?"

"I did. Well, Penelope brought one for you. I guess you invited her." I motion to the counter where I had set it. "It's a travel coffee mug. I didn't have the heart to tell her that you're too untamed to use it."

"Untamed?" He snort-laughs. "I like to let my coffee breathe. It's good for the taste."

It's funny how small events can magnify sounds you hear every day, like Dad's laugh. There's rarely a day that goes by where I don't hear it, but it sounds better today. "I have a present for you too, but in the bustle of getting out of the house today, I left it on the table. I'll bring it by later this week, if that's okay."

"Oh, that's fine. I didn't need anything. You know me, I didn't want a big deal made of my birthday." He waves his hand in a dismissive manner before tilting his head an angle away. "Can you hang out for a while and keep your old man company?"

The tips of my lips pull back. I see my dad most days. Even if he cuts back on work, I doubt seeing him so much is ever going to change. We've always been best friends. "Of course."

"Did you want some cake?" He gestures to the fridge.

I chuckle. "I had more than enough food at the restaurant, but thanks."

Dad matches my chuckle, but it fizzles out fast from exhaustion. "More for me."

"When does Mom get back?" I check my watch, noting it's an odd time of day for her to be gone, especially on Dad's birthday.

"She took her sister over to the mall. I told her I didn't need them sitting around here clucking. I want peace and quiet, so I can hear myself rest."

Sinking farther into the soft leather of the sofa, I fix my gaze on the TV. That's where I remain for the next hour until Dad's snores pipe so loudly, I can't hear the TV, and Mom returns, relieving me of my duties.

"Happy Birthday, Dad," I whisper under my breath as I close the door to their house and walk down the sidewalk. Still in a little shock, I would have never guessed this would happen today. It's certainly a birthday we will all remember.

It's dark in the hotel when I unlock the front door, letting myself in on Monday morning. It's been a while since I've worked alone. I find myself looking over my shoulder every few minutes, as if I'm expecting Dad to come rushing through the door.

He's okay. He's too stubborn not to be, but this incident is another reminder that he's not getting any younger. This job isn't getting any easier. He hasn't expounded on what he meant by "cutting back." Either way, I have a contract to get this hotel completed, and it seems like the job is getting bigger every day. I had messages from the hardware store saying the beams I ordered didn't come on their truck, and I should call in the morning when the next truck is due for arrival. It's disheartening, as that's the most pressing task that needs to be completed, but I can find many other ways to keep myself busy.

I grab my toolbox and lug it into the kitchen, where I set it right next to the erupted tile. The tiles aren't anything original to the hotel and not worth saving. They all need to be removed. This is the part of my job I loathe. It has nothing to do with restoring the character. It's just tile, and tiling is a lot of work. I bend over, dig in my toolbox for an extra-long tape measure, and my knuckles brush against a little round noisemaker.

It's no bigger than a fifty-cent piece. I picked it up at a hobby store a year ago and started hiding it at jobsites to drive Dad crazy. Over the years, it's become a running joke, and it seems to lighten the mood whenever we're in a rut. Grabbing the noise maker, I drag my gaze back to the cement, and my breath is heavy. I could use a laugh now, but Dad isn't coming in any time soon.

My gaze wafts back to the kitchen door and into the hall, still darkened. My mind drifts to Penelope, who should be coming in to "supervise" me any moment.

Suddenly, I have an idea.

Eleven

Penelope

Monday couldn't have come soon enough. I really should have stopped over here yesterday and worked, but I ended up taking a fast trip back into the city to check on my apartment, wash clothes, and get my mail.

Now, I'm rushing into the hotel, my forty-ounce water cup tucked in the nook of my arm. The familiar scents of sawdust and fresh paint greet me. I scan the front lobby, finding tools, pallets of wood flooring, but no Logan.

Light shifting in the hall pulls my attention down there. It could likely be a car driving by, but I slowly plod forward. "Logan?"

"Back here," he says, his voice hinting of a little morning rasp. It's deep and frankly makes him sound even more attractive. I sink my teeth into my bottom lip as I follow his voice down the long hallway when a series of bleeps blare.

My head jolts back. "What is that?" I'm terribly anxious around loud beeps. I immediately dig into my coat pocket, pull out my keychain, and make sure it's not my car alarm because that's exactly how it sounds. My alarm is off and now the sound is too.

Everything's quiet.

Hesitating, I stare down the hall, as I'm not sure what I'm walking into. "Logan?"

"Down here," he calls from the exact location as the loud noise. I have no idea why I'm so jumpy this morning. He's likely the one making that noise. I stride the rest of the way, entering the kitchen without pause.

"Good morning." My gaze lands on Logan, leaning over the floor where the cement had cracked.

"Morning, Boss Lady," His gaze flicks up to meet mine, and a spiral of electricity shoots through me. It's unexpected, especially this morning where I'm extra jittery. I startle and lose my balance and reach for the closest thing to steady me—the door.

"I'm not your boss," I mumble as my fingers barely graze the door when it's yanked back as if propelled by a string—and that exact same bleep blares again! I'm so taken aback, I stumble backward, knocking over the ladder that had been carefully stored against the wall. The ladder tips forward until it crashes with a slanted angle into the adjacent wall.

It's so much banging and beeping, I cover my ears.

Logan's voice cuts through the cacophony of sounds, steeped in a little too much innocence. "Are you okay?"

"I'm fine!" I pull my shoulders back, taking a deep breath as I stare at the door. With a string tied to the knob, it's clearly been rigged to spring back.

My attention cuts back to him—the only soul around—and a playful smile tugs on my lips. "Except for the fact you're trying to give me a heart attack. It's way too early for all this excitement."

He's smooth as he casually props a shoulder against the wall, a little smirk on his full lips. "A heart attack? That sounds serious."

I slide my hand over my heart, as if to prove how fast my heart is beating. Yes, it's still slamming against my chest. "Yeah, what's up with all the noise?"

Logan's lips tug higher into a feigned smirk of innocence. "I thought I'd test those trust issues of yours."

My eyes narrow as I search my brain for a reply, something playful, something witty, something smart, when another blasting bleep pops off. I startle so much my feet practically lift off the floor as my gaze slams back to the door. "What is that noise?" I shriek out in annoyance.

He throws his head back and chuckles as he strides to the door and points to a small round alarm hung on the back of the doorknob. "It's actually a running joke that Dad and I have to try to scare each other. When I found it in my toolbox, I couldn't resist." His smug grin only grows. "Sorry, but I'm not sorry, because you've been up my butt for days."

Despite my heart hammering against my chest wall, a chuckle brews inside. I bite my lower lip, trapping it back. "That was mean." I playfully turn on my heel, away from him and his toy.

Logan takes a long step forward. "But a little funny, right?"

My lips twitch, but I fight to hold them steady. "Maybe."

A mischievous spark in the corners of his eyes flashes, and I'm no longer able to hold back my smirk. "Just remember, you started this war."

"War?" The way his eyes sparkle even more when I laugh sends a zap right to my gut.

"Oh, yes," I spout back as I level my gaze with him, but he's tall. Much taller than me. He's standing close enough I have to tip my head back.

"Hey, what's that?" His hand rises as he motions to the wall behind me, but I resist. I'm not falling for his tricks again.

"Ah, more than likely another noisemaker."

"Nah, look." His voice lowers as he steps forward and retrieves the fallen ladder, pulling it away from the wall. "The ladder knocked a hole in the wall, which is really odd."

"Oh, no." My brow furrows as I twist my body to face my accident. This is why I don't mess around or play at work. It seems harmless, but in the end, it only creates more work. "I'm sorry," I mutter, my hand flying to the front of my throat as it suddenly feels dry.

Logan drops to a knee in front of the wall as he runs his hand along the edges of the hole. "Something must be off with this wall because a wall shouldn't crumble from an aluminum ladder bumping against it."

"I mean, it is a hundred years old." I run my hand over my hair and tuck back the loose strands behind my ears. His bottom lip rolls under as he tilts his head to the side and peers inside the hole. After a moment, he retrieves his phone, switches on his flashlight, and points it in.

"Just as I thought." His voice fills with wonder. "This wall is false. There's something back here."

"What do you mean?" My curiosity propels my feet forward as I try to peek inside. The way my shoulder rubs against his sends a knot to yank in my gut, but I'm able to ignore it as I threaten him, "I swear if this is another setup to scare me, you're going to die today, Mr. Legend."

"Mister?" His eyebrow rises as he gives me a side-eye. "Where did that come from?"

"It comes out when I'm serious." I'm only half trusting him now, but my interest is piqued, and I lean forward and stare into the hole. He's right. There is a small box. "I see it."

"See, I wasn't setting you up." After another quick look inside the hole, he peels back a little more of the wall, easily breaking it off with his hands. "This hole needs to be a little bigger," he says as he breaks off another chunk, and then he reaches inside to retrieve a small wooden box, about the size of his palm. With no markings or carvings, it looks rather unimpressive. Logan's lips curl back as he holds it up between us and whispers, "Treasure."

"Or a whole box of mouse droppings," I whisper back as I try to downplay my excitement. Inside, my heart ticks up a notch as this feels unreal. This hotel is massive, with at least twenty-five different rooms. The fact we found the one room with the single spot that had something hidden is mind-blowing. "Have you heard anything about this hotel having secrets like this?"

"No." He shakes his head, his eyes glued to the top of the box.

"Open it." Urgency infuses my tone, and I hover over the box, nearly pushing my forehead center over the top right next to his. Our faces are so close, I can feel his breath, but he doesn't flinch or step back like he minds.

He's intentional as he examines the box from all angles. There's only one easy way into it, and that's through the top. It appears to slide off. Logan places his hand over the lid, pushing it forward, and I hold my breath. Slowly, the bottom of the box is revealed as nothing more than the bottom of a wood box until he gets the lid about halfway off, and a piece of paper is folded up neatly and resting in the corner. "A note." I almost gasp while my heart continues to pound.

"Let's hope it's in English." He's careful to take the paper, handing me the box, freeing himself to open the letter with two hands.

"What if it's a treasure map?" I'm half-joking. I know nothing about hunting for treasure, but the more I mull it over, I could certainly use some. I'm that broke. It could be a miracle. His eyes rake over the page, and I hold my breath, half scared to look at it.

A sigh steeped in wonder slips out of his lips as he breathes out, "It's a love letter."

"For real?" I drop my gaze down at the writing. It's tiny and cursive with faded ink. In a couple of places, the dull paper is brittle, with little holes where the seam was folded. "Can you read it?"

He clears his throat and begins,

December 8th, 1905

My Dearest,

I'm sitting by the fire in our favorite spot, looking outside. The cold days are long, bringing in the dark nights early. I find the day to be even as I have much to keep me busy, but night comes, and my thoughts turn to you. Then my lungs forget how to work, forcing me to hold my breath. The place is so quiet. Even with everyone around me, I feel your silence. Some nights I swear I can feel your breath on my arm. How I long to embrace you again, to gaze into your eyes. You would make these gloomy days so much brighter.

How has it only been a couple of weeks since I've seen you? I find myself staring off into the air, doing nothing but re-membering you. I so deeply want to hear you whisper my name again. I can only hope you have these same feelings for me, and that when you return, we will finally be together.

I pray that time moves swiftly, and you don't forget about me. I long to cherish you forever. Please say you'll remember our love.

Until you return, I stay true to you. Only you will have my devotion and desire.

A. D.

Logan's words trickle away, and my jaw is left hanging nearly all the way to the floor. It's one thing to read a letter like that, but to hear Logan read it out loud in his sleepy morning rasp sends a shiver all the way up my spine. I'm literally speechless. I've never heard anything so beautiful in my life.

"I guess she really loved him." Logan's gaze is intent on the letter as he slowly refolds it into the original pattern and proceeds to return it into the box.

My knees are starting to ache from kneeling on the floor, but I'm a little too frozen to move. It's as if he reads my brain, and he rises to his feet, holding his free hand out to me in gesture to help me up. I slip my hand into his and ask, "What are you going to do with it?"

"I'm not sure. It's interesting. I'd be curious to do a little research." His lips align together, thinning out into a straight line in pause before he says, "I doubt any guests would be breaking holes in the wall. It had to be an owner or manager. There's an initial, and maybe I can look at the courthouse records for a surname to match." He lifts his shoulder, a curious smile lacing his lips. "Just for fun."

"Yeah, wouldn't that be interesting."

"Well." Logan's gaze drops back to the box before he pushes it toward me. "Do you want to hold on to this?"

My lips part as my gaze bounces from the box back to Logan's wide and patient eyes. "Me?"

"Yeah." He jerks his thumb over his shoulder back at the wall. "Clearly, I need to fix that wall, but I don't think we should hide it back in there. It seems like there's a reason we found it. Find some place safe to put it until we learn more about it." "Okay." I take the box, bringing it close to my body, as I feel the need to protect it. My mind is still reeling about how odd it was that we found this tiny box. "What are you going to do?"

"I'm going to do what I'm getting paid to do—get back to work." He sweeps his gaze away from me and plants it back on the ladder. With a swift motion, he picks it up and sets it back into place, getting right to work.

I guess that's my cue to leave, as I also have walls to scrub. I'm still a little jumpy. Not to mention curious. I don't want to get in Logan's way, but I wouldn't mind working a little closer to see if anything else turns up. Maybe I'll just slip out into the hall and see what I can clean out here. My eyes case up and down. Nothing but a wall and a couple of small windows. Washing never hurts anything, and I set up my mop bucket and get a fresh rag.

I've never had any proper training on how to go about cleaning, but I do what I can and stand on my toes, stretching to wipe the wall in a large arching pattern. The aroma of pine-scented cleaner quickly fills the hall, adding a lot to bring life back into this dimly lit place. We still haven't gained any power source, as we rely on the daylight filtering in through the windows, and Logan's generator for his tools. Logan's scuffing and random hammering behind me adds an odd comfort. The hotel is so big, and empty, I'm not sure I'd care to spend much time here if Logan wasn't around.

I finish the first long wall and refresh my water with sweat beading off my lower back. I untuck my neatly pressed blouse to let it hang loose, allowing air flow. After many hours, Logan comes out of the kitchen, his tool belt already removed.

"I'm going to take off for the day. I know it's a bit early, but I want to stop at the courthouse before they close at five." His gaze shifts to my pile of cleaning supplies. "Are you wrapping up too? I can walk you out."

My shoulders slump as I look back down the hall. I've finished with this part, but I don't have anything to do back in my hotel room, except scroll on my phone. I certainly don't have any clients calling for showings. If I want to get paid any time soon, my best bet is to keep cleaning. "I have the baseboards left here, and then I think I'm going to work on the lobby tonight. I should be good to take photos tomorrow. I can get all that uploaded online, and hopefully that starts to brings some calls in."

"Okay." He bobs his head and turns on his heel, calling back, "See you tomorrow."

"Bye." I wave and watch him stroll forward. As soon as he's out the door, I drop to the floor and crawl forward to wipe the baseboard. Everything is going smoothly, and I'm almost done when I hear:

Creeeek. Thud. Cruuump.

I freeze, squeezing the rag as I shift my attention down the hall. That noise did not come from behind me, where Logan had been working. It came from somewhere down there...

"Logan," I call, feeling silly as I watched him walk out the front door. Maybe he returned to grab something?

Silence.

It's likely an old hotel sound, like the place settling or the wind. I'm just jittery from Logan scaring me earlier. I roll my eyes and swipe the rag across the wall again.

Whrrrruhhhump. Thud.

I jump away from the wall, glaring down the hall. I clearly heard the noise come from waaaay down there. It was like a weird fan sound with a thud at the end, but the crazy thing is, this place doesn't have power, so there should be no fans.

Phssssh.

My heart slams against my chest, motoring hard as my brain runs through all the things it could be. I tiptoe to the end of the hall to make sure Logan shut the front door when he left, even though that's in the complete opposite direction as the noise is coming from. The lobby is empty, with nothing but dull late-evening light from the window casting a few creepy shadows across the floor. Maybe it's my imagination, but it feels like the air is a tad cooler. Goosebumps dot my spine as my gaze pulls to the exit, and I spot my car parked outside alone in the parking lot. I could leave and come back in the morning when Logan is here.

But what if something's waiting for me outside?

Because there really isn't any way for anyone to get inside.

What if this is how they are setting me up?

I run outside to get away from the noise, and *wham!*—they nab me.

My heart rams against my chest, and I slide my hand over my heart to steady it.

This is silly.

Breathing out a heavy sigh, I scan the place again. There's nobody here. There's nobody outside. It's just my imagination.

Clag!

That wasn't my imagination!

That was super loud, and now I'm shaking. It must be Logan playing another trick on me. This is what he does because he thinks it's funny. I almost chuckle when I think about how scared I got, and I whip out my phone to call him. "Wait until I think of a way to return this favor," I say to myself as I listen to the phone ring.

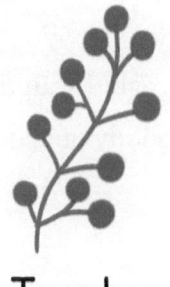

Twelve

Logan

First stop, the county recorder's office to get the complete list of hotel owners. I open the door to City Hall, and the smell of stale coffee mixed with dust mites wafts over me. A low murmur rises from two ladies standing near the copy machine in the corner. I take a few steps, arching my head as I scan the room for someone to help me. When no one acknowledges me, I call across the room, "Pardon me. I need the title records on that old hotel downtown. I'm doing a restoration."

"Ah, you're working at that hotel?" The older looking woman of the two says. "That's a big project." She moves over to her computer and hums as she clicks her mouse several times. "It's a bit of a long list. Is there something specific you're wanting to know?"

My gaze cuts to the other woman, still loitering in the corner, and she seems to be listening. Both these women look well past middle-aged, and they may know more than I do. "Since you asked. I'm especially looking for owners that would have the initials A.D."

"Hum, well, the current owner is Jin Park, so that's not him. Let's see here..." She hums some more as she clicks, and she speaks softly more to herself. "It's had a lot of owners, as it's struggled to stay afloat. It looks like a dozen or so people in the last couple of decades. Oh, wait—" she cuts herself off as she adjusts her readers to the end of her nose and tips her head forward, reading the screen. "Oh, that's interesting."

"What's interesting?" I lean over, trying to see her screen, but the angle completely seals off my onlooking.

"It appears it was vacant for ten years, after World War Two, but prior to that, it was owned by a Franco Dovenberg, so that's a D name for you..." Her voice trails off, as her lips continue to move while she reads quietly to herself.

"That's a long time for a building to sit empty."

"Oh, you know, that hotel has struggled ever since I was little. Since it's old, it's hard to maintain, and expensive."

"Right." She's not telling me anything I don't already know about how the hotel has struggled, but it feels different to hear it today, after I've spent time working over there. I tend to get attached to my projects, and I want to see this one thrive. My chest tightens as if she insulted one of my children.

"Say, now that I think of it." She pivots, turning back to the lady behind her. "The library maintains a digital archive of all the old newspapers, and you're likely to find out a wealth of information from those old reels if you want to know more."

"Maybe I'll stop there." I take a second to open the notes on my phone and type in the name Franco Dovenberg, and then I turn to leave, tossing a wave up behind me. "Thanks."

"It's my pleasure. I hope you get the place restored. It's a bit of an eyesore the way it is now."

"I'm trying," I murmur as I let myself out.

Back at home, I plop onto my chair and pop the top on an energy drink. Caffeine has long since lost its effect on me. I can drink it anytime and still sleep. I lean over my desk and type in the name: Franco Dovenberg.

Nothing.

Sighing, I scroll as nothing ever comes easy. Like clockwork my mind splits, half focusing on the screen in front of me, and the other half starts imagining who this person is. I love stories, especially real-life ones, bringing a bridge into where we are today. Being a hundred years old, the hotel must have some good stories.

I just need to find them.

To say it's a challenge is an understatement. I scroll, tapping on a few things that look like they might be interesting. A few obituaries from random places, but nothing I can use. Chasing a couple of leads, I don't break until I uncover another name: Ammoret Dovenberg, which would fit the A initial. She's apparently the daughter of Franco, the original owner, and that fits the narrative well. My fingers race over the keyboard as I type in search after search, looking for anything else.

My phone buzzes from inside my shirt pocket, and I take it out, sucking back a breath—Penelope. An image of Penelope floats to the front of my brain, her long silky hair framing her face as she looks back over her shoulder, ready to scold me for scaring her. I'm fast to smirk, ready to chuckle, as that was certainly a fun reaction. She got so mad. My chest proceeds to tighten as my mind seems to zoom in on her fiery eyes. She certainly looks cute when she's mad. Her pouty lips smashed together, and a single stress line pinned between her eyes.

I don't hate looking at her.

"Hello," I answer, ready to hear her voice.

"You got me," Penelope rushes out. "I was spooked for a minute, but I know it's you. You can come on out now."

"Come out of where? I'm at home." Sitting up straight, my gaze first drops to the time on my computer. It's about an hour after I left the hotel, and she clearly saw me leave. What's she getting at?

"Ha ha. Nice try." She laughs, but it's not her usual airy laugh. This one seems forced, and I can almost hear her cringe through the phone.

"What are you talking about? Are you still at the hotel? Is everything okay?" I stand, pushing my chair back in one swift motion.

"Yes, I'm still here, as you know. You're trying to scare me by making all that noise in the backrooms."

"No. No, I'm not. I'm at home." My brows lower as I register what she's saying. "Stay put. I'll be right there." I end the call already bolting out of my house. I jump into my truck and fire the engine. My tires skid as I slam the gas down, and I head back in the direction of the hotel. Tiny snowflakes flutter in front of my windshield. My visibility is fine, but they warn of slippery roads. I should slow down, but my heart is hammering in my chest.

I've walked every inch of that hotel several times and never saw signs of anyone even loitering around. It's been vacant for months. There shouldn't be anyone. Not during the day and especially this time of night.

Pulling into town at the above recommended speeds, I only slow once the hotel is in my sight. The parking lot is clear, except for her car. I screech to a stop right next to it and jump out of my truck, keeping my eyes peeled for signs of movement.

With a new layer of snow freshly fallen on the ground, fresh footprints would be easier to see, but there's nothing that catches my eyes. My gut lurches in warning, and I clench my jaw as I jog toward the front door. Yanking on the handle, I confirm it's locked tight as I had left it. No one came in this way...

Using my key, I let myself in, calling out softly, "Penelope!"

Footsteps echo from the hall, and I spin quickly as my heart about flies from my chest.

Penelope tiptoes forward, her shoulders slumping while she clenches her phone to her chest.

"You okay?" I ask, my focus splits between confirming she's okay, while also surveying all the possible ways someone could come into this room.

"I'm literally fine," she whispers. "It was you making a noise."

My jaw twitches as I move to the end of the hallway. The little battery run spotlights she's using are on, lighting a clear path forward, but my stomach crawls into my throat. Part of me says to get Penelope out of here, but since I don't know where the noise is coming from, I can't be sure someone isn't waiting outside for her. I could walk her to her car and tell her to go back to her hotel, but what if someone follows her? "You don't have any enemies, do you?"

"Enemies?" she scoffs, her brow furrowing. "Why would I have an enemy?"

"I don't know. You tell me. A crazy ex-boyfriend?"

"No." Her one-word answer doesn't satisfy my quest for truth. Something fishy is going on. It's probably not the brightest idea I've ever had, but my gut says to keep her close to me. "Stay right behind me."

Nodding, her lips pin into a serious line as she steps behind me. I stride forward, scanning in every direction for the smallest movement.

Nothing.

We make it to the end of the hall where it splits, heading into either the kitchen or to the guest rooms. I turn back to her. "Which way did the noise come from?"

"It's coming from back there." Her gaze stays locked on me, but her head tips toward the guest rooms. Grabbing my phone flashlight, I hold it out to examine my path forward. This hallway is carpeted, which would make footsteps muted and hard to hear.

No fresh snow traipsed in.

No sign of forced entry here.

"Maybe we should call the cops?" Penelope's voice is tight, but it doesn't distract me enough from noticing she's so close, I can smell her delicious scent. Under any other circumstances, I'd be unable to take my gaze off her. It seems unfair.

"We could." I pause, looking back at the direction we came. There's no sign of anything. I don't doubt she heard something, but it's likely the hotel settling under the pressure change that this current snowstorm brought. The cops don't have a lot of time to waste on stuff like that. "I'd hate to send them on a wild-goose chase. The wind's picked up a lot. It's more than likely something harmless—"

Thud.

My head springs back, and Penelope leaps forward, closing the small space that had been left between us as she now clings to my arm with both hands. Heat permeates from her body pressing into me, and I inhale. I can't say I hate that part.

"Any chance you think it's more rodents?" She digs her nails into my forearm, causing me to wince.

"I think it's safe to say those are gone." I focus my attention on where the noise came from. It's the room across from the hall—a room that should be empty. Keeping my voice firm, I call out, "You've got ten seconds to open this door, or I'm calling the cops."

Penelope inhales a sharp breath and hisses, "Don't you think we should tell him cops are already on the way?"

"Shh," I hiss back, as I don't believe anyone is there. I'm doing what I saw someone do on a TV show once. I fully expect that room to be empty. Tipping my head to the side, I listen.

Silence.

"See, it's nobody," I breathe out and attempt to slide my foot forward. Penelope still has a death grip on my arm, and she digs her nails farther, anchoring me back.

"Don't go in there," she whispers with urgency. "We need to leave and call the cops."

"I'm not going to waste a cop's time. It's seriously just the house settling—"

Thump. Screeeech.

"That's definitely scratching at the door! It's a ghost!" Penelope hisses, giving my arm another tug back as she sandwiches herself to my side. I inhale so sharply from the tingling sensation that ripples from my side; I'm getting lightheaded.

"It's definitely something, but it's no ghost." I could knock, but I've already called out a warning. I doubt it's human. "Do you have your key? Mine is in my tool belt."

With a huff, she reaches into her pocket, pulls out a master key, and slips it to me. I walk forward and slide it in the lock. Twisting the doorknob, I push the door forward a tiny crack and attempt to slip through. Immediately I'm met with a cold gust of wind and giant fur paws on my chest. "It's a dog," I exclaim, not scared—just thankful.

Penelope opens the door even more and gasps when she sees the almost-human-sized canine bouncing off me. "How did he get in here?"

Our gazes synchronize as we find the window pane has been completely shattered, glass all over the floor. "My guess is that happened after they sprayed the place, or he'd have been found or poisoned," I say as I look back.

The dog moves over to her, jumping on his hind legs, meeting Penelope almost at eye level as his tail wiggles so fast, he seems to be having a hard time staying balanced. He's obviously not shy, as he's quickly taken to her. "It looks like he's excited to be rescued."

"I bet he's starving." She's slow to pet him back, only putting one hand on his head.

"Get down," I holler at him, and he quickly obeys, sitting in front of her, his tail still motoring back and forth. "Look at that. He's trained. He has to be someone's pet." I focus my attention back on the dog. He's black with short shiny fur, and pointy ears. If I had to guess, I'd say a Doberman mix. He's wearing a thick red collar, and we're in luck because there's a tag. Stepping forward, I slowly bring my hand under the dog's nose, giving him time to sniff me. He flicks his tongue out to lick me, and I know it's safe to reach for the tag.

Pinsch Charming

"No address," I say, and chuckle as I add the last part. "But it looks like you caught yourself a prince. Were you looking for a Pinsch Charming?"

"Isn't every woman?" she says, moving her face closer so she can look too. "That's super cute. Like a play on pinscher, right?"

"I think so." I look back out the window, doing a fast eye sweep of the outside. There isn't anything else that would be suspicious. Then I turn back to them. "Yeah, I think it's safe to say Pinsch Charming is our culprit."

"What a relief." Another breath exhales from her lips. "What are we going to do with him? We can't leave him here."

"I have some of Dad's leftovers at my house. I can certainly load him up in the truck and take him to my place for the night." Twisting my wrist, I check my watch to confirm what I already knew. "It's too late to make any calls now. I can call animal control in the morning."

"That sounds okay." Her voice is monotone, but her breath is still coming out in uneven bursts, as if she's letting go of the stress of the event. She also checks her watch and says with exhaustion, "I could be done for the day. I'm ready to leave."

"All right." I pause, as I extend my hand to Pinsch, "You want to come with me? I got plenty of spaghetti at my place." He moves forward, but not to me. Instead, he parks his paws in front of Penelope.

"Do you know nothing about dogs? He'll be better off with me if that's what you are doing to feed him. Garlic is toxic to dogs." Penelope pats his head with a straight elbow, but his gaze is locked so intently on her, it's clear who he thinks he's going home with.

"Well, if I didn't think the hotel you're staying at would allow him." I attempt to reach forward to pet him, but he jerks his head away from me, all the while pushing his muzzle closer to Penelope.

Her eyes grow wider. "I think he's made his choice, and you are right. I'm not sure what I will do with him at the hotel, but I guess we will see."

"He looks like an easy keeper. Just feed him and let him sleep." I shrug, tacking on, "We can find a shelter in the morning."

"I guess if he insists." Her gaze lingers on him. On cue, he steps forward, nearly smashing his body into her legs as if to say he's going everywhere she goes.

"Hold on one second. I want to walk you out to your car, but I'm going to grab a piece of plywood and board up this window before something else crawls in."

"Good idea." Her gaze follows me, as I hurry back down the hall to the front lobby where I have a pile of mismatched wood. I find a piece large enough and return to the room to find Penelope and Pinsch in the exact same positions. She holds up her camera flashlight while I hammer a couple of nails through the board, securing it in place, and we all turn and drag our feet toward the front entrance.

I open the door, letting her walk out first, and then I pause to double-check it's locked. We start to cross the parking lot, but there's a niggling in the back of my head I can't let go. Turning my gaze to the side, I state firmly, "I know you don't need a babysitter or anything, but this place is awfully big, and there's a lot of potential hiding places. If it's okay with you, I'll be staying until you leave from now on. I don't like the idea of you being alone. You never know what could happen."

"You don't have to—" Her gaze is straightforward, focused on her car, and her quick steps don't slow as Pinsch is right on her heels, not taking his eyes off her.

"I know." I'd like to have a conversation about what happened. *Yeah, it was nothing, but it could have been something.* I reach forward, touching her forearm, hoping to slow her steps a little, and I add, "But I want to."

Her steps halt short of her car, and she turns toward me, her eyes soft but tired. After another long beat of silence she says, "Okay, fine."

Now that she's looking directly at me, I can tell this event frazzled her more than she let on. Her previously polished ponytail has become disheveled, with long wispy strands dangling in every direction, including a straggling one in front of her left eye. I hesitate at first, because I'm not one of those touchy-feely people, but she looks too exhausted to have noticed it. I reach forward, swipe after the longest strand of hair, and push it behind her ear. She stills, allowing me to do it, but her eyes laser on me as if demanding an explanation. "You had a hair blocking your face," I explain with a hushed voice. "I wouldn't want you to drive off with your line of vision blocked."

"Thank you." It comes out more like a question, but she doesn't linger, and she turns to the dog, "Come on, Pinch. Let's find some dinner."

"Don't hesitate to call if you need anything." I turn on my heel and call out to my new friend, "See you tomorrow, Pinch."

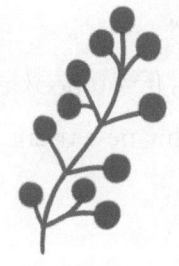

Thirteen

Penelope

Flipping through the channels on the flat screen, I snuggle in bed with Pinsch resting at the foot. I've never owned a dog, and I'm not quite sure what to do with him. I grabbed some kibble from the store on my way back. He gobbled up an entire bowl, and then we ordered room service. He seemed to enjoy the leftover bone from my steak I offered him.

He selected his spot, not having left it except for when a door slammed across the hall. At which point he proceeded to make a supervisory round of the room, growling at the door, and then came back to bed. He's definitely not a puppy. With a few gray hairs around his nose, he looks distinguished and wise and seems to wear out of energy fairly fast.

Yawning, my eyes water as I settle on some 90s sitcom rerun when a text comes in.

Vernon: We need to talk.

Pressing call on his name, I fold my lips in, waiting for him to pick up.

"Penelope." His voice is tight, hinting he's already holding back. "Were you planning to tell me about the rodents?"

"I handled it. They've already been taken care of, and I'm here, trying to hurry this listing along."

"Yeah, you are keeping secrets from me for almost two weeks. I thought you were down there having open houses and giving tours. I had no idea the place was on hold. I had to find out from Jin what you were really up to. We haven't had one call. Buyers are—"

"Buyers aren't calling," I interrupt because I don't need him telling me what's going on with my listing when I've been pouring my own sweat equity into it, "because I haven't been advertising it yet. I've pulled my advertising until the mess is cleaned. Trust me, I can handle it."

"Then why did I hear from the seller about the rodents before I heard from you?"

"I've been busy, and it slipped my mind." I bite my tongue, holding back what I truly want to say, everything about how I know he stuck me with the dump because he was luring me away from that condo. And he doesn't need to get started on who can't trust who, because I certainly don't trust him. I'm only holding on to this job until I sell this dump. I'll cash my commission check to start my own agency. "I'll do better to keep you in the loop."

"We will see about that." A quiet grumble echoes through the phone. "I'll be honest with you, when I agreed to this listing, I knew nothing about the infestation and the sheer amount of work that needed to be done, I think it's best if we encourage Mr. Park to let the bank take this off his hands."

I see his point. I agree this place is a dump—but I really need that commission. Without it, I won't have any seed money for a business. With the way Vernon shoved me aside on that condo, I doubt he'll be passing over any big listings any time soon. Plus, Logan swears he knows what he's doing, and oddly, I trust him. Maybe I'll regret it later, but for now, it's the last spark of hope I have. "I understand what you're saying, but these things take time to turn around."

"Well, don't let it take too much time," he grumbles. "I'll give you to the end of the month, and I want this place sold. We can't drag our feet on this. I need you back in the city showing these micro-units."

Swallowing deep, I let my hand float to my throat, and I hold it there as it feels grounding to grip on to something. *The end of the month. That's just two weeks.* That's an impossible deadline with all the work we have to do, but I'm not going to show any doubt. "That's all the time I need," I say in my most confident tone.

"I'm scheduling it now." His voice grows distant as he mumbles, "Open house in a week from Sunday, and if that fails, we start shopping for short sells..." His voice trails off and then *click!*

Pulling my phone from my ear, I stare at the blinking screen. He hung up on me. Anger bubbles in my throat. He's the one who talked me into this listing. I get he did it to swindle me out of that other deal, but he underestimated me. I'm not giving up because it's hard.

Images of the cement flooring erupting in the hotel kitchen flash to the front of my mind, causing me to take a hard swallow.

Nearly impossible.

I hate this situation so much; I want to yank on my hair and scream!

But Vernon doesn't deserve to have me react like that. I can't let him get to me.

My eyes have been opened to what's really going on with his business and how he's using me. I'm desperate to move on, and I'll do anything to make it happen. Adrenaline surges through my veins, pulling me more awake than I've been all day. If it wasn't after ten, I'd drive myself back to the hotel and take a second shift, but it's late, and Logan warned me about working by myself. Something I totally understand, but Logan doesn't need to worry about me.

My gaze drifts downward as the corners of my lips bend up in the slightest manner. He certainly had a sense of urgency when I called him, not taking no for an answer.

He was pretty sweet to do that.

Maybe I need to do better by showing my appreciation for all he's doing for me. Without him working so hard, my plans to quickly offload this hotel would be thwarted. Really, this entire sale is dependent on him. And since my entire fate as a successful real estate agent is now concentrated on this one sale, and my ability to break free of Vernon, that means my fate is dependent *on Logan.*

My eyes widen as even more adrenaline pumps through my veins. I'd better play these cards right, or I'll regret it. The music blares loudly from the closing credits on my show, and I'm a bit taken aback as I had nearly forgotten the show was even on. I hadn't paid attention to a single scene. TV isn't holding my attention tonight as my mind is reeling with so much pent-up stress. I jump off my bed and head to the window, pulling back the little curtain.

Snow is falling with lots of wind. Blah.

Turning away, I pace to the other side. It's a tiny room, taking me only about ten small steps. Pinsch stands in alert, seeming to be confused as to what I'm doing. "I don't know what I'm doing." Giving him a side-eye, I park both hands on my hips and stare forward into the bathroom mirror.

There's my stringy hair again.

Maybe I should avoid using conditioner all together, because it doesn't seem to do anything but make my hair look greasy. Stepping forward, I flip on the light and reach for my brush, running it through my hair several times. It's knotted, and I find more than a few good-sized tangles that only leave me more disgruntled. I've never felt this anxious before. This hotel project has me acting crazy, but as I struggle to get my brush through my hair, my hands begin to shake.

Is it even worth trying to save?

Maybe it's time for something more low maintenance, especially if I'm going to be trapped here in this low-budget hotel for the next two weeks.

I eye my toiletries bag.

I have some scissors in my bag somewhere.

Before I have a chance to argue with myself, I rummage to the bottom of my bag and pull out my pair of scissors.

It's only hair.

Really gross, stringy hair.

Plus, it will grow back.

A whimper pulls my attention outside the bathroom. Pinsch has parked himself outside the room, his head tilted. If I'm not mistaken, I would say it's a bit of a judgment slant. Do dogs judge?

"It's fine. I know what I'm doing," I say in a huff, even though it's an absolute stretch of the truth. I've never cut hair before.

But it can't hurt to trim it a little. Maybe it will give it some lift and body?

My hand is steady as I open the scissors and snip. I'm not even sure what I'm going for as I snip around my face, adding in some layers. It doesn't look terrible, and I start to recall it's been a long time since I had bangs. They might be exactly what I need to get my enthusiasm back. *Repositioning my scissors in front of my face, I snip again.*

I don't have a plan.

I certainly don't overthink it.

Strands fall to the tile floor. My lips remain tight—not upset, not emotional. Something in between. Maybe ready to stop being stuck. After several more snips, I set the scissors down on the counter and run my fingers through what's left. It's certainly lighter. Perhaps a little uneven?

I stare forward, aware my breath is coming in and out in uneven bursts. I'm not quite sure what that means, as emotionally I'm a bit numb. "What do you think, Pinch?"

A long whimper slips from his lips.

"I get it." With a final exhale, I flick off the light switch, heading back to bed. "You think I'm going to regret it in the morning, huh?" Following me on my heels, he jumps back on the bed. I slide in—taking care to pull the blanket up without stealing from him—then I lie down and add, "It's okay, sometimes I go a little crazy. It helps to release stress, and I've been really stressed this week." My eyes drift, closing tight, and I murmur, "Besides, I don't really have anyone to impress anyway..."

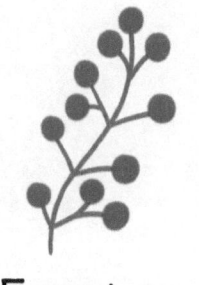

Fourteen

Logan

The front door pushes open with an extra creak this morning. It's likely as sick of the cold as I am. My boots lightly tap on the wood flooring, announcing my arrival, and a moment later Penelope peeks her head out of the hall. "Morning." Not even another second later, Pinsch Charming bounds around the corner, ears alert, and he crosses the floor, coming right up to me.

Offering a full smile to him, I bend to his level and scratch behind his ears. "Morning you two. You're awfully early. How did last night go?"

"Fine. No trouble at all." She nods and steps forward, lugging a mop bucket behind her.

Slinging my tool belt around my hips, I take a moment to secure it. She's quiet, but I do a double take as something's different about her. Wearing high-waisted jeans and a T-shirt, my gaze quickly dismisses her clothing as normal. Trying not to stare, it takes me a second to realize her hair is different. "You cut bangs?"

"I did." She blows upward, pushing them off her forehead. "I didn't think anyone would notice."

"They look, uh, you look great. Is something wrong?" Pinsch pushes his nose into my leg, asking for more attention, and I scratch behind his ears some more, loving the way his tongue drops out of his smile.

"Why would something be wrong just because I cut bangs?" She stares everywhere but at me, as she judiciously avoids eye contact, tipping me off further, she's really not okay.

"You did that to yourself?" I pat Pinsch a few extra times on the head. Turning my attention to my toolbox, I start to fidget with my tools, moving them in random spots, pretending like they need to be sorted. "I guess you never said you were getting a haircut...and nothing is wrong?" Pinsch must have figured out I was done petting him, because he sneezes and walks back to Penelope. She places her hand on the top of his head, looking a tad more comfortable around him than she did last time.

"Why would you think something is wrong?" She lifts her hand, combing through her bangs. "Do they look bad?"

"No, they look great. I just, you know. Whatever." I stuff a couple of screwdrivers into my belt and stand up straight. "I guess I'm assuming, but I have two sisters and giving themselves an unplanned haircut on a random weekday seems like the kind of thing they would do when they are manic, but that's clearly just a them thing."

"My boss called me last night," she rushes out as her free hand grips the top of her hip. "He was upset the place wasn't ready to show to clients, and the whole conversation put me in a mood. So, there." She flicks her hand out in a snappy gesture. "That's what happened."

I offer a smile—not a happy one—but the kind you give someone when you wish you could do more to support them, but you're not sure what can be done. I can clearly hear the frustration coiled around every one of her words. She's certainly trying hard to act as if she's not as stressed as she is, but she's not hiding it—at all. "A mood?" I can't help but smile at the way she downplayed it. She's even adorable when she's stressed.

She stops petting Pinsch and leans a shoulder against the doorframe, just another clue she's struggling with everything. "It's hard to explain, but I recently found out my boss is a scumbag, and he set me up by encouraging me to take this listing, so I was out of the city long enough for him to sell my best listing..." Her voice trails off but not before punctuating her sentence with a sassy eye roll.

"I had no idea—" We're interrupted by another sneeze, and Pinsch walks across the room and lays down in the corner.

"It's fine, really." Penelope shakes her head toward Pinsch and flashes half a smile at me. Watching her for a long moment, I suspect she's not as strong as she wants people to think. It's her eyes that give it all away. She's squinting, faking a smile, but the centers of her eyes are dull.

"Is it, though?" When she doesn't reply, I offer her a measured glance, yielding the silence to her.

"It sort of has to be..." One of her shoulders raises and lowers in a sluggish shrug. "Plus, I have a plan."

"You do?"

"Yeah, I do." She looks around the room, as if taking it in for the first time. "This place is massive. Yeah, it's a dump at the moment, but it's coming around. Despite my boss thinking this place is unsellable, I'm going to sell it and take the commission to walk away and become a broker and start my own agency."

When I don't say anything, because I sense she's not done, she goes off on the defensive. "It's not hard, and even if it is hard, I'm not afraid of hard work. It's all I've done for years. I can start my own agency, and then I won't have to worry about being scammed. I get to maintain all my contacts in the city and the life I built. I can do it."

"I believe you," I say.

"You do?"

"Yeah, I wouldn't be here working beside you if I didn't think this place had a second chance." I tip my head toward her, offering more encouragement. "Sometimes second chances are better than the first."

"Well, good." She turns in a half circle, positioning her back toward me for a moment while she scopes out the place again, and then whips her gaze back to me. "Do you have any updates on the timeline?"

"Uh." My gaze instantly averts down the hall to the biggest project, the flooring in the kitchen. "Well, if anything, I'm a little behind because my dad is taking time off, and it's only me now, but I'll get it done."

"Thank you." An emotional crack in her voice lingers, and she turns her back to me again.

"Say," I start and stop as I wait for her to turn her attention back to me. When she tosses a glance over her shoulder, I catch my breath. It's an excellent angle. Although all her angles are perfect. This one is especially gorgeous, because it highlights her high cheekbones.

"Yeah?" It's a bit of a sleepy sounding response, and she's patient as she waits for me to expound.

Dipping my fingers into my side pocket, I remove the sheet I printed with Ammoret's picture. "I did some research last night on the letter, and I think I know who our heroine is."

"Who?" A quizzical brow rises, and she pivots back to me, her lashes lowering as she focuses on the paper.

"Yeah, it wasn't too hard. The original owner's name is Franco Dovenberg, and he had a daughter named Ammoret Dovenberg—so I'm assuming that's the A.D." Pointing to the photo of her, I go on, "That also makes sense because that's when the building was being lived in, and not being used as a hotel, which would make it easier to put up false walls without, say, getting sued."

My bad joke about getting sued earns me a small smile, and I marvel at it.

"Wow, she's beautiful." Her voice holds a reverie. "So, no word on the man yet?"

"Well, I'm sure I can find him. I'll check the marriage records to see if she ever got married." Tipping my lips into a playful smile, I pretend to glare at Pinsch over in the corner. "I was interrupted last night before I had time..."

"Oh, about that. Thank you again—"

"Don't mention it." I offer a dismissive wave and add, "I was happy to help, and I'm glad it was a dog. Now I'm eager to solve our mystery, because the whole thing fascinates me. It's one thing to love someone that much, but I have to ask myself why they hid the letter in the wall. They clearly wanted someone to find it, which makes my mind reel even more, because that tells me there's more to the story."

"You really think they wanted people to find it? I would think it's the opposite, because the letter was hidden."

"It's hard to say, but I'm dying to learn more."

Penelope's lashes flutter, reminding me of butterfly wings, and it's all I can do not to stare. It's another tiny clue to how she's really feeling. "Hey." I lower my voice and step toward her. "Are you sure you're doing okay?"

"Just tired." Her lips tighten, as if symbolic of how she's sealing the rest of herself off. It's a normal response, considering most people aren't dying to pour their heart out to someone who's a mere work acquaintance. I get she's under a lot of stress, but I can't help but wish I could help. Not sure what I can do. She certainly didn't like my alarm prank. Then I get an idea, one I hope she'll accept.

"You haven't had enough caffeine yet today. There's a coffee shop down the block. How about we walk over, and it's my treat." Before she can rebut, I add "Usually, Dad makes coffee for us both. Since he's not here, I completely forgot to bring my own as well."

Pursing her lips, her focus shifts to the room, as if she can't bear to leave the work behind for even twenty minutes, and I go on, "We'll get it to go, and the fresh air might help you wake up."

A single worry line between her brow creases like she's about to decline, but to my surprise she sighs, saying, "That actually sounds lovely. Let me grab my coat."

She turns to go back down the hall, and my heart ticks up a notch, fluttering against my rib cage. "It's only coffee," I murmur under my breath to calm my soon-to-be-racing pulse. "With one of the most beautiful women I've ever seen…"

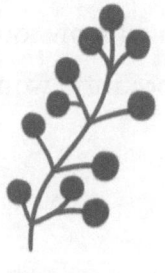

Fifteen

Penelope

With the morning sun peeking through the silvery winter haze, there's a rare, promising glow cast over the cobblestone sidewalks. Townsfolk bustle in and out of the quaint little shops with bundles of shopping bags and small-town smirks. Most everyone waves at Logan. I'm pretty much oblivious to all that is happening around me, because my body is on alert, completely attuned to the fact I'm walking shoulder to shoulder with Logan. Although I've been doing my best to avoid the attraction by keeping busy, now that we are out of the hotel, I can't deny there's this magnetism between us.

He's wearing an easy smile that matches his regular flannel shirt and denim jeans. "Do you always walk like you're being chased, or is this like a jumpiness that's left over from last night?"

When I laugh, a little puff of frozen air wafts out from my mouth. "This is standard New Yorker pace."

"Good to know this is normal. For a moment I thought you were embarrassed to be seen with me, and you were trying to ditch me."

"No, not trying to ditch you." A playful spark buds in my gut. "It's not my fault you're dragging your feet like an old guy."

"Old guy? Oh, so that's how you want to play this morning—a little sassy?" He juts out a good-humored elbow, tapping it with mine. "I'm thirty, which makes me *not old*. Although..." He takes a deep breath. "Since I've been doing construction for fifteen years, I'm well on my way to having the same old-guy back as my dad."

"Fifteen years." I calculate the math. "You must have started in high school."

"Technically, my dad was showing me around jobsites when I was in grade school, but I had to wait until I was sixteen to officially and legally work with tools. I worked in the summer while I attended university, but yeah, eventually I traded in my star basketball position for a tool belt, and it's all been history."

"Star basketball?" I give him a sideways glare. He clearly has the height to play, but there's a mischievous glint in his eye that tells me he's exaggerating. "That sounds boastful. I'm not sure I can visualize that."

"What, you don't believe me?" Logan stops on his heel in the center of the sidewalk, spreading his arms wide. "I mean, I still got a layup in me, but be warned, I might make you crush on me."

"No, I have rules about crushes. I don't have a crush on people for athletic skills." Despite my quick rebuttal with words, my body has a different reaction. A full fleet of butter-flies erupt in my gut, fluttering so hard I put my hand on my stomach. It's crazy to see him flirt like this. I guess getting out of the worksite does something to him. He's quiet, possibly offended, so I tack on, "Besides, you're more than likely out of basketball shape."

Dropping his jaw, mocking shock, he scurries to align his steps back with mine as I continue forward. "Hey, I'm not out of shape. I'm not a show-off."

We arrive at a corner store, tucked neatly beside a book-store. A chalkboard sign is set up right outside with a sign that says *Now Open* in crooked cursive chalk. My mouth waters as I can already smell the aroma of warm espresso and vanilla wafting out the open wood door.

Tipping his head to gesture me forward, I walk in first and he follows, saying, "So let me guess your coffee order. Something outlandish with ten ingredients but miraculously no calories and topped with a dollop of whipped cream?"

"How do you know what a dollop of whipped cream is?" Raising my brows, I admire his coffee lingo.

"Doesn't everyone? They used to sing about it in that commercial."

"I don't remember that." I jab my elbow into his, returning the favor he paid me earlier, doing anything I can to touch him but not make the yearning so obvious. It's like being this close to him makes my body crave touching him. Even if it's in a manner of teasing. "That must be one of your old-guy memories."

"Possibly." He gets in line, leaving a space in front of him, while gesturing for me to take it. I step in front of him and reply to his earlier question.

"So not outlandish, but just a banana cream latte with coconut milk."

"Sort of normal." He turns a critical eye on me. "Although, it sounds more like a mixed drink you should be having on a tropical island. Are you sure you didn't forget it's winter and you're not on an island?"

Snickering, we take a collective step forward as the line moves. "Yes, I'm well aware of where I am."

"Do you like your cup with a cute nickname on it?"

"Nickname?" I echo, not because I didn't hear, but these butterflies in my gut are going wild, and it takes all I can do to breathe evenly. "Why would you think that?"

"Well, Penelope might be a bit much for a barista to write, especially when the line is long. I can imagine you get into a bit of a spelling match as these Gen Zs aren't the brightest with phonics."

Unable to resist the tugging on the corners of my lips, I turn my head toward the counter, hiding my smirk. I'm at the front of the line now, and the barista looks up at me. "May I take your order?"

"Yeah, I'll have a banana cream latte with coconut milk and whipped cream."

"That sounds delicious." The young barista takes a moment to ring up my order and then grabs a cup and looks back at me. "Can I get a name?"

"Uh." I pause, because Logan is right. Penelope is always a struggle for these young kids to handle. I've long since given up on trying. "Just Lo." I feel Logan's heavy gaze on me like the lightest spotlight, and I struggle not to make eye contact.

She scribbles on the cup and sets it aside, then places her focus on Logan. "And for you, sir?"

"I'll have a caramel latte, and the name is Logan." Out of my peripheral vision, I see him pay.

When he steps aside, I stuff my hands in my coat pocket, join him at the drink station, and say, "Thank you for paying."

"I'm happy to pay, but you have to admit I was right about the nickname."

Finally, I let my gaze pull back to him and his sweet smile, and my heart skips a beat. It's been forever since I've allowed myself to banter with someone like this, and it feels great. Maybe exactly what I need to get past the bad mood I've been in. "I suppose I can admit it, but it's not like that was a hard thing to assume. Most people with longer names shorten it at times to make it easier."

"Well, now that I know your secret name, I'll be sure to use it," he says, winking. "I rather like that name, Lo. It even goes well with Logan."

I nearly sputter out my spit. I can't believe he went that hard with the flirting. Then I pause, he's actually right. Logan and Lo are adorable together in the cutest way, and now I'm grinning ear to ear. It's like one of those Pinterest couples.

They set our drinks on the counter, and we grab them and meander toward the door. Logan stands back, allowing me to pass first. When he falls back into sync with me, I look at him, needing to tame the flirting a little, because that last line still has my butterflies in an uproar. "How is your dad?"

"I talked to my mom last night on my way home from the courthouse. He's up and about, but a little slower than normal. If anything, his ego is the most bruised. He did mention I should thank you for the mug." He tips his head away from me before adding, "But I doubt he'll use it."

I sip my coffee absentmindedly as my brain doesn't seem to ever have a clear train of thought anymore. Logan looks my way with that half-smile he's been giving me all morning, and those butterflies startle again. "So, now that I know your secret name, is there anything else you care to share?" Logan's focus is on me, gentle and attentive.

A rush of warmth flows through my gut. I've never been one to talk about my personal life. I guess that's why working is easy for me. "Nah, nothing really." I hesitate, as I've learned when people ask about my personal life, I at least need to give them something easy. "Maybe I'm enjoying my time out of the office, and I appreciate your help."

His lips twist to the side, as if forewarning me that he's not giving up this conversation so easily. "So, you're not missing family or friends back home?"

"Nope." I pop the P, and feel my eyes grow wide as I already know what he's getting at. I've learned how to handle this question. It's best to be blunt, get it over with, and change the subject. "I don't have any family. Remember, I grew up in foster care. No big sad story or anything there. Just aged out." Everything rushes out fast, as it always does, before I expertly change the topic, "How's your coffee?"

"Good." Though his words are definitive, his tone is drenched with confusion. I easily ignore his tone. The faster I move on, the better.

"Mine's fabulous. Thanks for offering to take me. It's exactly what I needed. I might have to make this a regular morning stop."

His gaze flicks toward me, pausing for a mere moment before he says, "I think you're right. We should have regular coffee dates every morning."

I smile at him. It's a genuine smile, but it's mixed. For every part of this smile that's satisfied and happy, there's equal parts hesitation. It's not that I think Logan's a bad guy. I don't at all. It doesn't make sense to get attached to someone I'll likely never see again after I sell the hotel.

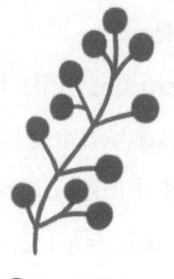

Sixteen

Logan

Back at the hotel, the late afternoon sun filters through the blinds, slanting rays of light over my newly tiled kitchen floor. I've been working steadily all afternoon with the goal of getting this done today. I diligently press the final tile into place and smirk as it fits like the perfect piece of a puzzle. A satisfied-but-tired sigh slips from my lips, and I sit back on my heels to admire the floor— clean, white, and *most importantly* level.

Tiling is my least favorite thing to do. I'm always happy when I'm able to subcontract this task to someone else, but with this entire job being so last minute, I didn't even try to bring in anyone else. I take the rag I've been working with and wipe the row of sweat off my brow, then retrieve my coffee cup. I've been saving the last sip for this moment, as it marks a job complete. Tipping my cup back, I swallow what is left, and my mind drifts—not to the tiles or the small mess in front of me scattered on the drop cloth. Instead, the coffee pulls my mind to Penelope and our morning walk.

Or should I say Lo?

Like seriously, her nickname is part of my first name. Hallmark can't plan it better than that. I can't resist an audible chuckle as I glance out of the kitchen doorway. I've easily gotten used to seeing her and Pinsch run past on their way up and down the hall, and it's been a while since I've heard any clattering. I toss my cup in the corner trash can and cross the room, aiming my ear down the hall. Nothing. "Hey, Lo," I call out, a smile tipping my lips into an amused grin. I love the way that little name rolls off my lips. "You still here?"

I doubt she'd take off without letting me know. When I don't hear her call back, I walk to the guest rooms, where she's been spending most of her time. Once I round the corner, I spot the ladder she's been using propped up against the wall, right next to an open guest room door. I pad forward, slowing when I get to the door, as I'm fully aware she doesn't like to be startled.

Learned that lesson the hard way.

Won't do that again.

It's a larger than average guest room with a king-size bed on one wall and a fireplace on the opposite. The dog we easily forgot to call animal control about, Pinsch, is napping on his side with his belly exposed to the front of the fireplace, like it's emitting heat. Penelope's in front of the stone fireplace on her hands and knees, one hand stretching along the fireplace, wiping out the soot. "It's too early for Santa," I joke.

Her head jolts before she glances back. "Don't worry, I've long left the days of wishing for Santa behind me." A cough bubbles out of her throat, and she rolls her hand into a fist, covering her mouth. After clearing her throat, she nods toward the fireplace. "You're just in time. You might want to look at this. I was cleaning, and I noticed one of the bricks is loose."

She sits back on her heels and runs the back of her hand across her forehead, more than likely to wipe the sheen of sweat, but she's oh so unsuccessful at that, and proceeds to smear soot across her head.

It's oddly adorable. I can't help but gaze at her cuteness when I step forward, crouching next to her so I can get a good look inside. "Hmm," I say, more to tease her than to satisfy my needs to make a sound. I run my hand over the white-painted bricks, pushing on each one until I get to the bottom row, and she's right. They do feel wobbly. I barely push on the corner one, and it shoots straight forward. "That must be the one that opens the secret passageway." I toss a look over my shoulder, only half serious as I watch for signs of the wall moving. I've clearly seen too many mysteries.

"Uh, I don't think that's supposed to do that." Penelope doesn't back away. Instead, she crawls forward, nearly smashing the side of her head into mine as she fights me for space, peering inside.

"Clearly this place has some secrets." My smile fades, and I pull out my phone, turn on my camera light, and shine it forward.

"What do you think it is?"

"Well, I'm hoping it's not another mouse hole." It's such an awkward angle with the hole being so close to the floor, the light does nothing to help. I stick my hand in. For a moment, I toy with the thought of pretending I got bitten by something—just to get a rise out of her, but my heart is actually pounding so hard in my chest, I doubt I could handle a startle like that. Plus, it would be mean to do it to her—mean, but also funny.

But mostly mean.

The hole is wide and deep. It doesn't take much, and my fingers brush against something small. "There's something in here," I whisper as I wrap my fingers around the item and pull it out.

We let out a collective gasp when we see it's the exact same wedge-shaped box we found in the wall. "It's another one!" Penelope rushes out.

It opens in the same manner as the first, and I don't waste a moment sliding the lid off. Another folded letter rests inside. With urgency, I retrieve the letter, pass the box to her, straighten the letter, and read:

My Dearest,

If you're reading this, then you know the heaviness has already grown so much that I can't ignore it anymore. Regretfully, I won't ask you how you are because after you read this, you won't want to share those things with me anymore. I desire with every fragmented piece of my heart you're well, and despite what I have to tell you, there will remain at least one tiny glimmer of hope in you that will continue to believe in true love.

With that, I'm writing to say goodbye. Please know this is not my decision.

They've made it clear I'm no longer allowed to write to you or see you. There's so much vengeance in their breaths when they speak your name, I'm afraid for your safety, and that's the only reason I am giving in. Please know I would never do this if I felt there was any other way.

Loving you was never a mistake. I would do it again and again for a thousand lifetimes. Even knowing I'll be heartbroken forever.

I won't ever forget you or the person I was when we were together. Our love will echo in everything I do for always. – A.D.

I whisper the salutation and focus back on Penelope. Heaviness lingers in the air. If I'm not mistaken, her eyes appear to carry a moisture that wasn't there before. We stare at each other for the longest moment, each of us digesting the pain in this letter.

Penelope blinks a few times, clearing her throat again, before saying, "I wonder what happened."

Emitting a deep sigh, I look back at the letter and take it all in again. "She really loved him. That's obvious."

"It sounds like maybe her family or someone wanted them to stay apart, like a modern Romeo and Juliet." Penelope breaks eye contact to stand, and brushes her hands off on her pants, seeming to need to put some distance between us.

"Let's pray it ended better for them," I murmur under my breath, refolding the letter, and returning it back to the box. After I slide the lid on, I stand up and pass the box over to her. "Do you want to store it with the other one?"

Her lips part. "You know, I never thought when we found the first one, that there might be another one. Do you think there's even more?"

"Possibly." I lift a shoulder, and she finally takes the box from me. "The way she spoke in the letter, she was writing to him often."

"Do you think he even got these letters?" Penelope stares at the box in her hands, rubbing the corner with her thumb.

"I would hope if someone loved me like that, I would have been told about it."

"Right." Her voice grows quiet, and Pinsch seems to finally catch wind of our conversation, stirring awake, punctuating his alertness with his signature sneeze.

"Well, good morning," I joke while I focus on him. "It's so nice of you to wake up when all the work is finally done."

Penelope chuckles as she steps forward, giving him a pat on the head. "I bet you're hungry." He tips his head back, locking eyes on her, and wags his tail. The look on his face confirms he's already taken to her.

I can't help but think I can fully understand why.

I clear my throat and turn toward the exit. "If you're ready to go, I'll walk you out."

"I had wanted to finish up here, but I should get Pinsch some dinner." After doing a quick scan around the room, she glances at me. "I suppose now is as good of a place as any to call it a night."

Moving in front of the door to wait for her, I try to act casual when I tack on, "Do you have any plans for the night?"

"Nope." Her lips whoosh to the side. "Just get lots of rest, so I can come back tomorrow. What about you?"

"I was thinking of going to the library to look through those archives. If you get bored, you're welcome to stop by."

Holding my breath, I gaze at her perfect pouty lips, hoping she gets the hint that the invitation isn't so much about finding more information on the letters—as it's only partly that. The question is more of a bait, as I casually throw it out and wait to see her reaction to hanging out with me in a non-work setting.

"Hmm." She squints at me, but it's not quite her fake smile. This one says she might be holding back... or at least that's what I tell myself. "I'll have to see if Pinsch Charming settles down after he gets dinner." The sweet smile forms on her lips as she lowers her lashes to the ground, adding, "But I'll try."

Try.

One single word.

It tells me all I need to know.

She feels this chemistry too.

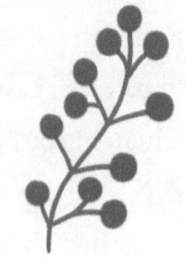

Seventeen

Penelope

The elevator dings right on cue, and the door slides open, revealing the library basement. Familiar scents of old paper waft toward me, sending me back to high school study hall. I've never been a reader and haven't slid even one toe into one of these book-infested buildings since school. It doesn't surprise me one bit it takes a sweet man like Logan to bring me back to one.

"In here." Logan's head pops out of the small room down the hall, and he waves at me. I move toward him, doing my best not to stare at him. It seems the more time I spend with him, the more his good looks are sneaking up on me.

He appears to have a signature way of wearing a shirt, and not just any shirt. It's always a flannel shirt with the sleeves rolled enough to show his sinewy forearms. I've yet to see the same one twice, as he has a wide assortment of plaids in all shades of blue to match his eyes. He has to do that on purpose because there's no way someone can accidentally buy an entire wardrobe to twin with his eyes.

And then his smile—easy and shy—it's the sort of smirk that hints of a lot of shared secrets even. It never fails to set the butterflies in my stomach into flight. "How's it going?" I ask, as I join him inside the little office. Evidently, he's been at this a while because the projector is already on, with a grainy image on the screen—a black-and-white photograph of a couple standing in front of the fireplace in the hotel lobby. "That's the hotel," I blurt out, a little shocked to see it in a photograph that's so old. "Is that our couple?"

"I don't know who the guy is, but I'm fairly sure that's Ammoret," Logan says in a hushed voice. "There was another photo a while back that was labeled Franco and his daughter, and this woman looks like her."

My feet slide forward until I'm in front of the only other chair in the room—right next to him. Lowering myself with my eyes glued to the screen, I can't take my eyes off them. She's wearing a dark dress. Although I can't make out the color with the black-and-white slide, it looks like it's velvet. Her light hair is pulled away from her face and pinned into loose curls, and her jewelry—like something royalty would wear—teardrop earrings that dangle almost to her shoulder.

The man is equally as classy in pressed slacks, a shirt tailored just right, and a blazer with tails. He has one arm wrapped around the woman with his gaze fixed on her, and his free hand grips the stem of a champagne flute. "They look like movie stars," I coo while noting their straight expressions. "But no smiles."

"Maybe they are avoiding the people who are trying to keep them apart."

Dry laughter falls from my lips. "It's sad, isn't it? They look like they could be so happy together, but we know it ended."

Logan's quiet for a long moment, staring at the photo. "Well, we don't know how it ended. We only have two letters. Maybe they were able to make it. Perhaps they ran away together, started a little family of their own, and lived the rest of their days in perfect love."

"I wasn't expecting that from you." My eyebrows rise into a skeptical arch. "You sound like a little bit of a romantic."

He shakes his head. "No, not at all. That's for people who want to get their hopes up and then get let down."

I give him a disbelieving look. "What are you, then?"

I honestly thought he'd brush the question away, because what guy wants to talk about love, but he doesn't miss a beat. "I'm what you call someone who roots for old love."

"Old love? Never heard of it."

"Probably because I made it up, but it's the love you see in this photo, not staged or done for social media. The kind of love my parents have and their parents. Not always perfect, but neither one of them ever even uttered the word divorce. They knew it was a forever love." His gaze slides down as he stares at his hands while pressing the pads of his fingers together. "Not this instalove stuff you see on TV that has everyone swapping relationships every few years."

"Interesting." I sigh softly while making an assumption. "Do you think there's a connection to why you love old property so much? You're just an all-around old soul."

Logan turns his face fully toward me, his voice low. "I never thought of it that way, but you're right. I've always preferred to think about a society that wasn't so disposable. Things shouldn't be wasted. People shouldn't be . . . forgotten."

He's talking soul, hitting me right in the gut, causing me to whisper, "I might agree with that."

"You do?" He stretches his hands over his head for a moment, leaning way back in his chair before dropping them back to the table, nearly brushing his hand on mine.

So near. I can feel the warmth permeating off his hand, and I stare at it. "What part do you agree with?" he asks.

The corners of my lips curl into a sensitive smile. "The whole concept of old love. I think if we had more of that, there would be stronger families."

Logan's voice is smooth, unwavering when he asks, "Is that what you want?"

Thick silence sweeps through the air, and my heart slams against my rib cage as his gaze connects with mine. "It would be nice," I finally manage. It's hard for me to think about since I came from the definition of a disposable family. Foster care left me in a different home every few months, as it was a constant loop of turnover. When I wasn't convenient, I was moved. That was no way to live. Deep down, I always yearned for a love that was forever. I never had a name for it—until now.

"Can you understand why I don't agree they didn't end up together? I think the letters we found are the start of their story, not their ending." He reaches forward and clicks the button of the projector to advance another slide.

Click.

The same couple, wearing more casual clothes this time—he's in dark suspenders and a bow tie, and she has a knee-length dress. Their hands are linked together with full smiles, almost as if the photo was shot while they were laughing. They're standing in front of the hotel again. I read the newspaper caption out loud, "Ammoret Dovenberg and her fiancé, Mr. Armond..." My voice trails off, and I blurt out, "We have his name! And they were engaged."

"We do," he affirms and pulls out his phone to jot down a note. "We can look up that name in the marriage licenses too."

I can't help but peer over his shoulder, the scent of cedar and musk wafting my way, and I stare at his note. "You certainly are rooting for them, aren't you?"

He quirks one of his eyebrows, holding it in pause. "Maybe it's them, or maybe it's you know, the whole idea that old love works out."

Goosebumps dot my spine, and I can't help but yearn for what they had. I look back at their photo, and I can see a spark in the center of the man's. "It's like he can't take his eyes off of her."

Maybe it was an accident, but it feels more intentional. Logan pulls his eyes off the screen, shifting his focus to me.

My heart slams into my throat.

This is a new look.

Something I'd never experienced before. This isn't his sleepy smile, or even his can't-help-but-be-gorgeous eyes. This is him shooting sparks right out of the center of his eyes, boring a trail of something gooey right to my heart.

The projector fan kicks in, humming loudly to cool the machine. The room has fast become overheated, but neither of us moves. A loud double knock pounds on the door, followed by someone opening it, popping in her head, and saying, "Oops, didn't know someone was in here."

We both startle, shifting our gazes behind us. The door is already shutting. Letting out a sigh, I return my attention to

Logan, heat flaming the tops of my cheeks. "Why do I feel like we were about to get busted doing something bad?"

He chuckles as he focuses back on the projector, clicking another photo forward. A smirk lifts the edges of his lips. "Speak for yourself. I'm on perfect behavior and have never been in trouble, nor will I ever be."

I struggle to keep a straight face. "Ha, we'll see about that. I bet if I asked your dad, he might be able to remind you of a time or two."

"He'll only confirm my sainthood," he teases, lifting his elbow enough to tap mine, sending a trickle of goosebumps up my arm. "Then you'll be out of excuses."

My brow furrows. "Excuses for what?"

Silence. Not even a little silence, but the projector fan switches off, leaving us in a heavy stillness. One where when he turns his face toward me, all I can hear is his breath so close to my ear. He reaches his hand up, in the slowest speed, and I watch as it nears my cheek.

Knock. Knock.

The door behind us flies open again. This time a woman with a gray bun pinned to the top of her head and large glasses pops her head all the way in and says, "Your time limit is up. There's a line of people waiting for this room."

When Logan drops his hand back to his side, he looks back to the screen. "There is?" Logan's tone drenches in disbelief.

He gets busy returning film rolls back into the bin and re-moves the one from the machine.

"We'll be right out." I stand and push my chair in, doing my best to tidy. She disappears around the corner, and I mumble, "Aren't we living in the digital age? Who would think there would be a run on the slide projector?" A giggle bubbles out of my lips right as Logan switches off the power on the machine and moves toward the open door.

"I wonder if she's making that up." His lips pinch together. We both move out the door, searching for someone—any-one—waiting outside, but there's no one. He dips his chin down, and whispers, "She's one of those old ladies with stuffy rules."

Tossing a look behind me, I see not a single person. I giggle again as we stride toward the open elevator. "I guess so."

Once inside, the door closes in slow motion, and I turn my attention to him. "Thanks for inviting me to join you. It was definitely worth researching. It will help me tell the hotel story better, you know. I can pull on some heartstrings to win some buyers."

His smile caves as he stares blankly at me. "What does that have to do with sales?"

"Nothing," I rush out, seeing him offended. "I mean, I didn't mean it like that. I enjoyed spending time with you. It's nice to see, you know, uh, the whole story of the hotel. Since we're working on it, uh, right?"

"You don't get it." His eyes narrow. Not unfriendly. More like a spotlight.

I open my mouth to defend myself again, feeling so embarrassed. "I do get it, and I didn't really mean it like that, it was something that blubbered out—"

"I understand what you meant." His words ring over the top of mine and are punctuated by the ding of the elevator arriving on the main floor.

Blinking, I take my gaze away from him to see a small gathering of people outside, waiting for the elevator. People are already starting to push in between us, and I walk forward, aligning my steps with his.

He's quiet.

I glue my lips shut, and we smile at each other the tiniest smile as we synchronize our steps, walking toward the exit. People all around, as this is the busiest floor of the library. Not a place to have a private conversation. When my fingers brush against the cool metal door handle, I stare at him—pained to leave the conversation like this. His eyes are wide, following my every move as I push the door open and smile back at him. "I'll, uh, see you tomorrow..."

"Sure."

I'm first to break our eye lock as I turn to walk the opposite way, but I can feel his gaze on me the whole way back to my car.

It definitely feels like we're both becoming more comfortable with each other, and even curious. It's too bad we don't live in the same city, because I could get used to seeing him.

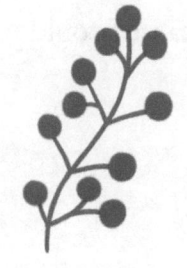

Eighteen

Logan

The next morning, I pull into the hotel parking lot next to Penelope's car, stomp on the brake, and slide my gaze to the clock on the dash—7:02.

I thought I was early.

Did she sleep here?

Plus, I thought I told her not to work alone.

Shaking my head, I mutter under my breath, "Stubborn woman," and yank on the door handle. I slide out of my truck, crossing the parking lot in a few brisk steps. When I swing open the door, I'm quick to spot Penelope behind the front desk with a dusting cloth. "Morning, Lo." I wait to see if she catches her nickname.

She remains with her back turned toward me. Her hair is pinned up in one of those messy hairdos that accentuates her neck and the perfect angle of her chin. It's an incredible view, and I halt, just marveling. "You're early."

"I could say the same thing to you." I come up to the counter, and cross my arms to lean on them. "Maybe I was in a hurry to get here because I enjoy the company."

Her lashes rise, pinning her gaze on me, and a flirty smirk grows on her lips. "If by company, you mean my boss from New York, you're in luck."

"No, I was thinking about you." I pause, running a hand through my hair, and add in my next breath, "But yeah, meeting your boss is interesting."

Her lips part for a long beat before she says, "Did something happen to you? Maybe you hit your head a little too hard because I don't remember you being this smooth a few days ago."

"It's clearly a defensive mechanism I picked up somewhere." The heated glare she gives me makes me shift my weight from one leg to the other. "What time is your boss going to be here?"

Twisting her wrist to check her Coach watch, she says, "Aw, I think with the drive maybe another hour. We have time to go for coffee, if you want."

I hike a flirty brow, mocking shock. "Now who's smooth?" She seems to pass a flicker of warmth from her eyes to me, and it makes my heart ramp up speed.

"You have no idea." Her lips tip even more into a playful smirk, and I'm obsessed. She doesn't have to ask me twice.

"Well, if we only have an hour, we'd better hurry."

"I'll grab my coat." She's already retrieving it out of what used to be a little supply closet behind the front desk.

As she walks forward, I scan the room. "Where's Pinsch Charming?"

"I left him on the back loading dock to hang out since my boss is coming. It's not a big deal or anything, but I didn't want Vernon to get any wrong ideas. Plus, I was thinking it's time I start making some calls. You'd think someone would be looking for him." Almost on cue, the dog barks, and Penelope smirks. "He'll be fine. He had two bowls of kibble this morning, half of my banana, and I might—or might not—have accidentally dropped my breakfast sausages on the floor right in front of him." I throw my hand up in a stop motion, adding, "But don't worry, it was lean and garlic-free sausage, so perfectly healthy for him."

"He basically has you wrapped around his paw," I tease as we move in unison out the front door.

"We're fine." She makes a dismissive wave in my direction as I lock the front door behind us. We trudge forward through the fresh powder, our boots stomping out patterned prints marking our trail. "I feel bad because he's well trained, so he must be someone's pet. I should maybe put some signs up."

"I can make some," I offer, feeling silly for not having done that already. With my dad getting hurt, and this project piling up on my plate, the thought hadn't occurred to me. "I'll grab a photo of him before I leave tonight and print some flyers at home."

"That would be great." The sigh she emits is a little heavier than one would expect for everything's "going fine" with a dog.

I can't resist another pry. "Are you sure everything is going okay with him?"

"With him?" She gives me a pointed expression as we both step to the side to make room for the oncoming pedestrians of the busy downtown street. "He's amazing, but maybe I'm on edge with Vernon coming. He's not one to visit me at work, and he's not exactly a fan of this project. It seems odd. I got this random text this morning."

"Did he say what he wanted?"

"No, just that he was stopping by, which frankly alarms me. This place isn't exactly on the way to anywhere, which means he's going out of his way to check in."

"I'm sure it will be fine. The place is looking much better, especially after I finished all the kitchen tile yesterday. Actually, it's perfect timing."

"You think so?"

"Yeah, I do. If anything, it gives you a chance to show him how hard you worked."

"I hope you're right."

"I'm sure that's it. If it is anything bad, he would have clearly given you a warning, right?"

"I don't know." She shakes her head, dropping her voice. "He's already proven he's not worthy of my trust. It doesn't matter what he did or didn't say. I'll wait to find out for sure once I see it with my own eyes..." Her words trickle off into a huff, as we approach the coffee shop.

"Are you ready for another banana latte with coconut milk, Lo?" I hang on to her neutral expression, hoping her lips turn up.

"That's exactly what I need." Her eyelids droop lower. It's the sort of sleepy expression you'd expect to see on someone when they first wake up, not after being awake for a while and taking a walk. I can't help but think she's getting run down working so much. Maybe her boss coming here is a good thing?

There's no one in line, and we walk straight to the counter. Without asking first, I tack on two muffins to our coffee order and then give her a side-eye. "Any last words before I pick out your muffin?"

"Oh, you didn't have to order a muffin."

"I didn't, but if your boss is coming, extra snacks are a good idea." I tip my head to the display case, snugly filled with baskets of muffins, each with puffed crowns and sprinkled with the perfect amount of sugar. My eyes pace to the banana nut muffins, an expected combo to her coffee, but I skip over them. I'd hate for her to get too much banana. "So, normally I'd say blueberry because it's the healthiest," I start to order, "but with the boss coming, I think you need chocolate. How about double chocolate muffins?"

"Sounds amazing." She smiles back at me, and the barista grabs two muffins, bagging them and handing me the sack, and a second barista sets our drinks on the counter.

We retrieve our drinks and turn back, walking in sync with each other as if it's the most natural thing in the world for us to go for a stroll together. I sip my drink, taking long pauses because it's very hot. She's more patient, cupping her coffee in hand, blowing on it through the little hole. Avoiding anything that makes her more stressed, I quickly set the conversation on something positive. "So, aside from work, what is your life like back in the city?"

"You mean there's supposed to be more than work?" She gives me a mischievous smile before taking the defensive tone. "I have hobbies. I just don't always have the time to do them."

"Okay, like what?"

"Well, for starters, I have an amazing apartment with a rooftop deck. I love sitting out there at night and staring at all the lights. It's probably one of my favorite things."

Scratching my chin, I maintain my serious expression. "Really?"

"Does that surprise you?"

I see her playing with the end of her hair, giving me a flirty grin, encouraging me to continue the conversation. "Yeah, I mean, that actually sounds relaxing. I didn't think you'd be the type of person who knew how to relax and sit still."

"Surprise, it happens on very rare occasions." We stop at the street corner, waiting for the light.

"That's fascinating, but I know something else equally fascinating." I open the bag, pull out my muffin, and then give her the bag. "Try your muffin."

She takes her muffin, and I wad up the empty bag and stuff it into one of the short trash cans that are perfectly placed on every street corner of downtown. Opening her mouth wide, her bottom teeth sink into her muffin first, and her lashes flutter. If I had to diagnose that flutter, I'd call it taste bud heaven. "Told ya." I don't wait for her to gush about their superiority. I already know. I take a huge bite of mine as the light turns green, and we cross the street together, both with a mouthful of food.

We walk the last block in silence as we finish off our muffins and cross the hotel parking lot—still with only our two cars. "He's not here yet," I state the obvious. "What do you need me to do to get ready for him? I can shovel the walk."

"Aw, that kind of stuff doesn't bother him." She unlocks the door, walking in first, and heads right to the front desk. Her gaze is almost frantic as she scans all over. After a long beat of silence, she says in a defeated tone, "I don't think there's anything we can do in the next few minutes that will drastically help this. Do whatever project you have next on your list, and I'll spend the next bit of time doing my last-minute staging."

"Well, if you think you're okay, I'll run to the hardware store to grab my beams. They are finally in."

"It might be a good idea for you to disappear before Vernon arrives." She nods as she continues to cup her coffee near the center of her body like it's a security object. "I'll text you if anything comes up, but I'm thinking he'll be here and gone before you return."

"All right." I toss a hand up as I turn on my heel and call back, "Good luck, Lo."

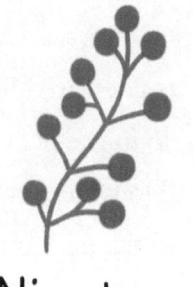

Nineteen

Penelope

I set my coffee on the back counter, feeling underwhelmed by this place. It's certainly a lot cleaner than it was a few days ago and has a nice pine-scented fragrance—well, except for that one room we found Pinsch Charming in. I don't know if he peed in there or what, but it has an odor. I just shut the door to that room, and plan to leave it that way. Normally, I save staging for buyers, but I don't think it will hurt for me to crack a window, and I can always light a candle.

My stomach is in such a loop of knots, I can barely think straight. I head back to the little coat closet and take out my bag, removing my "emergency" floral scented room spray and the single candle I have stored in there, because you never know what you'll find in these houses. I light the candle, set it on the back counter, and adjust it perfectly so the apple-pie fragrance fills the room.

I crack the window in the front lobby enough to let a light breeze filter in. Out of the corner of my eye, I spot Vernon's Audi pulling into the spot next to mine. My stomach loops into an endless spiral. I never used to feel like this when I saw him before. It used to feel like we were more of a team, maybe even the closest thing I'd ever had to a family. Ever since he pulled that deal out from under me, I'm unsettled.

Backing away from the window, I glance around the room again, not a thing out of place. If this was a showing, I wouldn't do anything differently. It's impeccable, right down to the fresh bowl of pinecones I plucked out of the yard and placed on the center of the coffee table. "Looks like a 'big pay raise to me,'" I murmur to myself while approaching the door to welcome Vernon.

He steps out of his Audi, his hair slicked back, showing the slight silvering above his ear. Though he's graying, it does nothing to age him. He has the kind of hair coloring that makes him look more distinguished, and frankly—wealthier. He's definitely handsome, though he's not my type. "Good morning, Vernon," I greet him with my shoulders back and one hand on my hip. "It's a pleasant surprise to see you out here."

"I'm more surprised than you are." He strides through the door, bringing in a cool gust of wind. I study his face, looking for a twitch or disapproving line, anything to show me a hint to why he's truly here. If he thinks he's stealing this sale from me after all the work I put into it, then he has another thing coming. "It smells like a coffee shop here."

Poof!

That's an odd sound that pulls my eyes wide open with interest. Like a puff of air, and my gaze immediately finds the cracked window, but that's normal, the soft breeze blowing the ends of the curtains enough for them to bounce back and forth off the wall. Out of my peripheral, I spot a glow on the back counter that wasn't there before.

Oh my!

The bottom corner of the wall calendar behind the candle has caught fire!

My eyes shoot out of my head, and I sprint over, snatch the calendar off the wall, and like a crazed idiot, I blow on the flame—only making it smoke more.

Without a second thought, I drop it to the floor, snatch my coffee off the counter, and toss it over the calendar. The flames disappear, while adding more smoke trails that fume out. The panic in my chest recedes, and I slowly raise my gaze back to Vernon. I quirk a sassy eyebrow and lead with, "That's what you get for insulting the smell. Now we enter the rustic campfire scent era."

He's smiling, a tight smile but a smile, nonetheless. "Like a pro, you always handle things."

Is that a compliment?

It can't be.

Narrowing my gaze, I turn back to the soaked calendar and the puddle of coffee on the floor. "For the first stop in this tour, I'll show you the janitor's closet, where I'll be grabbing cleaning supplies."

Chuckling and bobbing his head back to the candle, he says, "Not before I blow this out."

"Good idea." I take slow, even steps down the hall, wondering why this feels as if I'm about to go to a funeral, not show off the hotel I've been prepping for days. I used to look forward to talking to Vernon, running ideas by him and telling him my hopes and dreams for my future.

Everything has changed.

Vernon watches as I grab a few rags and some spray cleaner, and I make my way back to him, all the while my stomach is tangled in knots. "So, I should be ready to start some viewings this weekend," I say as I kneel in front of the puddle and begin soaking the coffee up with my first rag. "It's not perfect, but any new owner is going to have renovations of their own, and we aren't trying to overstep. Logan really is a genius when it comes to renovations. Aside from making everything safe, you can't tell his alterations aren't original—"

"Penelope," he cuts me off, his brows dipping lower in the center. "I tried to tell you this the other day over the phone, but I could hear how excited you were about this. It's clear you're in over your head. I talked to Jin, and he's motivated to move this place without the renovations. We've approached some chains. We're entering a bidding war. He doesn't need the renovations or the fancy candles for this one." He gestures toward my candle, still piping out smoke.

Now a glaring symbol of my embarrassment.

Confusion floods to the front of my brain. I've been carrying my phone with me everywhere. Jin never once even sent me a text that hinted of this. "I'm lost." I pause to swallow and then start again, "He's my client, and I've talked to him about what we're doing. He hasn't even hinted—"

"He didn't want to hurt your feelings." Vernon raises his chin, smugly staring down at me. "He knows how hard you were working, but he came to me—"

"He came to you?" I spit out, my words trembling while my pulse rockets, thundering in my ears. "Or did you reach out to him?"

"Uh." Vernon's head shakes, filling in for his lack of words, telling me the truth of what really happened. "I don't remember exactly—"

Standing upright, I raise my gaze, blazing. "This is my client, and you went behind my back."

He offers a half-weighted shrug. "I found a buyer. My company has a reputation and letting properties foreclose is not one I'm willing to use as my tagline. Keeping our reputation strong is what matters."

"What matters?" I'm surprised I don't stutter as my breath comes out in uneven waves. "You stole this from me. Now you've done this twice!"

Vernon stands silent, his slick grin spreading across his face like cancer. "Sometimes clients don't share the same vision as an agent. That's what was happening here. You were emotional, and Jin noticed that. He wanted a sale. It was better that I took over."

"Emotional?" I snap back, my words picking up speed. "Is that what you call treating people fairly and being honest in your business dealings?"

His jaw flaps open, ready to mansplain. I narrow my eyes, unwilling to hear another word from him. He hasn't the slightest clue what he did when he made an enemy out of me. I may not be one to play dirty, but he knows I will outwork him and win my way. *The honest way.* "You're threatened by me."

He guffaws, too forced, while averting my eye contact. Then, in some weak display of faux concern, he touches the tips of his fingers on my forearm. "Calm down."

I snap my arm back, instantly recoiling. "Don't ever think you can touch me." His lips only sneer wider as he swipes his hand through the side of his hair, smoothing down his effortless wave. By now I recaptured my own flickering smile as I see through his façade all too clearly. Parking a hand on my hip, I point my own smug glare at him. "You may be my boss, but I'm the one who signed the contract on this one. I'll handle my client. And when I sell this place—and I *will*—I'll take my commission and be on my way." I raise my hand, gesturing toward the door, heart pounding, a tiny smile still tugging at my lips. "You may leave. I don't need your toxic behavior here."

He mutters something inaudible but eventually spins on his heel, not looking back as he strides out the door. My hand finds the front of my chest, and I hold it there, trying to calm the racing pace of my heartbeat. That wasn't exactly how I planned this meeting to go. In a way, I'm not surprised. I also oddly think it's what needed to happen for me to see clearly where I'm going...

Far away from Vernon and his real estate company. There are better things for me, even if I must make it happen alone.

I'm not scared to be alone.

Always have been.

Twenty

Logan

Unbeknownst to Penelope, I snuck through the back door and crouched in the kitchen, listening to everything her jerk-hole boss said to her. It was hard to resist the urge to run down the hall and punch him. I was completely enamored with the way she held her ground. As soon as I was sure the coast was clear, I pad down the hall to tell her how proud I was of her. I find her frozen in front of the window, staring out as Vernon's Audi squeals out of the parking lot. She seems to be lost in thought, because she doesn't look back when I walk up behind her and the floorboards squeak.

*I have to admit when I first met her all frazzled over the mice,
I didn't think she had that fire in her, but now... I just marvel.
Not only is she stunning but she's tough.*

After a beat of silence, Penelope jerks the curtain closed,
like it had personally offended her, and spins around, locking
her gaze with mine. My heart skips a literal beat. Her expression—half pleased, more than half determined, and fully
gorgeous—puts me in a chokehold. I'm eager to brag about
what I saw. "You were impressive."

Her gorgeous grin slowly peeks out, creasing the dimple
next to her beauty mark on her left cheek. "What did you
see?"

I arch a focused eyebrow. "I didn't see anything, but I didn't
need to. I heard it all from down the hall. You were brilliant.
Not too mean but strong enough to assert yourself. I'm thor-
oughly impressed."

Her lips pinch together as if suppressing a laugh. "At least
one of us is impressed."

I cock my head to the side and peer at her. "You should be
too."

Her gaze lowers to the floor before slowly rising back up.
"He tried to steal my client."

"I heard that." I lower my tone, easing off the banter. "From
the sound of it though, it's not a done deal. Maybe if you
reach out now, you can intervene. Once your client hears
about the love notes, and what an absolute marketing gold

mine to get magazine and blog features that will blow this place up, he'll be glad he stuck with you. You're offering a legacy. Vernon only wants a quick buck."

Her straight brow softens into a natural curve. "So now you're my business coach?"

I chuckle, loving how we're able to converse about this like friends. "Not at all. You certainly don't need me. You handled everything perfectly. I'm just here to admire you."

Penelope triple blinks, and I wait for her to laugh my compliments off, but she doesn't. "Thank you." Her tone is strong, almost as powerful as when she was speaking with Vernon.

"For what?"

"I'm not entirely sure...maybe everything." She folds her arms across her chest, not to cut me off, but in a weird way it makes her appear even more approachable. "For not trying to step in and talk over me."

"It's not my job to do so. I knew you had it." Twisting my lips back into a flirty line, I tack on, "But if you ever do need someone to defend you, I'm happy to do so."

Our gazes hold on to each other, as if testing the other, and a flicker of heat kindles between us. I could say so much more. Like how adorable she is when she's mad and she pushes that pouty lip out. How I find myself staring at it. How I'm secretly glad for myself that this deal wasn't swiped away from her, because it means I can continue to work with her—for now.

I could go on and on, but I don't.

Because she's not a woman who needs a confidence boost. She clearly can handle everything she needs to do, and I'm happy to be here, along on her journey.

"I finished up the last of my tasks." I hike a thumb over my shoulder, pointing back down the hall. "I replaced that guest room window panel. I'll change out that last beam tonight after you leave, just in case there's any safety issues. Then I think you're ready to show the place." My voice cracks, as I waver between admiring her and already missing her.

"Oh." Her lips form a perfect circle, and I struggle not to stare at them. "That's great news. I'll be able to share that with Jin when I call him."

"Yeah, I don't think any of our efforts are wasted. Like I said before, once he hears about the love letters, I think you can convince him to stay the course."

"Right." Her words are quieter than normal, dropping into a low murmur, "Now to find the perfect buyer."

"Well, if this was a Hallmark movie, you'd buy it, move out of the city, run the place as your own, and fall in love with the handsome man who helped you fix it up."

"Ha!" Her head jerks back as she adds another chuckle. "Like that's happening. I have no funds to buy a place like this."

It's not lost on me that her first rebuttal is about the bank and not about falling in love with me. "The bank has lots of money."

"Yeah, they aren't going to lend any to me when I have no idea how to run a hotel."

"Well, then I think your next best bet is to scope out a local buyer, one you can sell this story to. If we can convince them they need it, we can make the connection to Jin and prove Vernon wrong for good. You can still fall in love with the local handyman—"

"Great idea." Her tone is sarcastic. "Do you happen to know any local billionaires who want to buy a hotel?"

"Billionaires who want to buy a hotel...no." I steel my chin, acting like it totally didn't sting that she so easily dismissed my flirtation. Maybe she's distracted with everything piling on to her plate, but it still deflates my ego. Even so, I'll do everything in my power to help her. "You should start with calling your client to make sure he isn't double playing you."

"You are right." Her lips purse out. "I'll take care of that right now." She whips her phone out of her pocket, determination washing over her expression. She presses the contact number and puts the phone to her ear, glancing my way and then averting her attention to the floor. "Yes, hello, Jin? I know this is random, but it's about the hotel. I was speaking with Vernon. He seems to think you're about to sell to a chain. I've been working on it, and I would hate to see it sold to someone who—" She stops talking abruptly, and listens before saying, "It's not moldy. Did Vernon tell you we found mold?"

There is a long pause, where her brows bunch together, and then she adds, "I'm not in trouble with my business. I'm calling because I thought maybe you will understand the real opportunity. This hotel has these secrets that we're uncovering—" She stops, rolls in her bottom lip as she listens, and then a reluctant sigh drops from her lips. "I understand what a money pit the place has been, but it will be worth it."

Another long pause, and then: "What do you mean you're meeting Vernon for dinner? He just left here," she says, but the phone has apparently gone dead because she drops it to her side and flashes me a look of forlornity, speaking in a small voice, "He hung up on me without giving me a chance to explain what is happening here." Penelope's brows lower in concern as she stares off into space. "I think he's going to need some more convincing."

"I can be very convincing." I tip my head forward, hoping she gets my drift. "How about we go for a drive?"

A mischievous spark gleams out of the corner of her eye as she nods her head. "I'll drive."

Twenty-One

Penelope

With the way my heart is slamming against my chest wall, I grip the steering wheel like it is the safety cord to my parachute. I absolutely feel like I'm free-falling.

"Relax, they're probably just networking," Logan says gently, his deep voice warm enough to distract me for a few seconds. "You know, trying to figure out what future projects they can collaborate on?"

I give him my best I'm-not-buying-it look, but it only makes his smile tilt wider. "This is *not* networking." My eyes fix on the glow of the restaurant up ahead like it is the scene of a crime. I try my best to slide down in my seat as I get ready to drive by the front of the place. "This is poaching. And I swear—"

"Lo," Logan interrupts, calmly and maddeningly reasonable. "You can't drive while crouching down like that. You'll get pulled over. Not to mention killed."

I give him a huff and sit up straight, right as we align with the front patio. My stomach turns, like my body has some homing detection system. Sure enough, he's there. "He brought him to my spot. This is where I take my clients," I say with a groan. My lips whoosh to the side. When exactly did I become a groaner? This whole experience of dealing with Vernon is making me act completely out of character. Dragging my hand down my face, I whimper, "If I lose Jin, I lose my commission. I won't have the seed money to start my own business."

"We don't know what they are talking about yet." Logan's face presses to the glass on his window as he also studies the scene. "We need to get closer. Can you find a parking spot?"

"Can I find a parking spot on one of the busiest streets in New York City?" I turn the corner and head to the private parking lot, reserved for patrons. There are no spots left, and I drive to circle the block to get another glimpse of them. I groan again, this time adding a healthy thunk of my head slamming against the back of my seat. "Logan, I'm spiraling. I'm spiraling and spying. This is not what emotionally stable people do."

"Well, if it makes you feel better," Logan says, his voice filled with amusement, "I'm having fun. I guess I like emotionally unstable women who double as spies."

My breath catches, but not from his exact words. It's the inflection in his voice—firm, as if stating a fact more than teasing. I turn the corner at the end of the block again. For a moment, the only sound in the car is my thudding heart. Or maybe there's other sounds but I definitely can't hear them.

"You know you don't always have to do everything alone." Logan's voice is barely above a whisper. "You don't have to fix everything by yourself just to prove yourself."

I swallow a hard swallow as now my throat is dry, and a tad scratchy. I swallow again, making sure I'm not getting sick.

No, not really sick.

Just terrified of this conversation. I squeeze the wheel tighter. "I'm not trying to prove anything."

"Aren't you?"

Someone starts to back out right in front of me, and I slam on the brakes to wait for their spot. Logan's head goes flying forward, springing a smile on his lips. I take a hard left, and eagerly kill the engine, grab my things, preparing to take this spy mission inside. When I open my door to get out, Logan's unmoving, sitting in his seat staring at me. "What's wrong?" I ask, unsure what comes next.

But before I can get the words out, Pinsch Charming—who I forgot was sleeping in the back seat—launches himself into the front seat, landing squarely across my lap.

Laughing as the dog licks my cheek, Logan smirks. "See? Even he thinks you don't have to do everything alone. He wants to help too."

Holding the dog back with one hand, and swiping at the slobber on my face with the back of my other hand, I can't help but let a giggle leak out. Maybe everything isn't completely falling apart. Having Logan and Pinsch here is lifting my spirits in a way I didn't really ever feel before. Maybe—just maybe—some things are finally starting to fall *into* place.

Now if I can talk to Jin. Everything is going to be fine. I pat Pinsch's head. "Stay right here. I can't take you inside, but if you're good we'll find you a pup cup on the way home." I crack the window and shut the door. Logan and I approach the sidewalk at the same time.

"Get down." He motions to the ground as he squats and slides against the building. It's one of the funniest things I've seen in a long time. Since I was already holding in a giggle from Pinsch being silly, it's insanely hard for me to control my laughter. Following his lead, I crouch low and scoot along the wall behind the row of artificial greenery placed near The Hideout's patio. It's obvious because it's January, and the leaves are bright green.

Logan waves me forward and whispers, "Stay quiet and low. The patio is right on the other side of these bushes."

"You know I've been here many times, and I never noticed these aren't real shrubs." Perplexed, I stare forward, marveling at how clearly I see plastic stems on each leaf and twine wrapping the leaves to a chain-link fence. It should be nothing, but it seems like another veil being lifted on what I thought was my reality. "Everyone and everything is fake," I mutter under my breath.

"Shh," he says again, placing his finger to his lips.

Zipping my lips, I peer through the plastic leaves to the patio and shiver. It really is too cold to dine outside, even with the heaters the restaurant uses. I try holding my breath to stop the little visible puffs of breath coming out of my mouth, before they give away our hiding spot, but I can't hold my breath forever.

Maybe I'm not this desperate?

I've worked my tail off to get where I am with this company. I've already lost all my trust in Vernon. I need to walk away, but a part of me burns to catch him in this act of trust betrayal, to prove that he's the scum I already know he is. He'll never admit it and never apologize. I don't think I need that from him, but it's finding that closure. I'm not the one closing the door on something I worked so hard to open.

So, I huddle behind my shrub and peek out, scanning the patio for Vernon using my favorite dining spot to steal my client. I like to sit adjacent to the window, so I can glance in and people watch everyone inside. Sure enough, Vernon's changed his jacket to his deal-making sport coat, and he's sitting across from Jin. I hiss, "That's them!"

"Get down!" Logan places his hand on top of my head, physically moving me to a lower position. We sonorously drop to the ground, causing a bustling with the fake leaves. "He could recognize you, but he doesn't know me. I'm going to get a photo for evidence."

"What if he saw us?" I hiss again, and then shut my mouth when another cloud of breath flows out of my mouth from the frigid temps.

"This is how we die." His tone is serious, but a glimmer sparks out of the corner of his eye. He stays perfectly aligned behind his shrub and stares forward, holding his phone in front of his face with the camera on. "From the gardener mistaking us for part of the shrub."

"I doubt there's a gardener. These bushes are totally plastic. There's no need to trim them," I whisper-shout as I reach for the metal fence pole in front of my face. "Look, it's just a fence with plastic leaves—" but then cut myself off.

The nearest waiter pivots, turning his gaze toward us. I hold my breath, and crawl farther into the bush. I'm so close to the fence now my nose is pushed against it as I chant internally, "It's the wind. Please think it's the wind..."

It's not my lucky day, because the waiter takes several steps forward, and he is clearly focused on something. Before I can avert my gaze, I'm making direct eye contact with him. I drop my jaw open in shock and assert, "Abort the mission!"

Logan jumps up, pulling me with him, but I'm too entangled in the branches to get up with any ease. Instead, I so ungracefully slam my face into the fence post. My lips part from the sheer shock and adrenaline surge, and my bottom lip catches the fence post with enough moisture to stick.

"Let's run." Logan grabs my arm, attempting to yank me up, but with my lip attached to the fence post, I screech out sounding like some sort of animal getting murdered. All eyes on the patio shift in our direction.

Oh crud, I'm cooked!

There are not times to sit around and cry.

There are times to rip the Band-Aid off. It stinks to be me right now. I take a deep breath, sucking in all the courage I have because I'm going to rip my lip off. Placing one hand on the pole to steady myself, I hold my breath while jerking back on my head.

And I'm free!

Without wasting another breath, I push back off the pole to scoot out from underneath the fence shrub and take Logan's hand hovering over me and allow him to help me up. *Everything is happening so fast, but I happen to notice he's a very handsome hoverer.*

As soon as my hand slides into his, a sonic boom zaps up my arm. I don't doubt if we were in any other situation, I'd freeze from all the butterflies whooshing around my gut. My heart literally shoots rockets into my throat, and it's pounding out alarm sounds, telling me *to run!*

Hand in hand, we take off, scurrying along the outside perimeter of the place. My lip flames in heat as I pick up my pace to jog, steering away from the restaurant. Once I'm down a full block, I let out a defeated moan. "I can't believe you talked me into that. That was my favorite place to eat. I can never show my face there again. We didn't even get a chance to confront Jin before we got busted."

"Talked you into it?" He's wearing a full smile. "I didn't even know that place existed. You drove me. Plus," he holds his phone out in front of me. "It was worth it because I got an incriminating photo. When he denies he went behind your back, we have evidence."

Exhaling several times, I wait for my breath to even, letting everything that happened in the last few hours sink in there. I can't believe I stooped to this level. I was so determined to prove Vernon can't be trusted. Shaking my head at the fake leaf still attached to my jacket, I brush it away, wishing it was that simple to brush off this embarrassment. Logan has to think I'm insane... "What do you think? Should we head back to the hotel?"

His gaze pins on me with the most serious concentration lines between his brows. "I think I need to tend to your lip."

"What?" My cheeks heat, my eyes threatening to shoot from their sockets. I know we've been flirting, but that's super direct. Plus, that waiter could be chasing us. "This is not a good time for kissing," I hiss.

"Kissing?" he echoes as his brows bunch together, nearly crisscrossing. "Your lip is bleeding. I was wondering if there is a drugstore nearby."

As if on cue, a coppery scent swirls in my nostrils. My hand finds my throbbing lip, and I brush my fingertips against it. When I pull them away, fresh blood is on them. That's not good. Now I'm even more embarrassed about my random kissing assumption. "My apartment is a few blocks." I motion to the north.

"Sounds good." He nods in agreement. "Let's grab Pinsch, and we can stop there."

My feet align with his, oddly, relief flows from my gut into my breaths. It doesn't make sense. I didn't solve my problem. Vernon's still back on that patio stealing my client, and I didn't get to even talk to him. I've likely lost the last paycheck I'll get. When I look a little further inside, my relief isn't centered around Vernon. It's a feeling I experience when I look to my left and see Logan walking next to me. I'm getting used to his company and his friendship. Maybe I'm not winning at life. I'm actually really sucking at it, but it feels nice to not be alone while I fail.

"Thank you for not being weird about what happened." I lead the way up the cement steps to my sixth-floor apartment. "I'm good with public embarrassment for one day."

"You have no need to be embarrassed at all." Logan walks with Pinsch, following along behind me, as we round another corner and start the final flight of steps. "I admire you for how you're handling this whole thing with Vernon."

"Admire?" I echo, smashing the pads of my finger to my lip to stop the trail of blood from oozing down my face again. It stings like white-and-blue fire, but I freeze my face to prevent showing any signs of my physical pain.

"Don't sound so surprised," he calls from behind me.

We make it to the top floor, and I cross the hall to my apartment, taking the time to unlock the door. Unsure of how to respond to his kind words, I'm quiet. He's more than likely saying that to cheer me up. Nobody in their right mind would admire a lunatic who accidentally freezes their face to a fake bush.

"Come on in," I say, waving him forward as I push the door open. "Welcome to my humble home." Pinsch Charming scrabbles through the door first, his tail wagging at top speed, and he pauses to loiter in the little foyer with a cautious tilt of the head. Logan follows him, taking in my micro space with a smile. It's not unusually small for a New York City studio apartment—maybe three long steps from one side of the room to the other— but I'm proud of it. I bought this place with no help from anyone. It's my one safe place.

"It's cute," he says, turning back to me after doing an eye sweep of the place. "And exactly what I pictured."

"Let me guess," I say, walking toward the only other door in the place, my bathroom. "You imagined confined, overpriced, and that my bedroom doubles as my living room, and my desk is also my dining table?"

Logan's easy laugh rolls out. "Exactly."

A chuckle rolls out of my mouth as I understand the absurdity of it all. I love living in New York. I can't imagine being anywhere else. I motion to the neatly made futon pushed up against the only window. A white down comforter is folded and laid over the armrest, and an assortment of purple-and-gray throw pillows are perfectly positioned to look as if I had tossed them into place. "You're correct. As you can see, over here you'll find my living-slash-sleeping area. I like to refer to it as my sit or slumber suite."

"Nice." He walks over to look at the photos taped above my bed. For a moment, I pause. I'd forgotten those were there. They aren't anything too personal, but they also aren't anything I show people. "These yours?"

"That's my mom and me. The only photo I have of her before she passed." My breath grows shallow as it always does when I speak about my mom. Turning away from him, I pretend to check on Pinsch, who has found a spot to lay right in front of the door.

"You look like your mom." His words sting the piece of my heart where I've desperately tried to tuck all those memories away. "And you were young in that photo. It must have been hard to lose your mom at that age."

"Like seven or so." By seven or so, I mean seven years and six days. I still remember everything about the week of my birthday so perfectly. It was the week everything changed. One day, I was celebrating my birthday and posing for that photo, and the next week I was in foster care, living a nightmare.

"What is the black heart for?" Logan's fingers hover over the black heart I scribbled directly on the wall above my pictures.

"Ah, it's hard to explain." I scratch an itch that isn't on my chin as I ponder if I should tell him exactly how weird I am. "It's, uh, just...I use a black heart as my symbol. I obviously have a heart, but people have sort of used it the wrong way, like Vernon most recently. There's a string of people before him, mostly from growing up in foster care," I speak quickly, hoping my explanations satisfies his curiosity.

"So, when you said before you don't have any family, you really meant it, huh?" He's still staring at the heart and does something I never would have expected. He places his palm in the center of it. His hand is large enough that he nearly covers it all, and I stand back and watch in horror as I'm now wishing I hadn't opened my apartment up to him.

"Not that I'm in contact with," I try to talk, and pretend I don't notice how carefully he's still examining my drawing. "I think I have an uncle or two, but I was little when I was put into the system, and I guess I've always had the attitude that if they didn't care to keep tabs on me when it would have mattered the most to me, then I don't really need to go banging around on those closed doors now." Desperate to divert the conversation, I take a step toward the wall and speak in my best tour guide voice. "And here we have my world-class kitchen. One stove burner that doesn't work if the bathroom light is on. Don't ask me why. A mini fridge that works, but since I don't cook, all you will find is bottled water and my coffee creamer. But the microwave is unbeaten."

Logan leans one broad shoulder against the wall, a playful smile grows on his face. "So, you don't ever use that kitchen."

"I mean..." I glance around sheepishly. "Define 'use.' Do I make food from scratch? No." I channel my best Vanna

White as I gesture to the microwave again. "But it's an excellent resource for heating up leftover Chinese food"

"I'm impressed."

"You should be. As you can see, it's a very exclusive floor plan. Sure, it's not much, but it's mine." I offer a sheepish smile that tugs at my lip, causing me to wince.

"Oh, your lip." He must have caught my wince and motions to the bathroom behind me. "Did you say you had a first aid kit, because it's bleeding again."

"Surprisingly, I do have one." I go into my bathroom to grab my kit, since that's the sole reason we stopped here. I catch a glimpse of my face in the mirror and almost gasp. I didn't realize my lip had bled that badly. Dried blood is smeared on most of the lower half of my face. Logan never said a word. I grab a towel from the rack, run it under warm water, and attempt to wipe the blood off.

To my amazement, Logan comes up behind me with his arms outstretched. "Can I help you?"

My overindependence kicks in, and I move to block him from coming into the bathroom. It's silly to need help washing my face. The look he's giving me is so tender, my heartbeat kicks up a notch, causing me to hesitate. Before I can do anything else, I find myself handing the towel over to him.

His fingers brush the tips of mine. I can't help but think he is intentional as he holds his hand in pause for a heartbeat too long. Warmth floods my body, freezing me in place as he raises the towel almost to my lip. "This might sting."

"It already does," I whisper with a weakened voice that is not from the pain, but from the heated way he's looking at me. Logan's smile is soft as he places his thumb to rest against my chin as an anchor, and the rag touches my lip—warm at first, then turning to a dull burn. I inhale sharply but don't flinch. His hand is gentle. Oddly, even though it burns, his touch calms me.

"There," he says quietly, his eyes flicking from my lip to my eyes, holding my gaze as if tasked with the job of discovering a deeper layer inside them. I've never had anyone stare at me like this—so deeply, as if they are truly seeing me. Goosebumps dot along my spine. Magnetic forces take over my body, begging me to lean closer to him. "You are all clean," he whispers as he hands the towel back. "And still beautiful."

My heart slams against my chest so hard, I no longer feel my lip throb. I can't find even one single word to mutter. "Maybe don't try that stunt again." His voice dips low and attractive. "I kind of like your face the way it is."

My breath catches in my throat. He continues to gaze at me, letting the words settle between us—gentle and warm as the remnants of his touch linger on my chin.

Warmth floods my chest and travels up my neck and into my ears. I literally feel my ears glow. This tiny bathroom is barely big enough for one person, let alone two packed in here together, sucking up all the air.

It's hot in here!

He doesn't back away, and to avoid getting lightheaded, I take the only tiny step I can backwards.

Thunk.

That was me, and I yelp as I topple backward—tripping on the corner of the toilet and landing squarely in the shower.

Logan freezes as if dumbfounded. "Lo?"

From inside the shower, my voice actually echoes. "That was...planned. Obviously. I'm continuing the apartment tour with a fast look inside my shower. You can see how I keep the tile so expertly clean with Scrub and Bubbles."

He steps forward, laughing as he draws back the shower curtain and peeks in. "Are you okay?"

My cheeks flush even warmer, but I manage to steel my shoulders back. "Like I said before, the place has an exclusive floor plan. Everything is right at your fingertips. This shower here is like one of those automatic ones, you don't even know you entered it."

Logan's shoulders bounce as he struggles to keep a straight face. "Is the tour over, or are you seriously trying to die today?"

"Oh, no. There's more." My eyes narrow into a playful slit. "Help me up, and I'll show you the best part of the apartment."

He reaches forward, offering his hand. "Here." Again, our hands connect hungrily and linger together as he pulls me up. My balance is slightly off. I'm sure it has nothing to do with this new weakness in my knees or how his arm brushes somewhat intentionally around my waist to steady me. And suddenly, amid the laughter, the room heats into a sauna again. This time, the lighting even seems to morph into a glowy warmth, making the moment feel almost magical.

"I think," he says while I'm still all too aware of his hand still on my waist, "this is my favorite apartment I've ever seen."

"Oh, you haven't seen anything yet." I give him a look, half-embarrassed, half-flirty. "Wait until you see the roof..."

Twenty-Two

Logan

Lo is still brushing her fingers against her lip when she stumbles out of her bathroom and stops in front of her futon. "Okay, I'll show you my favorite place, but you should feel special because I've never brought anyone else up here before, and you have to promise not to laugh."

I can't help but chuckle. "I don't know. After that toilet flip, I don't think I can make that promise."

"Please, that was all planned as it's the easiest way to enter the shower." She playfully rolls her eyes, and steps on the stool in the kitchen until she reaches a handle on the ceiling and pulls on it, opening the door to bring down the attic-style stairs. They unfold until they reach the floor, and she starts to climb them, calling back, "Follow me." I'm quiet as I trail her. She pushes open the metal door at the top. The city opens up like it's one of the best kept secrets for those who can see it from this view.

It's not a fancy deck—no firepit or lounging furniture, just some worn pavers—but with New York as the backdrop, that's all anyone needs. My jaw drops as I watch the horizon bathed in the early evening sunset making everything golden. The skyscrapers appear to be burning on one side, and the city doesn't slow as people and cars bustle below us. She plops down on a cement ledge that runs the length of the roof, leaving enough room for me to sit too. "And now you know why I needed this apartment," she says with a content smile.

I select my spot, purposely positioning our shoulders so close, they almost graze against each other. I wouldn't have to sit that close. The deck is small, but there could be room for me to scoot over. I can't help but want to be near her. When I glance at her, the soft glow of the sun hits the side of her face so perfectly, she looks like a movie star doing some cameo on stage. Yet, her expression opens in a way I hadn't seen before. It's not the silly one from downstairs when she was doing her tour. It's almost also not the business one from back at the hotel. Something tells me this is really her.

My chest constricts, not in a way that demands medical attention, but like it's drawing a boundary for me, warning me what I'm about to say might change things. I'm not scared to tell her how impressed I am by her. If I'm honest there's something deeper than being impressed brewing inside me. It's how I can be so close to her with our shoulders almost touching, but it's not near enough. "It's perfect," I finally manage to say.

She smiles her authentic smile. "I know."

"So, question about that black heart." I purposely pause there, giving her time to react. She didn't seem like she wanted to speak much about it earlier, but I've got a few questions.

Her throat twitches from a swallow. "Yeah, go ahead."

"You said something about how it was from the people who mistreated you. You made it seem like it was mostly foster care situations, but you haven't really spoken about romantic relationships. I'm assuming you don't have a boyfriend, since he's never around, but I don't know." I blow out a breath as I struggle to find the right words to ask how it all ties together. "You work a lot. I guess, I'm wondering if you think you'll ever let yourself fall in love."

She smirks, leaning back as she crosses her arms and peers over at me. "Wow, that was some deep questions for a guy who's *assuming* I don't have a boyfriend." She lets that linger in the air for a beat before tilting her head. "You're right. I don't have a boyfriend, and I work a lot. As far as the black heart goes, of course it's there as a symbol of all my failed relationships. And as for falling in love, I guess . . . it always feels more like risk than like I'll receive any benefit." Her gaze flicks to mine, playful but direct. "Are you volunteering for the position, or making conversation?"

"I like it here," I say, and then I wince when that doesn't sound right. "I mean; this day has been strange but oddly good. It may seem sort of random, but I need you to know it's been great."

She turns toward me, all the light firing behind her, and she looks like an absolute goddess as her eyes pace over my face.

"I'm starting to like you," I say, slower this time. "You're funny and smart and strong, and you stand up for yourself. You froze your face to a fence, and you fell into your shower, and somehow that made me like you even more. And you're actually lucky you froze your lip, or I'd definitely try to kiss you with that sunset..."

Her lips bend into a stunned smile. "You like me because I fell over a toilet?"

Chuckles bubble up from my gut, and I drop my head into my hands, and rub my forehead. "No. I already liked you. That pretty much sealed the deal."

"I'm starting to like you too." Without warning, she leans her head over, pressing her cheek into my shoulder, causing my heart to ramp up in a way I could never be prepared for. She whispers into my arm, "I'll take a rain check on that kiss..."

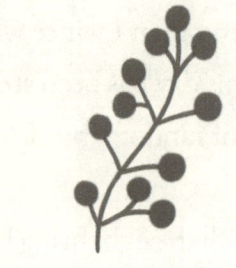

Twenty-Three

Penelope

Back in the car on our return to the hotel, the hum of the road noise fills the car, padding the awkward silence that's gone on with all the words we dared not to speak, including us almost kissing. Outside, the moon rests lower tonight, bringing in a silvery glow. I keep my hands on a perfect ten and two, even though I haven't driven like that since I passed my driver's test in high school. It's as if my whole body is alert to the mood changing between us.

Pinsch took extra time to settle into the back seat this trip as he already had enough napping. He mostly seems content to stare out the window, but that might be because I sacrificed an old pair of flip-flops I'd found at my apartment for him to chew on. He's not chewing as much as he's holding them in his mouth, pretending he's captured some prey.

Logan appears more at ease, one elbow propped against the door, casually leaning. He hasn't said much since we left my roof deck, where we'd sat a little too close and joked about kissing.

Where nothing actually happened.

Yet it feels like something shifted.

Now every other thought is about us almost kissing.

"So," I clear my throat, eager to fill the thick silence, "Thank you for coming with me to spy on Vernon. You certainly didn't need to, but it was nice. I appreciate you doing that, even though we didn't actually confront him or convince him of anything."

He smirks. "The pleasure is all mine. I'm glad I got to see your exclusive bathroom tour."

I catch the teasing in his eyes, but I also sense something else. That quiet question neither one of us dares to ask.

What is happening between us?

It burns in my chest in a way that feels like I'm living more than dying. Yet, I can't bear to bring it up. I'm too vulnerable. "You should feel privileged you got such a fantastic tour," I tease, raising my chin.

"I do," he says, hanging on to the last word like he isn't quite sure if he should add a joke or not. His voice grows quiet. "I'm honored you shared your space with me."

Working overtime all night, my heart takes a traitorous shift—ramping up even more. It's too overpowering, stealing a pending word from my mouth. We drift back into silence when we hit a clear long stretch of highway.

Out of my peripheral vision, I see him shift in his seat, leaning closer toward me, his hand moving over on our shared armrest like he's about to reach for mine. I tighten my grip on the steering wheel, and he pulls his hand back to his lap. "Tonight was nice." He's quieter now.

Not used to being so open, I hesitate. He seems so confident to pass compliments my way. It's not something I've ever found easy to do or share. I'm more comfortable with teasing, so I stay in that lane. "Aside from freezing my lip off, it was."

He smirks again, bringing his hand back to the shared armrest. "I almost—" He pauses. "Never mind."

My heart throbs in my chest. I know what he almost said. I know he almost kissed me and almost reached for my hand. Something inside me beats like a bass drum, warning me to pull back.

Maybe it's the timing.

Maybe I'm terrified.

Okay, I am terrified.

But not of Logan.

Logan hasn't given me even one single reason to be terrified. He's one of the sweetest most gentle men I've ever met. It's like there's this looming invisible border with a giant warning sign on it that says, "Once you cross this line, you won't be able to keep your walls up anymore."

I'm not sure I can change things between us.

Because once I get a glimpse of what something more would be like, I wouldn't be able to give that up so easily, and we live two very different lives, in two very different places. I've worked so hard to build my life in New York. I can't turn my back on that dream.

After hours of silence, I turn into the hotel parking lot. Except for Logan's truck, it's empty. A single glowing street-light in the corner lights the dark sky like a promise, or maybe something worse, a warning. My tires roll to a stop, and it feels like the seconds are taking hours as I shut off the car and proceed to remove the key.

He's staring at me with such intensity, it almost takes my breath away when he whispers, "Penelope."

I slowly turn to him, my quivering hand clenching my keys.

His lips part, then close again. A long beat of silence passes. As much as I had told myself I don't want to change anything between us, because I now wholeheartedly believe it could ruin me, I yearn for him to hint at something.

On cue, Pinsch jumps out of the back seat, tail wagging as he lands on my lap. "Look who is excited to be back home." I find his favorite spot behind his ears to scratch.

"I guess so." Logan says, his voice light and airy. "It is pretty late."

Even though an ache in my chest pulses, I manage to smile. "Yeah, I'm definitely ready for bed."

"Yeah, me too. I'll see you tomorrow. Goodnight." Just like that, Logan climbs out of my car, not changing a thing between us. I'm left with a lap dog that doesn't know he's not the size of a lap dog, and he won't stop kissing my face. At least someone wants to kiss me.

Twenty-Four

Logan

I'm looking forward to the aroma of fresh paint and sawdust that greets me the next day at the hotel. I had a restless night, where I couldn't close my eyes without seeing Penelope's soft expressions and flirty eyes. Part of me feels we are on the same page, heading toward something amazing. The other part of me is cautious, reminding me we are working together. She might just be extra nice to me right now because of how much I'm helping her. My brain is warring with my heart. If my heart had its way, I'd have not only told her how much I was falling for her yesterday, but I'd have kissed her.

Sighing, I duck under a low hanging extension cord plugged into a generator that is currently off. My boots aren't exactly quiet as I stride forward, and Dad's voice calls out, "Logan." Not having expected him back here anytime this week, I startle and turn toward his voice. He's standing outside the kitchen door with his tool belt hanging off his hips, his open coffee cup in hand.

"Look who's back," I greet him, as I stuff my hands in my jacket pockets and shake my head.

Appearing extra stiff, Dad walks forward while motioning to his cup. "I brought the thermos of coffee. It's on the kitchen counter."

"That's good news." I knew he wouldn't stay gone long, but I'm doubting he's all the way better. I study his hand placement as he sips out of his mug. Sure enough, his other hand presses into the small of his back, like he can't stand straight without the added support.

I grab my tool belt and focus on that. "Did your doctor say it is okay for you to return with your back like that?"

I'm not surprised by his eye roll. "I don't need some white-coat-wearing prissy tellin' me when I'm allowed to work at my own business with my own back."

"You're a little hunched over still, Dad."

His eyelids droop lower than normal as silence swoops in and settles, heavy like those support beams I installed. "It's hard to let go," Dad says with an exaggerated sigh. "I'm not ready to retire. What am I going to do all day? I'm not the type to sit around the house." He crosses the kitchen, setting his cup on the counter with a little extra force. "I built Legend Builders. It did more than put food on the table. It gave me an identity. Plus, it was an awfully good income, putting you through architecture school. It's been a good life."

"I know what you built." I hope to infuse my tone with enough empathy he cheers up. "I've watched you hammer nails since I was in kindergarten. Remember how I used to sit in the cab of your rust-bucket Ford and watch you for hours? You don't have to tell me what this business is to you. I was there when you left before the sun was up, only to come home to dinner being over, and all you had was leftovers wrapped in tinfoil. I see what you've done. It's not lost on me." I look at Dad—really studying him as I think that's what this really is about. He needs some recognition for all the hard days. "But I also can see you're not standing straight. You lucked out this time. You'll likely heal up, but if you keep pushing your body like this, you risk damage that won't heal."

"What am I going to do?" Dad's jaw clenches and un-clenches. "Just sit around and wait to die?"

"No. Nobody is ready for that to happen. You let it be someone else's turn to do the heavy lifting. You find a way to do this a different way. Maybe you teach. Or consult. Or just go fishing every day. I have the best dock on the lake waiting for you to enjoy it. I think you might be surprised by all the things you will find time to enjoy if you let it happen."

Dad stares past me, out the kitchen window. "It's going to be hard." His voice is low. "I'm going to miss the work, but I think I'm going to miss seeing you every day the most."

"Dad." Surprisingly my voice cracks seeing my dad like this. He isn't one to ever be emotional. "That doesn't need to change if you don't want it to. You're always welcome to come say hi and bring my coffee."

"Perhaps." Dad pauses as he retrieves his coffee cup again. "I'll maybe take the rest of the winter off. You know winters are hard. Muscles are stiff."

"That sounds like a great start." I stare at him, waiting for him to make the first move as I hate rushing him. I can tell, by the way he avoids my direct eye contact, he's fighting back emotions.

Eventually Dad emits one of his famous grunting sighs. "I hate when you're right."

"I might have learned some stuff from you." I smile. When he doesn't say anything else, I have an idea. "You know. If you want a project to work on that won't hurt your back, I have something I can share with you."

He quirks an eyebrow. "You do?"

"Yeah, I can't believe I haven't mentioned it yet, but Penelope and I found two different love letters in the walls. They appear to be from the same person. We did a little digging and found a name, but I know if a person had a lot of time, they could find more. It's really fascinating."

In the background the sound of the front door shutting draws my attention, and my gaze cuts to the hall in search of Penelope. Her heels click on the floor, echoing as she calls out, "Morning."

"In the kitchen with Dad," I call back.

We listen as her heels click some more, and she smiles faintly as she steps in, brushing snow from her shoulders. "Boy, who ordered more winter?"

Dad's focus shifts to her, and he smiles bigger. "I don't know, but it looks like the day got a lot brighter since you walked in."

"Dad." I know what he is doing, but I'm too late to cut him off He's not one to flirt with anyone. He's happily married to Mom. This is what he does when he's getting ready to play matchmaker. He's been gone a few days and missed some things. He doesn't have a clue about the chemistry budding between me and Penelope. I don't need him buttering her up for me.

He ignores my tone of warning, and winks at me. "If you'd stop being so stuck in your past, you'd see how much brighter it was in here too."

Penelope tilts her head, giving me a curious smile, but she stays quiet.

Dad stares at me before shifting his gaze to Penelope and then back to me. It's like he's a mind reader. The glimmer in his eyes grows. "What did I miss?"

"Nothing," I murmur.

Dad's grin grows even wider, hinting he's catching on. "Well, if you want my opinion, those goofy grins on your faces aren't nothing—"

"About the love letters," I cut in, as heat flames on my cheeks. I focus on Penelope, filling her in on our morning conversations. "Dad's taking some time off from work, but I was encouraging him to research those letters. Do you still have them?"

"I do." She motions to her handbag strung over her arm. "I have them in my purse right here." After taking a moment to dig at the bottom of her bag, she retrieves the two wooden boxes and hands them over.

Dad takes them and immediately locks on to the craftsmanship. "Wow, look at that box. You can tell it's all handmade, and the lid had to be carved perfectly to slide in like that."

"Dad, open the box," I urge as I really don't care about the box itself.

Grunting, he slides off the lids, reading one letter at a time. With so many questions still circling my mind, I can barely hold in my words. Dad doesn't seem as confused as I would have thought. When he finishes the second letter, he simply folds it up and returns it to the box, handing it back to Penelope. "So maybe neither one of you have heard about the legend surrounding this hotel, and how it got its reputation for being a special place for Christmas celebrations." His chuckle is light, braided with hints of nostalgia. "People called him Bellamy, but that might have been his last name. I'm not sure if I ever heard a first name."

"Bellamy?" Penelope echoes.

"From what I remember, he certainly wasn't rich. He was a working man, hired to help look after the place. He was good at fixing things and making things, but every winter, you'd find him back in that workshop behind this place. Back then it was used more as a stable, but he liked to disappear back there and make toys out of the scraps he collected all year."

"Wait a second," I cut Dad off as I can already see where this is going. "This sounds like it's headed toward a fairy tale. I bet you're going to say people thought he was Santa."

"Nobody thought he was Santa. That's silly. He liked to make things out of the scraps and then open the stable to the folks to come and pick out what they wanted. You know, the families who had fallen into hard times. It wasn't a secret. Everybody knew it was him, and that's how this whole place got its connection to Christmas. Eventually they coined his little workshop The Toymaker's Stable."

"What does that have to do with the letters?" I ask, feeling like Dad is making this up.

"Well, rumor was that he was in love with the oldest daughter who grew up in this house. I guess after her father found out, he ran him out of town." Dad inserts a chuckle and shakes his head as he adds, "That didn't stop him from coming back every Christmas to hand out toys." He pauses to swallow and then adds in a lower tone, "I don't think he ever married. He spent his life being known as the Toymaker that loved his boss's daughter."

"That's heartbreaking," Penelope says, her voice quieter than ever.

A sharp bark echoes from outside, just on the other side of the kitchen wall. Dad angles his head toward the window, and then back to me, his eyes narrowing. "Why does that dog sound so close?"

"We found a stray dog in one of the rooms. There's a tag, and it says his name is Pinsch Charming, but no address."

"So, you kept him?" Dad's question comes out more like he's solving a riddle.

"We didn't officially keep him. We haven't found his home yet. Penelope's been taking him back to her hotel at night, but he seems to prefer it here. Like this is home. He's a great dog. Well trained and the hugest eyes you've ever seen."

Dad's bottom lip rolls in as he strides to the window and nearly presses his nose to the glass to peer out. "Good-looking dog there."

"He is, and he's very well behaved." Penelope agrees with a proud mama smile beaming on her lips. There's no way she can deny she has bonded with him.

Dad returns his gaze to me while rubbing the bridge of his nose. "You know I always wanted a dog, but your mom's allergic."

I grin, a little relieved, which is odd. I'm not sure why I feel like I'm fifteen again and trying to sneak a pet in. "Yeah, we are planning to call animal control, eventually. I guess we've been so busy, and he's so well trained, we've been putting it off because we're enjoying him, but he clearly belongs somewhere."

Dad tips his head back to the window again, sighing. "Maybe I'm wrong, but he looks like he belongs here."

"I was a little afraid of that." Penelope walks forward, peeking out the window too. "What are we going to do with him when the place sells?"

"He'll let you know what he wants to do," Dad says as he backs away from the window while hiking his thumb over his shoulder. "Say, back to those letters. Something popped into my head. I'm reminded of when I was replacing that trim." He walks toward the exit, waving us along, "Come with me for a moment."

"What did you find?" Penelope's fast on his heels, and I'm nearly sprinting.

"I noticed one of the boards is shifty. I thought it was junk like the rest of this place. I was going to tack it back down, but I got hurt before I could. Now I'm wondering if it is meant to do that."

We walk to the front lobby, and he points to the small piece of trim next to the fireplace. "There's an odd smaller piece of trim cut out and pieced back together. Dad bends over and presses lightly on it. I can't believe my eyes, but the section of trim falls forward, swinging inward, and there's no wall behind it. "It's a secret compartment." Dad marvels as he bends even more, trying to see inside.

I crowd the hole as well, digging my hand in, searching for the box. Inside is a narrow cavity that is big enough for my hand to fit inside but no extra space. Just like I had thought...a small wooden box. "There's another one," I exclaim as I produce the box, holding it out in front of us.

Dad's breath catches as Penelope gasps and says, "Read it."

I already know what it is, but it doesn't stop my hand from trembling. This box is covered in a lot more dust than the other ones. I take a moment to brush the top clean before I slide it off in the same manner as the other lids slid off. The letter is folded exactly as the first two, and I flatten the sheet out to read the cursive letters looped across the top of the page:

"My Dearest, I'm writing with trembling hands to tell you I've lost all hope of us ever reuniting. Father has announced he expects me to marry Eric Vonderwell. According to Father, Eric is an excellent match for me and has enough farmland for us

to live many generations. I do not love him. I love you, and I
refuse to marry a man who isn't you.

You once asked me before if I could run away with you. I was
too frightened of my father, but I no longer care. I wish to run
away to you.

Tomorrow is December 24th, and I declare at the first light,
I shall take the narrow path behind the stables, as you had
planned. If your promise still holds, meet me at dawn. I have
some money, my mother's locket, and my Cartier brooch that I
managed to hide away weeks ago. I'll retrieve them, and we can
sell them to start our new life.

Praying you'll be there in the morning,

A.D.

"Wow," Penelope's voice holds a heavy awe. "If we know they never married, then what do you think happened? Did she run away by herself?"

"Hard to say." I raise a shoulder and lower it.

"Wait a moment here." Dad holds up his index finger, inserting it into the air. "That letter said she was going to meet him on December 24th. That's the day the toymaker always came back to the stables. Every year..."

"Do you think he was coming back to meet her?" Penelope's voice pitches in excitement. "Would he really hold out hope all that time?"

Wonder seeps into my chest, as I really don't want to believe any other thing would be true. "I think he was. Maybe he gave the toys away as an excuse to bring him back here, but he was secretly waiting for his true love."

"Isn't that the most heartbreaking thing you've ever heard," Penelope's voice dips down at the end as her eyes lower back to the box.

Another loud bark pops off from the backyard, and Dad arches his chin to gaze out the window. "I might need to go introduce myself to this little feller out there. What did you say his name was?"

"The tag said Pinsch Charming," Penelope replies, her feet still cemented to the ground, as if she's too stunned to move.

"I love that name. So clever. Say, I'll be right back." Dad walks forward, letting himself out the back door. As soon as the door slams behind him, I turn to Penelope. "Dad always brings coffee when he works. There's a thermos you can share too. If you like it's in the kitchen." I motion down the hall back to the kitchen, but she's still, and her face is pale. "Is something wrong?"

She doesn't answer or move to acknowledge I even spoke to her. Slowly, I take a step toward her. As I watch her so still, and void of her usual sassiness, my heart seems to crawl in my throat. When I can't stand the silence any longer, I say, "I'm here if you want to talk about it."

She blows out a shaky breath, before saying, "It's really nothing, but hearing how she was waiting for him, and then maybe how he came back every year waiting for her, and they never reunited." She shakes her head. "It triggered something inside me." Her words break up before they fall off, and suddenly she's choking on tears.

I blink, unsure of what my place is, but I can't stand to see her cry. Clearly, it's jogged her own past heartbreak. More than likely some jerk who gave her trust issues. Anger bubbles from my gut all the way to my throat, but I stuff it back, refusing to let her see that. Instead, I move another step forward until I'm close enough to pull her into an embrace. I hesitate, my hand trembles as it hovers over her hip. I don't want to assume, but my heart begs me to hold her. I gently let my fingers graze her waist. "He's not worth it," I say, unsure of who's got her so upset.

Her breath hitches, unleashing more tears. "It's not a man like that...it's my father. He left right before my mom died. From the time I was little, Mom and I both waited for years for him to return. After she died, I knew in my gut he'd come back for me. He had to because I didn't have anyone else. I couldn't fathom how he would leave me to become an orphan. Obviously, since I grew up in foster care, he never returned. I thought I was over it, but I guess not...It's stupid to cry about it now. It was so many years ago."

"It's not stupid at all. He's your dad, and you loved him." I raise my hand near her cheek, offering comfort, and she instantly leans her face into my hand.

She sniffs as she wipes her eyes with the back of her hand. "Sorry, I didn't expect to be so triggered by that story."

"You don't have to be sorry, and please don't be. You're human."

Penelope's gaze catches mine, but her voice is barely a whisper, "Thank you for not saying I'm crazy."

I quirk a small smile as the silence in the room starts to feel different. She doesn't back away from me. I place my thumb on top of her cheekbone and swipe away her tears, one at a time until the last one is dried up.

She seems to study me, and my heartbeat ticks up a notch. I watch her watch me, and her gaze shifts from my eyes to my lips and back again. There's a long beat of silence, where I'm not sure what to do next. With no more tears to wipe, I let my hand drop back to my side, not touching her, but close enough to feel the warmth from her skin. The tension that's been building for the last couple of days rises between us. Or maybe it's been there longer than that? I think it budded the first time I saw her, and those morning walks to the coffee shop didn't help. We both felt it on her rooftop. That's undeniable.

I risk a bit of a flirty smile. "I never had a chance to ask how your lip was feeling today."

Her smile softens. The air is thick with possibility. It's like we're pulled together by an invisible force, both of us leaning forward at the slowest setting. I can't stand to rush the moment, and I pause when her breath starts to mix with mine, and I whisper, "Are we really going to do this?"

She returns my whisper with a breathless, "I think we are."

"You know if I kiss you, you're going to have a crush on me." I'm slow to slide my hand along the small of her back, drawing her closer. She seems to melt into my arm as if she needs the support.

"Remember, I have rules about crushes..." Her words fall away as our lips finally cave together into a perfect and patient kiss, like we both expect to have years to practice.

She pulls away first but allows her forehead to fall forward until it reaches mine. I hold her for so long, I forget what time it is, as it seems the holding is what she needs the most. After the most beautiful lingering moment I've ever shared with another human being, her pocket vibrates. "Your pocket is calling," I whisper when she makes no attempt to move.

"I heard it, but I didn't want this moment to end." She sighs heavily—and dramatically IMO—and witheringly says, "I hate I have to get this right now, but it's my boss. I'm sure he's going to tell me he officially stole Jin..."

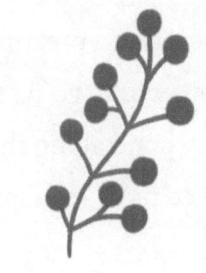

Twenty-Five

Penelope

Masking my heartbreak and frustration, I force an energetic voice, "Hey, Vernon."

"Penelope," his slimy, used-car-salesman voice wafts through the phone. "I got some great news."

I could certainly use some great news, but I know that great news from Vernon simply means it's great news for *him*. He's not capable of celebrating anyone but himself, and I hold my tone steady. "What is it?"

"Well, good news for me, anyway," he boasts and my brow bends down. I called it. Great news for him. "Jin has accepted an offer on the hotel. Super 7 Economy Hotels has agreed to purchase the property for a quarter million—"

"A quarter of a million?" I cough. That's a mere fraction of the asking price. My hand flies to my chest, as my heart literally screeches to a stop. To prevent my hand from trembling, I squeeze my phone tighter. It's not even about the commission at this point. They couldn't have found a slimier hotel chain to scoop it up. Super 7 Economy Hotels practically come with bedbugs. If I had known they were going to buy it, I would have left the rodents. I get this hotel is old, but it's so much more than its age. It has so much history and value beyond its years. Super 7 will never honor that. My voice is tight. "You know this is my listing and my client. I don't appreciate you going behind my back."

"You know how it is. The longer a property sits on the market they lose their value, and the rumors of rodents got out. There wasn't anyone else standing in line. You weren't getting it sold, and it was headed to foreclosure, which I can't have on my agency record."

Rising fury floods my veins as my face heats, and I take a deep breath. I should maintain professionalism. Play the game, so to speak. But I've done that for years. I've finally hit that proverbial wall.

I can't do this anymore.

I can't suck up to Vernon.

I can't pretend he's doing the right thing for the community or even Jin.

I certainly can't work for him anymore.

Hotel commission or no hotel commission, sometimes you need to take a stand. My eyes are literally burning when I spit out, "You know what, Vernon? I'm done."

A snarky chuckle comes through the phone. "Come on, now. Don't get all sassy. This is a win for you because it's a win for me."

My head tilts to the side. Who even says stuff like that? A win for me because he wins? I've never met a more egotistical man in my life, and statements like that only fuel my certainty. "Yes, Vernon, I'm done. If you want to play these games and call them 'business,' go ahead. That's not how I do business. I have integrity."

Another chuckle blasts through the phone, this one a little haughtier. "What are you even blabbering about? It must be your time of the month again, huh?"

A hiss slips out of my mouth from the sharp inhalation. I don't hesitate to end the call and drop the phone to my side. My heart pounds in my ears, reminding me I just quit my job and have no income... Oddly, my breath becomes lighter, and the weight that's been pressing on my shoulders for weeks seems to almost lift. Maybe it's an adrenaline thing and will likely come back heavier later, after I've had time to process everything, but as of right now, I don't care about the consequences.

I did what was right.

"You quit your job," Logan's voice breaks the silence, startling me, as in the heat of the argument, I'd forgotten he was even here. I turn around, facing him. My first instinct is to keep my face hard as I'm strong. I know I'll get through this, but one look at his downturned lips and soft empathic eyes, and I melt. "I guess so."

I wait for him to drill me about what my plans are to do next. Nobody in their right mind would quit a job without a plan, but he doesn't. Instead, he pulls his lips into his easy grin and says, "I'm proud of you."

With my head held high, I grin my biggest smile back. "Me too." I let out another heavy breath as I scan the place, not quite sure what to do with myself. It doesn't make sense for me to stay standing here when I quit. If I had been in the office, I would have stormed out to make a big scene, but I'm not in the office. I'm in this hotel, which I've grown very fond of. I'm standing next to Logan, who just kissed me for the first time... "I, uh, guess I'm done here."

Unprepared for the tears that stack up behind my eyes, I blink several times. So much emotion comes flooding to my brain. It's not even about quitting my job. I wasn't ready to leave this place or Logan—not like this! I stare at Logan. "Thank you for all your help. I'll make sure you still get paid..." My words fall away as my voice cracks, and I squeak out, "I'm sorry, I had no idea this was going to end this way."

He opens his mouth to speak but then closes it before any words come out. When he opens it again, the words that come out are even and controlled. "How about I help you make your final rounds to lock up."

"Yeah, I don't think I have much to do as I cleaned everything. Maybe I'll make sure there aren't more dogs hanging out." It's hard for me to tear my gaze from his. There's so much left unsaid between us, especially now. I honestly don't know what to say. Hopefully something will come to my mind. I force one foot in front of the other and walk forward.

The afternoon sunlight shines brighter than it has since I've been here, coming in through windows, casting long shadows across the floor, and I follow them out the door. For a long quiet beat, I pass another look to him. The tension isn't uncomfortable, but it's there. "I hope the buyers appreciate what they are getting," Logan says in a casual way.

"You did excellent work."

"We both did." We couldn't have walked any slower through the hotel, checking the place one last time. He collects his dad's thermos, returning it back to Jerry, when he finally comes in from playing with Pinsch. I say goodbye to him one final time. His dad leaves out the back door, and Logan and I return to the living room, where he lingers in the doorway, almost shyly. "Ah, it seems like almost yesterday when you nearly burned the place down with your candle."

I laugh, enjoying how he joins me. "It was yesterday." As soon as the laughter dies, my smile fades. I'm suffering to hold back emotional tears. I sulk to the coat closet and grab my coat.

Logan comes up behind me. At first, I thought he was going to offer to help me put my coat on but instead, his hand finds my forearm. "Are you really okay with this?"

"Of course. Vernon is a jerk. There's no way I can still work for him..." My voice trails off as a tidal wave of emotion slams in the back of my throat. I squeak out, "It's the best thing for me now to get back to the city and start over, and move beyond Vernon and his shady deals."

"What if..." Logan reaches forward, placing his finger next to my hairline. Something in the air shifts. Something gentle and raw as he proceeds to brush my hair back behind my ear while he whispers, "What if someone here accidentally fell for you."

Taken aback by the sweetness of the moment, I swallow. My chest constricts. I fell for him too, but it really shouldn't matter because I can't stay here. "Logan," I whisper, "my life is in New York."

"I know." His lips press together, and we stand arm's length apart, taking each other in. "You know if this were a movie, you'd buy this hotel, and we'd run it together, falling madly in love with each other, and have so many babies we'd fill this whole place up."

I look down, trying to hide the sudden rush in my eyes. Call it timing or life or even bad luck. There are many reasons why it's absurd. "Well, you're welcome to buy it. You'll need more than a quarter of a million to outbid Super 7. I'm sure you won't have any problems finding some lucky woman to marry and fill the place up with kids."

"Yeah." His reply is soft. "She won't be you."

I blink harder than I've ever blinked before, ignoring how sweet he's being. "So, I hate to ask but I don't have room for Pinsch in my apartment, and he seems to be content here. Do you mind checking on him for the next day or two? I'll call animal control to have him picked up."

"I'll make sure he's taken care of. Actually, from the way my dad's eyes were gleaming, I think I already have someone to help me with him. He might be exactly what my dad needs for his new retirement." He nods slowly, holding his lips together like he wants to say more.

I shift my weight from one foot to the other. With no other reasons to wait around, I reach for the doorknob. "Thank you again for your help. Not just with the house but for coming to spy on Vernon yesterday. That was sort of fun."

He nods once, deeply. "Thank you for trusting me with the place and for the...almost..."

A beat passes.

I let out a contented sigh, ready to start to put closure on this whole experience. I twist the doorknob, cracking the door open enough to let light spill in. We step out together. Everything feels like it's happening in slow motion. I pull the door shut behind us and force a satisfied smile. "That's it."

"I guess it is..." Logan stares down at me, his eyes wide. "It was a pleasure working with you. If you ever need any more work like this, don't hesitate to look me up. Or if you're in town, let me know."

"For sure." We share a quiet exchange of smiles. Not sad ones. More like the ones that come easy after time spent together getting to know each other, with enough tension to make direct eye contact feel like an electric zap to my heart.

Ting. Ting. Ting.

I freeze, lifting my ear into the light breeze as the sound happens again.

Ting. Ting. Ting.

"Did you hear that?" My voice is quiet as I'm still trying to listen. The night air is still, with hardly even a car out for traffic. I definitely heard something sound like it was coming from the side of the hotel. "It sounds like Santa," I joke, trying to lighten the mood. "Maybe he's coming to save us."

"I heard it too, but I can promise you it's not Santa. That was coming from down by the old stable." Logan's face darkens as he quietly sets down his toolbox and steps in front of me while he scans the grounds. After a moment, he peers back at me. "Why don't you get in your car and lock the door. I'm sure it's nothing, but I should check."

"Absolutely not. There's no way I'm staying here alone." I grab on to his arm, hooking my hand through it to assert my position next to him. "If you go, I go."

His fast glance in my direction hints of an oncoming protest, but he nods to the side of the hotel. "Let's walk this way."

Trudging forward, we round the side of the hotel, the one area I hadn't spent any time working on. There's nothing down there but deep snow drifts and a shuttered-up old stable. A crisp wind cools the tips of my ears as it stirs the evergreens that dot the landscape. I'm about to make a joke when we halt at the same time, our gazes slamming to the ground.

Footprints!

Not just footprints but huge, big man boot prints. They are fresh and lead all the way to the stable. "Someone's here," I gasp as my brain fires alarms at me. "Nobody is supposed to be here."

"These weren't here this morning." Logan bends low, studying the prints. "Do you think it's Vernon?"

"I highly doubt it. His ego's too big to bring him back to this little city, and I just got off the phone with him. There's no way he'd make it out here that fast."

His hand instinctively brushes against the small of my back as I continue to cling to his arm. My heart is slamming against my chest. "I've been here for over a week and never had the urge to go inside that old stable. Why would anyone want to trespass? You need a tetanus shot to even go in there."

Logan's jaw twitches, as he draws me even closer. "Do you know what's even weirder?" He doesn't wait for me to guess. "Pinsch didn't bark, and he's in that loading dock, or at least he should be."

"We need to go get him now."

"Yeah, we need to check on him." We trudge a little faster around the side of the hotel until we reach the fenced loading dock. As expected, Pinsch jumps up in excitement, coming right over to greet us. "Hey, Pinsch." I lower my hands under his chin to scratch him as his body wiggles in excitement. My heart hammers against my chest as I keep an eye on him, and the other on the surroundings. "Did you see anyone come back here?"

Of course, his answer is to wag his tail faster and jump on me again. I take that as a no and turn my attention back to Logan. "I think we should call the cops."

"You always think that."

"I do not, and what do you mean by that anyway?"

"You said that the night we found Pinsch. Can you imagine how silly we would have felt wasting some police officer's time for an adorable dog?" Logan nods toward the stable. "You can certainly go lock yourself in your car and take Pinsch with you while I check things out."

"No," I affirm, standing straight and moving closer to Logan again. "I will not be left alone, and Pinsch can come with us. Safety in numbers."

"Whatever you think."

We plow forward, and goosebumps dot my skin when I see only one set of footprints going in. "You do realize there are footsteps going into the stable, but not out..."

"Maybe they have a groundskeeper who is still on the payroll to keep the place up while it's on the market," he says in a chill voice. "Who knows, maybe they notified him they were selling the place, and he came to get some personal things before they change the locks. You know, I'm sure it's all logical stuff."

"You sure have an active imagination." My throat is dry as I cower next to Logan while Pinsch cowers next to me. We have to look insane, the three of us hovering in front of this little building.

"Says the woman who said it was Santa."

"Yeah, Santa would be better than this. This is actually creepy." The closer we inch to the stable, the more I decide it's a bad idea. The roof overhang sags low over the door, giving it an extra layer of concealment. The whitewash paint has long been gone. Rotted gray boards are exposed with only one single window next to the door, it's obvious the glass has long been shuttered and gone, making entrance to the place easy, as one could climb through the window. "It looks like the stable's been vandalized more than once," Logan says.

"Can't imagine they'd find anything but a mold infestation in there."

"Right." We pause at the door, right where the footprints end. The door is closed, but there's no evidence of a forced entry. "They had to have a key." Logan steps right up next to the door. "I'll knock."

"Great idea. Give them time to prepare to kill us."

Shaking his head, he raps on the wood a few times, calling out, "Anybody in here? I see your footprints."

Silence.

"If it was Santa, he'd leave through the chimney. Do you see a chimney?" I joke to lighten the mood. Logan doesn't even flinch, grasping the doorknob and pushing on it. When the door doesn't budge, he slams his body against it, forcing it.

"Now we look like the aggressive ones."

"It's fine," he mutters, his voice rasping. "This wood is so rotten; it will crack. As he speaks, the door unlatches and creepily floats open.

My eyes feel as if they are about to pop out of my head. I don't know why I don't run the opposite way, but there is a weird magnetism that pulls us in unison to peer inside. Except for the small amount of light coming in from the window and the now cracked door, it's dark. The scent of dust coats the air, but that doesn't stop Logan from lifting his jacket to cover his mouth like a mask and stepping forward.

A vision of me locked safely in my car with Pinsch while we jam out to Taylor Swift and let Logan handle the superhero stuff floats in my mind. Maybe I was being a little stubborn when I dismissed that option early? Right now, it feels like a perfectly valid option I should have weighed a bit better. "You see anything?" I call in, not because I want to go inside, but I also don't want to stand out here all alone.

"Rusted tools and dirty rags on a workbench."

"Oh, that must have been the toymaker's bench." Curiosity buds, and I lean my head inside, peeking around the corner of the doorframe. Afterall, toys aren't scary.

The bench is nothing more than a thick slab of disfigured wood. It's darkened, I assume, from decades of storage. Maybe it's against my better judgment, but I take one tiny step forward and squint to make out the tools. There's a tiny knife with a rusty blade. I know better than to touch that, but my gaze hooks on the small magnifying glass sitting next to it. With a sturdy wood handle, it looks to still be functional. My lips curve up when I see a row of the tiniest glass jars pushed up against the wall. Each jar is filled with something different, from screws to colored buttons, and even glass marbles. "Wow," I whisper as I study the jars, my mind placing each item on a toy. I can see the little wooden wheels on a train set, and the buttons would look adorable on a rag doll.

"How fun is all this." I've lost my fear for the place, and I take another step inside. Now I'm so close to the bench, I touch it. It wobbles with an audible creak in the wooden legs, but it's so intriguing. "This bench belongs in a museum," I whisper again with my gaze locked forward. I've lost sight of where Logan even is. When he doesn't reply, my gaze rises. All I see is Pinsch sitting studiously at the door. A whimper leaks out of his mouth, but he doesn't investigate farther inside.

"Nobody's here," Logan confirms as he walks back in front of the open door where I can see him.

"But the footprints?"

"It seems impossible for them to only be one set, but as you can see, this place is tiny, with only one room. There's no place to hide, and no one is here."

"There must be another exit." I take my phone, turn on the flashlight, and scan the walls. "He slipped out a back door or something when he heard us coming." I walk forward, the floorboards wailing under my weight—which makes me pause. I don't love that, but I keep walking. "Maybe it's like one of those old rooms with a secret passageway. We just have to find it," I joke, examining the walls for signs of a book or something that sticks out.

Logan chuckles, brushing cobwebs from above his head. "I don't think this place is big enough for secret passages."

Not ready to give up yet, I step even farther inside. Each footstep makes the floorboards groan, and I'm questioning all my life choices. Maybe I should give up dairy? I mean, I get this place is old, but I'm not that heavy. My thoughts fall away when my foot breaks through the floor, and I drop and scream, "Ah!"

"Lo!" Logan darts over, dropping to the floor where I'm straddling between two levels. One of my legs is in a small hole, while my body has fallen to the floor. "Are you okay?"

Wiggling my toes, I slowly pull out my leg. No longer trusting the floorboards, I'm careful not to move too much. "I think so."

He reaches around my waist, hoisting me to standing, not letting go once I'm back on my feet. We have the same idea, as we stare down into the hole my foot had cleared. Then we exchange a look. "Are you thinking what I'm thinking?"

Logan's gaze goes back to the hole. "Only one way to find out."

He drops to his knees, shining his phone flashlight into the hole. I stay right on his hip, leaning inside.

Darkness.

My voice returns to a whisper, "It's some sort of a cavity."

"Do you want to reach in?"

"I already took a turn, which means it would be rude of me to go again." I bump his elbow with mine. "Your turn."

He leans forward even more, studying the hole before he slips his hand into it and exclaims, "No way." I'm speechless as he pulls out a small wood box, exactly like the others. "Another one," he whispers.

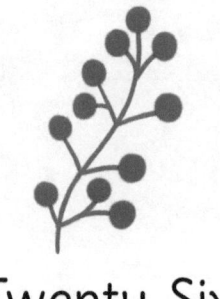

Twenty-Six

Logan

We exchange another look, our eyes wide with disbelief.

"Get the letter," Penelope impatiently urges. Unable to contain my excitement, I'm already sliding the lid off the box. Just like the last time, my fingers are unsteady. I've always had the steady hand of a carpenter, but I'm not cut out for this heartbreak stuff. There's a letter exactly where the others have been. I flatten it out, and read,

My Dearest Ammoret,

It's midnight, and your father's bedroom light just went out. I long for the day when I don't have to write these letters in secret, but for right now at least, this is how it must be. I talked to your father today, and he forbids me from talking to you again.

Though I don't agree with him. He wants you to have the life you deserve with riches and comfort, and until I can provide those things for you, he'll never approve.

I'll never believe love is something one needs to be protected from.

I will wait for you.

I understand if you give up, but I never will.

I am not leaving you. Not in my heart. Not in my hope. Not in our dreams to live a life together.

I will be where I've always been.

Yours.

Waiting for all life,

Forever your beau

"Wow," Penelope's jaw drops as her lashes flutter, appearing to blink back new moisture. "I would be sick to my stomach if I were her. He loves her so much, and it's not fair."

There are a lot of things in life that aren't fair. I'm not one to argue with that, but I can't help but feel ill as well. This letter has put me in a mood. One where all I can think about is how a few moments ago, I was kissing Penelope. Now we too are saying goodbye, but really, we aren't forced. Not like this. Maybe we are letting our own stubbornness get in the way, but a few hours' drive is nothing compared to what these two lovers went through. I clear my throat and ponder how to tell her my thoughts. It shouldn't be hard. We already kissed, so she has to know I have feelings for her. "It sort of makes you question why people—"

Her loud gasp cuts me off, as she points to the box and exclaims, "Look! There's a key inside. What do you think that's for?"

I turn my attention back to the box, and spy an iron key—old, ornate with a carved vine of flowers rounding out the handle. It's absolutely breathtaking. "That's definitely not a door key. It's huge."

"Maybe it's symbolic. Like he gave her the key to his heart." Her breath is shallow, bringing in dreamy inflections.

"They sure like their scavenger hunts." I breathe out a sigh of frustration. I have no idea how to find out what this key fits. Off the top of my head, I didn't find any random locked cabinets or anything at the hotel.

Glancing around, my gaze pulls back to the hole in the floor. Without giving it another thought, my eyes narrow and I reach back in. I can't feel anything, but my arm isn't long enough to reach all the way to the end of the hole. "I'm going to make the hole bigger," I say as I start to break away at the boards. Since they are already weakened, they easily crack off.

"I'll help." Penelope joins me, breaking off pieces of crumbling wood. It doesn't take long to reveal the shallow space beneath us. It's perfectly square, appearing to be made for a secret storage space.

With another box down here!

Penelope gasps, pointing as I see it. "Look!"

I'm already removing it, but this box is different than the others. It's metal, and much heavier than the other three. It's clearly an old safe because it has a giant lock on the front. It doesn't give us pause though, because it is unmistakably shaped to fit the old key. I hold the box between us and focus back on her. "You can do the honor of unlocking it."

"What do you think it is?" Her lip pinches together in indication.

"That's the only way we can find out."

She slides the key in and, as we both expect, it fits perfectly, giving a satisfying click when she turns it. The lock is released, and the lid lifts. "It works," she squeals in a hushed voice.

I'm blown away by what's happening and pause to catch my breath. She reaches forward, and we lift the lid together. I'm watching her first, enjoying the wonder on her face as her eyes swell round and her jaw drops. She's literally speechless, and I lower my gaze to see why.

There's a giant wad of money, an antique locket, and a Cartier brooch.

My lips part with awe, as my mind flashes back to the earlier letter about how Ammoret hid those things to help fund their new life. My heart sinks to a new level of low, drowning out the last of my hope that they ever made it out together. "It's her savings," I say, now blinking back my own tears. I'm not a crier. It's impossible not to feel like my heart is split open when it seems like these two went through so much.

Penelope's hand finds her chest, as she's watchful, not daring to touch the items. Her perfect lower lip trembles. Not enough to be obvious, but enough that I catch it before she sucks it in, trapping it behind her top lip.

There's sufficient light coming in from the door for me to latch on to her side profile. I study her skin, paler than normal. Perhaps she's cold? More than likely she's feeling as I am. Gutted. My hand actually burns as I fight the urge to reach out to her. Not that I can fix the situation for this couple, but I can do my best to comfort her. Stealing a kiss earlier felt right, but that was before we knew our time was up. Now it feels a bit more like I'd be using her for a moment of respite.

She blinks in the slowest setting. A tear falls on her cheek, catching the light before it slips. I'm no longer thinking about the letter. It's all I can do not to grab her and kiss her again. Kiss her sadness away.

In a hushed voice, like I'm praying, I say, "You're so beautiful."

A sharp sigh slips out of her lips, and her eyes shut fast and tight. "Don't say that."

"It's true." She's close enough I can touch her. I wouldn't need to take even the smallest step. I don't bother her though, as she seems to need space.

After many long moments, she lets out a sigh steeped in disappointment. "I really wanted to believe in this, and them. Like somehow, they made it happen."

"We still don't know how it ended."

"This is pretty clear to me. It says she found the letter and reburied it with her savings but never needed the money because she never left."

"Maybe it worked out in secret. Maybe they continued to see each other clandestinely over the years when he came back to make his toys. You never know."

She tips her head to the side, like it's weighing too much to hold up high. "It's a beautiful thought."

"It is." I lick my lips, an idea seeds inside my head, and now my heart is hammering against my chest. "Do you know what else is a beautiful thought?"

"What's that?"

I point to the wad of cash. "It looks like you have enough deposit money to start your brokerage."

She straightens her posture, placing a hand over her heart. "I could never take their money."

"I think you should." I speak slower now. She has to see how hard she worked for this hotel, and she got no commission. It's the only thing that's fair.

"It's not mine. It doesn't belong to me. It would clearly belong to the owner of the hotel, and that's Jin—"

"Who basically side railed you out of the contract he signed."

She stares at the cash for a beat before shaking her head. "It doesn't matter. It's not mine."

"I think they want you to have it."

"Who?"

"Ammoret and her toymaker. Think about it, how did we find all those letters, including this one with random footprints and no person. This hotel has existed for decades, why did no one else find the letters?"

"I don't know, but I'm not taking what doesn't belong to me." As soon as her words are out, she rolls her lips in, as if to seal off this conversation.

"They wanted us to find the letters," my voice ticks up in excitement as it all makes sense now. "They knew we'd be able to tell their story. I'm happy to preserve the letters and add them to my blog. I'm sure a museum will take the jewelry, but nobody needs to know about the cash."

Her eyelids lower as she stares at the ground. "It's dishonest."

"Maybe it is, but do you think Jin deserves it? He's a billionaire, who screwed you over. I think you're meant to have it, to help tell the story of this hotel and the love that existed between these walls, even after it's converted to a Super 7."

"Maybe I'm meant to use the money, but that doesn't mean I can take it and open a brokerage. How does that help them?"

"How do you want to help?" I ask, my brow furrowing together.

"I know it seems crazy, and I can't believe I'm saying this. It's the last thing I ever wanted, but to me, as I look at that money, it feels like I'm meant to use it to save the hotel. I can keep it as is, especially now since I know Jin went so low on the asking price. He's practically giving it away."

My heart, which had been puttering too hard against my rib cage slams into a screeching halt, skipping a beat, and I stutter, "A-Are you saying you want to buy the hotel?"

"Well, I still want to start my own brokerage, but I don't see how that would be hindered by this. When I think about letting this place go to Super 7, after everything we've learned about Ammoret, my chest hurts. Not just because of their love story, but because of everything that's happened." She turns her attention fully on me, her eyes shining bright. "I don't need a hotel. It's certainly out of my scope of practice, but it's Pinsch's home, and it could be my home, at least until we have time to figure things out. And maybe you'd want to come around some too."

Stunned, I blink as my heart does a triple backflip. I can't believe this is happening. All my reservations about how she feels about me spill away. I step forward, asserting my position next to her. "Are you being serious now or randomly brain-storming?"

"I…I'm serious. I agree with you. Jin doesn't need that money. He barely stepped foot in this place, and he would have never found it. I also don't think it's mine to use as I want. We were led to it for a greater purpose. I know for a fact Super 7 would level this little stable to dirt. I don't think Ammoret would want that. I can't think of a better way to use the money. Of course, it's not going to be enough. I'll have to get a loan for the rest, but if I can find a bank to get behind me, I'll go for it. Not for me, but for them."

If my arms were burning to touch her earlier, they are on fire now. I can't resist picking her off the floor, spinning her around. She laughs so sweetly when I do.

I'm laughing too when I set her down, my voice cracking when I say, "I'll be honest. I was pretending I was fine with you leaving, but I'm falling apart. I don't want you to leave. It's all for selfish reasons too. I know you deserve your brokerage, but I really want you here, because I could seriously fall for you." "I feel the same way." She beams back the most beautiful smile at me. "And are you saying you'll help me with this dump?"

"Put it this way. You will have a hard time getting rid of me."

"I hope so." Her eyes sparkle back at me for a long beat before she lets out an exasperated sigh. "I wish I could stay here now, but I need to beat Jin before he signs more papers, or my plan will be thwarted before we even start. Maybe I'll give him a call now and see where his head is. I don't think he was the one in a hurry to sign. I think it was all Vernon." She already pulled out her phone and presses it to her ear.

I walk toward the door, where Pinsch is still relaxing. He seems comfortable at the hotel, like he knows it's his home. He stares at me and sniffs at my feet. "What do you think, Pinsch. It looks like our lady friend might be sticking around for a while longer. I bet you're happy about that."

He leans forward, licking my shoes.

"Not sure you want to wash those. They aren't that clean." He huffs out a signature sneeze, and I scratch behind his ears. "Well, I'm excited to have her stay…" I stop talking because I hear Penelope behind me. Averting my attention to her, I ask, "What did he say?"

"Nothing. I didn't get to talk to him. His secretary said he has meetings all day. I must make an appointment with the earlier meeting being next week. I can't wait that long."

"So, what now?"

"Back to New York."

"This is starting to feel like *Groundhog's Day.*" A chuckle leaks from my lips as I clearly am enjoying the turn of events. "We just came from there."

"If I walk into his office without an appointment, he'll have to see me."

"Did you want me to go with you?"

She sighs, looking back at Pinsch, who I'm still petting. "I appreciate the offer, but I don't plan to stay long. Maybe one night, and it would actually make me feel better if you were here, keeping an eye on Pinsch. We still don't know where the footprints came from. Maybe someone will show up?"

"Nobody's here," I blurt out as my eyebrows furrow. "We both know that, but if it makes you feel better, I'll keep a watch over everything. I can also make sure no one from Super 7 shows up, even though I doubt they'd be here that quickly."

She scans the stable again. "I'd love to stay here and look a little more. Who knows what else we'll find, but I need to leave if I'm going to stop Vernon. I'll call you if there's good news."

She starts to walk forward, but I must make something crystal clear in case she has even a sliver of doubt. "You can call me if there's bad news too."

"Huh, why?" Her words seem to overlap.

I stare into her eyes, not blinking. "Because I want to be there for you."

Her eyes soften as the corners of her lips curl up into a gentle smile, and she throws up her hand in a nonmoving wave as she starts to walk away. "Deal. I'll call you either way."

Twenty-Seven

Penelope

If you'd have told me even a month ago that I would be crouched on the top floor of Jin's Midtown office building, waiting in the shadows behind a plant like some looney, I'd have laughed out loud. Today, however, this feels like a logical thing to do. I'm getting awfully good at spying. Today's plant, a lovely and tall palm. There's nothing artificial about this one, as it has a light woody scent wafting off of it. Though, I really wouldn't care if it smelled like garbage because it's perfect for me to hide behind.

Looking around at the sleek, modern furniture and the large windows with breathtaking views, I get a sinking sensation in my gut. Jin's decision to offload that hotel quickly makes sense. I mean, it's decrepit, falling apart, and out of the city. It was never a good investment for him. He's not one to mess around with historic buildings. He craves fast and shiny things.

Good thing for him I know someone who is a perfect match for that building.

I hope it's not too late. The elevator door dings open, and Jin steps off, strolling past his secretary, heading down the hall. Using it as coverage, I pick up the plant and scurry along after him. He reaches the end of the hall, opens the glass door to his corner office, and I glide in next to him. His gaze slides over, and he immediately puts up a hand. "I need to hire a security guard, don't I?"

My foot freezes midair, hovering like I'm some cartoon as I peek my head through an opening in the leaves. "Not if you start taking my calls."

"Look, I know you're disappointed, but I don't care to waste more time on that money pit."

I hold up my hand, flashing five digits. "Five minutes is all I need. *Please!*" I didn't plan for my voice to come out squawking in pure desperation. It is so forceful it startles both of us, and his head jolts back.

"Five minutes while you go over another hundred-thousand-dollar renovation quote with me? No thank you."

"No more quotes. Your heart wasn't in renovation, and I understand. That's why I'm taking it in a new direction. I want to buy it from you for the same price Super 7 offered you."

A heavy sigh leaks out of his throat, but I don't give him space to speak. "It's undervalued, but if you're practically giving it away to someone, you might as well give it to someone who cares about it."

A curious smile buds at the corner of his mouth. "You're saying you can come up with a quarter of a million dollars?"

"I'll figure out a way to get a loan. I might have to call in a few favors, that I'll more than likely regret." My voice drops into a low murmur as I recall the last time I called in a favor and ended up wearing an alligator costume to a charity ball when it was my turn to return the favor, but some things are worth it.

He starts to pivot on his heel, turning his back toward me. I'm losing him, so I rush out, "I've got some, uh, savings I can use for the down payment. You won't have to worry about the money. The point is, just please let me buy it for the same price!"

"What are you planning to do with it? It's a dump."

"Maybe you didn't hear? I quit my job at Vernon's brokerage. I still plan to do real estate, and yes, I don't have a plan for the hotel, but I have time, and I'm rambling but please give me a chance to keep that hotel local and historic—the way the town needs it to be." I don't say the last part, the way

Ammoret wants me to keep it for her. He doesn't need to think I'm talking to ghosts because he'll surely blow me off.

He parks one hand on his hip, offering a heavy sigh like it's the only thing he has effort left to do. "And what were you planning on doing with my plant?"

My eyes swell huge. I'd forgotten I'm still pretending to hide behind it. I quirk a silly smile. "I tried everything I could to get past your receptionist, but she's like a hawk with *zero* chill."

"All the more reason to hire my own security guard," he murmurs to himself.

Since my cover is obviously blown, I lower the plant to the ground. "To be honest, I hated that hotel the first time I saw it. I saw the same dump you did, but Vernon talked me into taking that listing. Although I'm suspicious of his motives now, I've spent a lot of time there. I've uncovered a secret history that involves one of the most beautiful love stories. I'd love a chance to tell it. If the hotel gets sold to Super 7, we both know they will gut any history, and everyone loses."

His hand finds his chin, and he rubs the five o'clock shadow that runs along his jawline. "You really don't think financing is going to be a problem for you? Because I want this off my books."

I shake my head. "Not a problem at all."

My gaze races around his face as I wait for a tinge of a smile to tell me he's on board. His expression stays neutral, and his voice lowers into a grumble, "You're lucky I like you. I should call the cops for trespassing."

"That is not trespassing—" Before I can come up with a logical excuse of what to call this, he sticks his hand out, offering a handshake. "Work on the details with my secretary."

That's it!

Pinching my lips to steal back the squeal I want to shriek, I remain poised as I take his hand, and firmly say, "You got a deal."

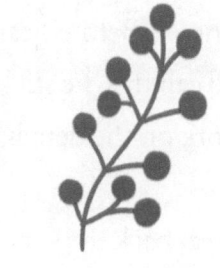

Twenty-Eight

Logan

The lake's still frozen solid into a wide stretch of glassy ice. Dad's been finding it difficult to be still and rest, unless he has someone to keep him company. Yet, his back is not ready for a full day's work. Despite his dislike for fishing, I talked him into sitting out here to get out of the house. I dragged a pair of folding lawn chairs over, parking them near our fishing holes. Even with the chair, Dad's more hunched than normal as he holds his rod in front of him, the line disappearing into the smooth water below.

I've been checking on him regularly. We haven't had one of our chats since he stopped working. He's quiet, unlike how he normally is when we fish, and his breath is heavy, almost weighted, coming out in slow clouds. The silence that's gone on for the last hour hasn't been awkward—it's the kind of silence that says what he's feeling without him needing to say any words. *His whole life changed, and he's not sure what to think about it.*

"How are you holding up?" I keep my voice casual. "Are you and Mom getting along?"

Dad quirks an eyebrow. "I sleep in, I wake up stiff. I try to do those stupid stretches the doctor gave me. They don't work. Then your mom forces me to go for a walk. That only takes up the first hour of the day, and then I go crazy."

"It'll get better." I smile faintly. That's exactly how I pictured his days going. There'll be an adjustment period where he doesn't know what to do, especially since he's still healing. "Maybe it's time to pick up another hobby. I mean, you only fish because I like it. What's something you can do that you like?"

He gazes out at the lake like he is seeing it with different eyes. "You promise not to laugh?"

Surprised by the sudden upbeat change in tone, I look over at him. "Of course."

"You know me, I love woodworking. Frankly, that's all I know. I can't imagine a world where I don't work with my hands. I wake up in the middle of the night smelling the sweet oak. I'll never get that out of my blood, so I've been carving, just small things that I can work on while I sit."

"Wait. Seriously?" I sit up taller from the shock of this news. "Since when do you do that?"

"It actually started with that wood box you found," Dad says, sheepishly. "I got to looking at it and realized there wasn't much to that design. It's fascinating how it held up all these years, decades really. Quality items will do that. So, I've been making little boxes, and carving things into them. Initials, funny sayings, and one with our wedding verse on it." His eyes flick to me. "Your mom made me make that one..." He snickers, but I can hear the love braided into his tone. "And all because of the monkey I made that came out looking like your aunt Bridget when she's having a bad hair day. I had to point it out, but your mother didn't find my humor funny."

My smirk grew wide from his honesty. "Why didn't you tell me?"

Dad gives me a pointed look. "Didn't think you'd care. You always see me as the guy with the drill and the bad back."

"I do," I say. "But now you're the guy with a drill and a little box collection. That's kind of awesome."

Dad pulls on his line, checking the bobber, even though it hasn't moved all morning. Then he nonchalantly turns to me. "So, that's my secret. Care to tell me yours?"

Swallowing, I about brush off his inquiry with a chuckle, but his eyes sparkle in that special way that tells me he already knows.

How did he know?

He's my dad.

We've always been close like that.

I can't believe I'm doing this, but I take a breath and let it out. "It's Penelope."

On cue, Dad's eyebrow finds a new elevation. "What about her?"

"She's smart. Funny. She likes her coffee banana flavored, which arguably is the most disgusting flavor, but I can't begin to find it gross because I'm finding everything she does to be adorable. I think about her more than I should, and she's back in New York right now, trying to buy that hotel."

Dad gives me the same patient look he wears when his drill makes a noise it shouldn't. "It's interesting that she wants to buy it. What do you think about it?"

Shaking my head, I resist the urge to hang it low. She's taking on an absolute money drain, but it's impossible to explain to someone what this journey has been for both of us. Even though it seems like a bad investment, it feels right. On so many levels. Not just professionally, but like it's meant to bring us together. I'll do everything in my power to help bring the place up to par. I don't doubt it will be a success. The hotel isn't what's bothering me. I'm confident in my ability to work hard. "I worry it's not going to be good enough for her."

By *it*, I totally mean me. That's what I'm really thinking about. I worry that by continuing to work close to her, I'll fall so hard. Then she'll decide this was an okay gig for an in-between thing, and head back to the city the first chance she gets. I'll never recover.

Dad's huff is something between a laugh and a sigh. "Logan, you're a builder. You built everything from skyscrapers to Matchbox cars when you were little. You know how these things go. You start by planting on a solid foundation. Don't rush that part. Don't start laying things out without having a plan. Once you get that perfect, the rest is easy, but it starts with a conversation." He winks at me, leaning over. "And you're not going to destroy the whole thing with one conversation. It's the foundation."

A nervous laugh leaks out of my throat. "Yeah, this is so much different than building a matchbox car."

"It's only different because it matters more." Dad's free hand covers his heart in a humble gesture that makes my stomach twist. "That fear you feel? It means something's real there."

Dad holds my gaze, no teasing in his eyes now—just quiet encouragement. A lifetime of love packed into a single fatherly look. "Besides," Dad mumbles with a humored inflection, "if she turns you down, you aren't out anything. Still single without any fish."

When I laugh, my shoulders fall a little, releasing some of the tension that has been there all morning. "You're so encouraging."

"That's what I'm here for." Dad claps a hand on his knee. "Now c'mon. Let's get these poles out of the lake and head back to the house. Your mom's making lasagna."

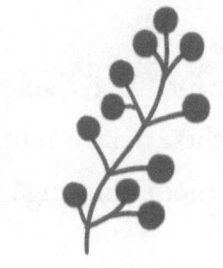

Twenty-Nine

Penelope

More snowflakes are falling from the sky in what seems to be a never-ending supply this year. We had an early winter, and at this rate, I'm already overwhelmed. It's definitely settled in. Even with all this snow, I experience an easier breath as I unlock the front door to the hotel. It still needs so much work—more than most sane people would take on—but I've grown attached to the place. Regardless of how much money it is, and how much work is ahead, it feels right.

The right kind of right too.

It's an even breath that comes out when I think about it, which is odd for me because I'm normally up and down in my emotions, and a whirlwind of stress. Everything about how

Ammoret laid those letters out, like they were meant for me to find them, has me at peace. I feel her hand in all of this, guiding me. I don't doubt there'll be more secrets to uncover as I move forward, and I welcome them.

I don't have the door latched behind me before tires crunching in the snow avert my attention back out. A truck pulls next to my car, headlights slicing through the snow flurry. The door opens, and out steps Logan.

So much for the peaceful and even breath.

My heart slams in my throat, thrumming out beats like a high school marching band that forgot how to stay in rhythm. He hurries over, his face flushed light red from the icy air or perhaps anticipation.

"I did it! I convinced him to sell it to me," I call out, unable to wait until he asks. Snowflakes blow in at an angle, catching on my eyelashes, and I blink them away. "I'm the new owner!"

"I knew you would. I don't think anyone can say no to you." Logan halts hard, only a few feet from me.

"Well, maybe Vernon, but he doesn't count," I say sarcastically.

He raises his gaze to study the place while he peels off his winter gloves with a grin. "You are now the proud owner of a half-frozen, half-gutted money pit that might still have mice in it. Congrats!"

"Or maybe it has more money?" I shoot back, eyes shining. "And love letters and you can't put a price on that." I sigh.

No amount of teasing is breaking my smile today. Maybe it's adrenaline that will crash in the morning, and I'll feel all the stress. As for right now, I want to celebrate, and I have the perfect plan. "Do you remember when you talked about those Christmas balls they used to host here?"

"Yeah."

I don't pause for him to reply longer than with a single word. "I want to bring that back. This year, and just in time for Christmas as a grand opening."

Logan stares, speechless for a moment, before blurting out, "Wait. You want to host a ball? Here in this dump?"

"Yeah, I planned it out. We *open* with a Christmas Eve Grand Ball." My hands fly with excitement as I speak. "We'll use the big Christmas tree that's already decorated. It'll be like it used to be. But we have to get it done fast. I mean—*really* fast. I'm officially broke now, so unless we open by Christmas, I'll be eating noodles for New Year's."

"Noodles for New Year's has a nice ring to it."

"Stop." I laugh. Even starvation can't stress me out. Everything has worked out so well this far.

"You're serious?" Logan runs a hand down the side of his face. "Do you not remember what the inside still looks like?"

"I remember," I say, standing up even taller. "So... will you help me?"

He takes a slow step closer—his eyes sparkling as the snow flies around him. "I'll help you," he says finally, "on one condition."

I tilt my head as I detect heavy flirtation in his tone. "Oh?"

"You go to the ball with me."

The words leave his mouth easily. They certainly aren't what I'd expected, sending a ping right to my heart. I blink, not because it feels bad, but it puts me in a vulnerable position. Sure, we've done an awful lot of things together lately, from working together, getting coffee together, and hiding behind fake plants together, but this feels like he's asking something else. I hate to assume, but I can't help but hope. "Like... with you?"

"With me," he says, holding my gaze even. "As my date."

I tried to be coy, holding back my smile. It's no use, as a full smile spreads across my face. It's honestly more than I would have ever hoped for. "So, you'll only help me save my financial future *if* I go to a magical Christmas ball, in a hotel that I now own, with you?"

"That's the deal." I can't believe it's even possible, but his gaze morphs to one that's even softer, sweeter, and heavy on the flirting, with a mischievous glint sparking out of the center of both of his eyes. And that handsome smirk I missed while I was gone but now love fills in at the perfect angle.

"Well, when you put it like that, how could I say no?"

"Good. Then we'd better get started. We've got a ballroom to bring back to life."

He steps forward, bumping my shoulder against his as we turn toward the building, and I say, "I already made a schedule. It's going to be tight, but I think we can get it done by Christmas. Do you think we can pull it off?"

"With you?" He glances at the shuttered-up windows that still have rotted wreaths from last year, and then back to me. "I don't have a single doubt."

"Not just me," I speak over him. "Us. We're a team..."

Thirty

Logan

The hotel is smelling better and better each day. Gone are the musty odors and dust motes that were here when I first entered this place. Now a blend of pine and lemon polish—an oddly comforting mix—wafts through the air. Footsteps echo distantly from somewhere upstairs as the newly hired housekeeping crew bustles through the halls, scrubbing, dusting, and making rooms, that haven't seen a guest in over a year, shine like they are new again.

I stand at the edge of the grand ballroom, my hands even at my sides, surveying my work. The original chandelier glitters with fresh candles, which I have to say was backbreaking work to get those all in there. After Penelope's candle incident earlier this month, I knew better than to use real candles. Only fake ones for her from here on out.

The once-dull floors polished up well. Now they emit a sheen under the warm light. At the far end of the room, the Christmas tree towers to the ceiling, every branch carefully trimmed and draped in ribbons, glass ornaments, and strands of twinkling lights. It's a sight to see, but even with all the beauty before me, it's nothing compared to the beauty who walks in.

Penelope.

She's carrying the tree topper. The golden star that I removed so it could be properly cleaned, but she must be done with it. She looks up at the tree, then at me. "I can't believe we pulled this off."

"I think," I say, placing my ladder in front of the tree and holding it steady for her, "it's going to be the most magical night of the year."

Holding the star as if it's something sacred, she steps up on the ladder, her brows pin together in concentration, and she carefully steps up another step until she can reach the tallest branch. She seems to be holding her breath, when I tease, "Don't worry, remember if you fall, I got you."

"Don't make me want to fake it just to be in your arms again." She laughs as she adds the tree topper, and then steps down, not stopping until she's back on the flat floor. Brushing her hands on her jeans, she says, "That day you caught me was my best day at work ever."

My heart ramps up. I pretend she doesn't have this overwhelming effect on me, but for the most part, I'm a goner whenever she's around. I still think about that moment way more often than I should. "Moment of truth," I say softly with reverence as I reach for the cord and plug it in.

The soft gold lights blink on simultaneously, bathing the ballroom in a warm glow. The star spirals out light in the most spectacular pattern. It's like something out of a dream. Penelope gasps as her head tips back, taking it all in. "It's gorgeous!"

She's staring at the tree. It's every bit as beautiful as I knew it would be, but it's nothing compared to her. I can't stop staring at her. "Yeah," I say barely louder than my breath. "It has nothing on you."

When she looks back at me, I don't give her a chance to look away. I lean in slowly, giving her enough time to realize what my intentions are. She can certainly stop me, but there's never going to be another more perfect moment to finally kiss her again. We've both been dancing around this for days as we rushed to get everything on "her schedule" done in time. I can honestly say, I got every single thing completed on her list with barely any time to spare, but for the little time we have left, I know what I want to do. I've been holding this kiss in so long my knees actually shake. My heart ramps up, beating against my chest wall, but I'm committed to this, and I watch her closely for any sign that she's not ready. She must be feeling the same way, because she leans closer too.

Her lips meet mine with quiet certainty. She wraps her arms around my neck, pulling me into the kiss. All the noise from the housekeeping crew, and the old creaks of the hotel—all of it disappear, and I melt into her lips.

As much as it pains me to do so, I pull back before the kiss is anything but sweet. Penelope's light laughter surprises me, as she bats her lashes playfully. "That was nice, but certainly not on the schedule."

I grin as I find my fingers brushing against her lower back. I can't not touch her. "I added it." My lips burn for another kiss, but I resist because I have something else in mind. With my hand still resting gently on her waist, I whisper, "I've got something to show you."

"Oh no." Her head jerks back. "Should I be nervous?"

I take her hand, smoothing my palm across hers before I lace our fingers together. We've never actually said we're a couple. Something definitely happened to me when she agreed to stay. Neither of us are dating anyone else. We were both so frantic about getting this place open, we sort of put any romance on hold. Even though we haven't spoken about it, I feel comfortable taking her hand in mine as if she were mine, especially now that we finally completed our second kiss. "I've been working on those old letters. I've framed them and it may seem sort of cheesy, but I set up a small exhibit with those newspaper photos we found. I'm going to unveil it to the public at the ball."

Her eyes widened. "I can't say I'm surprised, but I have no idea when you found time to do that. I haven't given you a break since you took this job."

"Truthfully, I mostly worked on it in the middle of the night after I finally went home from here, but it's been so worth it. I feel this connection. I think they set us up, and it's the least I could do to honor the love they had and shared with us."

She's quiet for a long time before brushing her thumb over my cheek. Goosebumps erupt on my skin where her finger has touched. I could seriously stay like this forever, marveling in the way that feels. After a while she says, "That's the most romantic thing I've ever heard,"

Shrugging, I downplay any credit she's giving me. "I figured if this hotel gets a second chance, it needs to be centered on that. All the love contained in these walls."

It's her turn to lean toward me, and she sweetly rests her head on my chest, inviting me to wrap my arms around her. Being a full head taller than her, her head gives me the perfect place to rest my chin, and I stare at the lights on the tree. "I'm really glad you bought this place," I murmur as my heart seems to pump fuller of flutters for her.

"I'm really glad you made it feel like home," she whispers.

I wish I could tease her to lighten our anxieties. We've poured everything we can into this. Although I believe in her, there's still so much that can go wrong. I'm all seriousness when I ask, "Are you ready for the ball tomorrow?"

"As ready as I'll ever be..."

Thirty-One

Penelope

The chandeliers glow above the sea of velvet and satin dresses. Evergreen garlands wind around the pillars, and glass lanterns illuminate the hallway and grand staircase. I couldn't have planned a better backdrop as the never-ending snow this winter has brought us once again gently falling flakes outside the tall arched windows.

Inside everything is warm, cozy, and I could argue...magical.

Standing inside the ballroom's grand archway, my breath catches in my throat as I pinch myself. I can't believe this is even the same place I first saw two months earlier. I spent an hour getting ready, curling and pinning up my hair in a fashion I would normally never wear. Feeling ultra-festive, I added a touch of red on my lips. I worry I'm overdressed, but as I scan the room, those thoughts flitter away. Everyone is dressed in their best holiday attire.

Logan approaches from across the room. I smile when I see his blue flannel shirt tailored perfectly. He seems to be searching the room but when our eyes connect, he stops in the middle of his step and stares like he's meeting me for the first time. With our gazes still connected, we both walk toward each other, closing the distance until he's close enough to reach for my hand. "You're going to make me forget why we came here tonight," he murmurs.

"You won't forget, because I can remind you. I dragged us into an impossible renovation schedule to revive a dying hotel on a shoestring budget. Now I'm spending every last red cent I have to throw this ball. My financial security lies on how things go tonight," I tease. "Does any of that ring a bell?"

Warmth radiates from the gentle way he squeezes my hand, and he adds a devious smile. "That was only part of it. The bigger reason is because I wanted to dance with you in a satin dress."

I start to reply, but the music stops, telling me it's time for the next thing on my schedule. It's a planned intermission. Logan turns, gently pulling me forward, where the velvet curtains have been drawn.

"Ready?" he whispers, a cautious glint in his eyes.

I nod, keeping my attention on him. This is his moment.

He pulls the cord.

The curtains sweep open.

A sleek glass display case stands a little clandestinely in the corner. Inside, under soft golden light, lay the letters.

With edges curled and much of the paper yellowing, they aren't in the best of shape. One of them has a corner torn off, but all those flaws make it feel even more miraculous. Logan added a small silver plaque beneath each one with the location of where the letter was found. And beneath each letter is the box in which the letter was hidden. "I arranged the letters the same way we read them," he whispers to me. "So they can have the same emotional journey we had."

I skim over the ink, not needing to read any of them. I've read them so many times, I've practically memorized them. "It's perfect."

"Well, not exactly perfect." He smiles earnestly. "I think it's the way Ammoret would have wanted them. This way they won't be forgotten."

People step forward, and I back away, giving them space to experience a little of the magic of this place. I wasn't prepared for the emotions to be this strong. So much is riding on this night. I swallow hard and steel my face, as I observe the crowd.

Logan leans toward me, whispering again, "Can you feel it? This place is coming back to life."

With my overwhelming emotions clogging my throat, I manage to say, "You did that."

The air between us shifts, heating. He leans down, kissing my temple in the sweetest way. "We both did." I'm such a sucker for the sweet little kisses. The butterflies that never sleep when Logan is near erupt in my stomach. The music begins again. Slow and low. Logan extends his hand with his palm open. "I believe you owe me a dance."

"I can hardly wait another second." It's easy for me to walk forward with him. There really isn't anywhere I'd rather be. The room seems to narrow to just us. We begin to step in the kind of dance where each movement is a gesture of affection.

One of his hands settles on my lower back while the other holds mine. "You know," he says quietly, eyes locked on mine, "this always has been my favorite building. Now I have even more reasons to add to my list."

"It's officially my favorite too," I barely get my whisper out before he leans in, stealing a kiss full of everything that has been building between us. It ends before I'm ready for it to end, and he pulls away, leading me in a few steps before the music ends. I hold my breath as I scan the room, trying to read the vibes. To my surprise the crowd claps.

Tears of joy spring to my eyes.

I have no idea what the future of this place holds.

At least tonight is a success.

I'm about to step off the dance floor to check on the security guard at the front door when an older woman grabs my forearm, her eyes brimming. "We had our wedding dance here decades ago. We never thought we'd dance in this room again. Thank you."

Such a simple statement but my heart swells so full. I look back at Logan, who is beaming at me, and I return my focus to the woman. "It's my pleasure to bring this place back to life, but I wouldn't be here without my partner, Logan." I motion toward him.

Oddly, he steps forward. I think he's going to shake the woman's hand, but instead he surprises me, by grabbing a champagne glass from the nearest waiter and nearly shouting, "Everyone!" The room falls into hushed whispers, and Logan goes on, "I want to say something before the snow buries us all in here until spring."

A hearty chuckle ripples through the room. I find myself smiling wider. Logan glances my way, his expression soft. "As you all saw, this hotel was crumbling. Literally. And Penelope put her mind into bringing it back, but she didn't just bring the hotel back—she brought back its story. Its heart." He raises his glass higher. "To you, Penelope...for taking the chance on this place, for calling me and begging me to take a job I didn't want, because I didn't know I needed it...And for all this Christmas magic."

The crowd erupts to applause. I cover my mouth, hiding the fact I'm biting my lip hard. I'm clearly not fighting my feelings for Logan anymore. I freely let the butterflies take over. They are so fierce, sometimes I feel them in my bones. I lean toward him, hoping to let some of his warmth wrap around me. He embraces me and whispers into my ear, "Hope you're okay with toasts. I've got more planned for New Year's."

My heart stops. Everything about this evening is more than I could have ever planned. That success doesn't even compare to the feelings in my heart. More than anything, I hope that now we finally have this place up and running, we can slow down and figure out what we are to each other. I'm falling so in love with Logan. I hope he's feeling the same way. "I can hardly wait to hear it," I say.

Thirty-Two

Penelope

New Year's Eve finally brings a clear night with no chance of new snow. Calmness washes over me. With guests eating in the dining room, Logan surprises me by setting up a private dinner for us in the conference room that's usually reserved for meetings. I sit across from him at the long table, and the aroma of roasted garlic and herbs linger in the air.

Expecting to see him relaxed with all our days of work behind us, I find something completely opposite. Logan is fidgety, as he keeps checking his watch and his lips pinch tightly. It might have to do with the surprise he said he has. Whatever it is, he's acting weird.

Aside from the fidgeting, he looks handsome as ever. It's almost unfair. Wearing his signature flannel shirt with the sleeves pushed up to his elbows, top buttons undone. His dark hair is ruffled a little in the front, adding to his rugged and handsome look.

And me?

I'd stood in front of the mirror for several minutes, adjusting the black velvet dress I'd impulsively bought from a downtown boutique. It's not my usual style, but I'm expecting tonight to be special, if not pivotal, for us.

We aren't friends anymore. We haven't made anything official. We've been lingering in some middle ground I don't know what to call it. If I'm reading Logan's vibes right, he's definitely going to ask me to be his girlfriend. My gut twists as I can't help but wish it happens tonight.

"I hope you saved room for dessert." he says as he stands and disappears back into the hall that leads to the kitchen.

My stomach flutters from the anticipation of what he might be bringing back. I call after him, "Actually, I'm getting full. I'll have to pass, but I'm totally ready for my surprise..."

He returns carrying a small plate, the kind usually reserved for something you don't want to share. He lowers the plate in front of me, revealing a little round tart with thin banana slices arranged like flower petals on top. A dollop of whipped cream tops it off. "It's coconut cream filled. If I got it correct, it should taste like your morning coffee."

My chest cinches in the best possible way, and all I can manage is, "Wow."

"So, that means I did well?"

"You always do." I take the fork, peeling back the corner and lift it to my mouth for a nibble. The filling meets my tongue first. It might be the most delicious thing I've ever tried. "Amazing," I say, as I dig my fork back in for another bite. "Do you want to try it?"

His lips pinch together again, and he wags his hair. "No, I'm good. That's not my preferred food combo, but I'm happy you like it."

I take another bite and smile as I chew. "I feel bad eating in front of you."

"Don't feel bad. After everything you've done these last few weeks, you deserve a treat." He takes my hand, holding it on the table, and I eat in comfortable silence. The only sound is Christmas music filtering in from the dining room. Well, that and the thrum of my heart trying to beat its way out of my chest. The dessert is a nice surprise. Something tells me it's not *the* surprise, and I don't know how much longer I can handle this tension.

After I finish my dessert, Logan leads me up the steep back staircase. Still confused about why we are going this way, I hang on to his arm. This staircase was reserved for staff back in the day, and it's the one thing that hasn't been replaced. It creaks under my weight, reminding me of the floorboards

of the workshop, and those actually gave out. Swallowing
my memories, I follow him to the last door on this floor.
My brows pin together as even more confusion buds in my
chest. Unless he's going to push me out the window, there's
nowhere else to go. "Where are we going?" I finally ask. I'm
ready to pull him back in the direction we came. He's not
going to get me to jump out that window. I laugh out loud at
the thought because he obviously never would do that.

But still...there's nothing here.

"You'll see." Though he's quiet, the inflection in his voice
is excitement. "Close your eyes."

I do, and I allow him to guide me a few more steps all
the way to the wall. The air is colder now, and I sarcastically
say, "Just as I suspected. You are going to push me out that
window."

"No, never." His hand is on my lower back, as he leads
me even closer until I can touch the window, and he says,
"Open."

Before I open my eyes, I take a moment to dramatically
cross my hands in front of my chest, to be playful. As soon as
my eyes pop open, my breath catches in my throat. I'm looking out the back window, the one I never pay any attention
to—there's a rooftop deck on the other side of it! "How did
that happen?"

Logan steps forward and pushes the window wide open. "I
wanted to do this for you the whole time, but I wasn't sure

how to go about it, because the hotel roof is so slanted. Then one day I noticed this window was a fire escape, which means it's bigger than the others, and opened all the way, leading to the first-floor roof overhang. I was a little skeptical about the condition of the roof below, but it passed all the inspections. I knew I had to do it." He holds his hand out, ready to help me step out. "Come on."

I playfully narrow my eyes as I take his hand. "You want me to go first, so you can push me over, right?"

"No, absolutely not. Stop being so silly."

I step out and immediately turn in a circle, taking it all in. He'd added wooden railing around the small rooftop, but he didn't stop there. Little lanterns are strung along the railing, illuminating the deck with dots of amber. A small gas firepit glows from the middle, and a wicker love seat with thick blankets and throw pillows sits in front of it.

"Logan." I pause, as I can say a lot of things to him. I can tell him this is completely unnecessary, and I didn't expect it. He already knows that. I can shower him with praise, but he's not the kind of guy who needs that. I can tell him this is easily the sweetest thing someone has ever done for me, but he doesn't wait for me to say it.

"You told me once," his voice remains steady, "your favorite thing about New York is your rooftop deck. That was where you dreamed your dreams. I didn't want you to lose that. I hope this is acceptable."

"I don't know how you did this without me finding out."

"It was harder than I thought it would be, especially since you moved in." A satisfied chuckle slips through his lips. "At first, I thought I could work at night when you left, but you started to never leave. So, I did most of it the other day when you went back to New York. I've been sneaking the furniture up while you ran errands."

I've literally run out of words. I never even imagined a special place here at the hotel. Leave it to Logan to make sure it happens. I step closer to him, grabbing both of his hands while I rise to the tips of my toes to kiss him. He's a willing participant, bringing his lips down to meet mine. Our lips tangle together slowly at first. The perfect kiss to say thank you, I see you, I'm so hopelessly falling in love with you.

When we break apart, I'm breathless and only able to whisper, "I will never be able to find the words to tell you how much this means to me, but thank you."

"I know what it means. Now you have a place to watch the lights." He motions to the loveseat. We sit together, taking the time to tuck the blanket around us, and he pulls me close to his side, wrapping an arm around my shoulder.

But beneath the celebration, something stirs—a weight I've felt since we had our grand opening. I haven't dared utter a word. "You know, I still have my apartment in New York," I say right as a cool breeze picks up. I draw the blanket up while

I lean my head on his shoulder. "And about those dreams. I still plan to open my own brokerage, but I didn't plan this."

He keeps his gaze on the stars. "Neither did I."

"The grand opening went so well, I've got reservations booked out for two months," I say. "I should have enough cash flow now to hire a manager. I've been thinking about that a lot lately. Hiring a manager makes the most sense, especially since I don't have a clue what I'm doing anyway."

I want him to say something, weigh in a little, but he stays quiet. I get being silent is his thing, but my brain throbs as I war my options with myself. Maybe he plans for this to be a temporary thing, and he's content not to make a big deal about it? "So, I guess, if you think it's not a bad idea, I'll put an ad out for a manager, so I can go back..."

"You could," he says so simply my heart actually stumbles.

"Is that what you want?"

"I know you've got dreams, and I'll be the last person to get in the way of those. But if you're waiting for me to give you a reason to stay..." He finally moves his gaze to connect with mine, causing my heart to skip a beat. I want for him to plead how much he wants me. He doesn't. He says something better. "Stay because you want to."

"I want to stay..." I close my mouth as I wait for the right words to say. At some point staying is going to slow, maybe even stop my progress with my brokerage. "I could delay moving back until spring," I throw out to see his reaction.

At this point, I'm sad he's not trying to convince me to stay, but I get it. We had an unspoken understanding that I will leave when the hotel is ready. "I don't want to do anything that's going to mess up your plans. I know you're busier now with work since your dad retired, while you're also trying to steer the business away from the heavy construction to preservation. I get that you have a lot going on too. What do you want me to—"

He cuts me off by bringing his face down, pulling me into a kiss—fierce and tender and impossible to ignore—saying exactly what I need him to say without saying anything.

I pull back, my eyes searching his. I don't need any other confirmation. "Okay, then. I'll stay," I whisper. "I'm already here. I might as well take my time to hire a manager and make sure they get trained."

Maybe it's my imagination but Logan lets out a deeper than average breath. The alarm I'd set on my phone goes off, reminding us something else is happening. I retrieve my phone, shut off the alarm, and then turn my focus back to him. "Happy New Year, Logan." There's a formality in using his first name I didn't expect, and happy tears spring to my eyes.

He doesn't wait to tip my face toward him, kissing me again even slower this time. Off in the distance, the city shoots off fireworks, but neither of us looks up. I certainly don't need to see them. Everything I want is right here.

The following morning, I stand in the lobby with a mop in one hand, a spray bottle in the other, and a mental list packed in my brain. I survived the grand opening Christmas Ball and the following blur of the week between Christmas and New Year's. Actually, I more than survived. Sales thrived and look promising for the next few weeks. Now comes the unglamorous part—deep cleaning and taking down the decorations. "It shouldn't be too bad," I say to myself as I'm determined to stay focused until the job is complete.

The back door slams a little louder than it should. I already know who's walking up the hallway. Logan, with his slanted grin and his sleeves rolled up, and a black insulated vest over the top of his flannel shirt. "You know," he says, his tone playful. "Now that you have a housekeeping staff, you could have them do this, so we can spend the day binge-watching whatever nonsense we want."

"I totally could." I sigh dreamily, as that sounds amazing. "But I'm trying to stash as much extra money as I can." I extend my mop and go after a spot on the floor, not wanting to get distracted.

Logan doesn't miss the chance to tease me and he points behind me. "You missed a spot."

"I did not." I move the mop in the other direction, so he can't inspect my cleaning. I'm laughing because working with him makes it always feel like I'm not really working.

He leans in without notice, stealing a kiss. My reaction goes against everything I want in the moment, but I put my palm on his shoulder, pull away, and hiss. "Logan, I'm working, and that's not very professional. A guest could totally walk by."

"It's not like you can get fired." His eyes glint with his mischievous smile. "There has to be some benefit to being the owner."

Do I want to toss this mop to the floor and run upstairs to our private deck and snuggle for hours? Yes. I would love that very much, but I also have standards to uphold. "I have to work right now."

"Me too," he croons as he leans even closer, whispering right near my neck. "I'm actively working on making you fall in love with me."

Goosebumps spiral up my spine, and I almost drop my spray bottle. "Well, that's good to know." I continue to push the mop back and forth, fully aware of how close he is to me.

"Just warning you," he says smugly. "We already completed level one and that was flirting. You passed, by the way."

"Oh good," I scoff as he makes getting anything done nearly impossible. I'm not upset though. It's the opposite. I'm laughing when I ask, "What is level two?"

"Definitely kissing. So much kissing. I'm going to kiss you until you stop pretending you aren't falling in love with me."

"Logan..." My voice comes out sounding a tad tired when I speak, even though butterflies are going crazy in my gut. This whole situation is confusing. Even though we spend all the time together we can, we still haven't spoken a word more about this going on any longer after I leave, and well, I can't imagine how hard that's going to be if we are in love with each other. "I'm trying to work—"

No warning this time just his hands cupping my face and his warm lips, that taste faintly like peppermint, crashing into mine. My body stills, except for my lips, which are actively kissing back, and my heart—which clearly hasn't gotten the memo that I'm leaving in the spring—my heart is getting attached to this sweet man as much as I try to tell it to stop.

I pull back and playfully scold, "You can't just—"

"Watch me." He leans in again, brushing his mouth against mine.

"Logan—" I drop the mop and the spray bottle because I need the use of my hands to push him back. I'm fully playful and laughing when I say, "I'm working—"

"And I'm falling in love with you." His voice is dead serious. "And I know you're scared to say it, but you are falling in love with me too. And I want you to know, even if you make me mop stupid floors when there's good TV on, I'm not going anywhere. Even if you do leave, we'll make it work."

I open my mouth but then close it right away.

He's right. I'm falling so in love with him. I find it hard to breathe when I think about going back to New York. Every time he touches me, it seals us together a little more, and it terrifies me. He's become ingrained in my brain and in my heart. When I think about going back to New York, it feels like I'm leaving home.

He is fast becoming my home.

But I can't tell him that.

It's scary. It's only going to make it hurt worse when I do leave. Instead, I rise to the tip of my toes, and kiss him back, not playfully or even lightly. When I finally pull away, he grins his crooked smirk against my lips. "So... you're on board with level two?"

A chuckle bursts out of my lips. I don't care what level we're on. He can call it what he wants, as long as I don't get my heart broken.

The next day, I walk on my tiptoes as I listen for Logan. His drill hums steadily, and then it stops. That's my cue to go in. Nerves loop knots in my stomach. He's been pulling out all the stops to be sweet to me, always full of surprises and willing to help me do anything. I figured it was time I step it up. I can keep secrets too. Thanks to his dad I got this one done in record time. "Hey," I lean into the lobby, and he looks up from the trim.

"Hey, you."

I don't know how he keeps his secrets because I can barely keep a straight face. "Can I borrow you for a minute?"

His eyes narrow as if suspicious. "I thought I was already being borrowed when I was asked to fix this trim?"

I walk forward, grab his hand, and then hoist him up. "Come on. It's your turn to be surprised."

"Uh-huh." His eyes widen. "I should warn you that I don't do plumbing—ever. I might be falling in love with you, but that doesn't translate to toilets."

"I trusted you when you made me close my eyes to find my patio." I quietly coax him forward. "It's your turn. Trust me with this. Close your eyes."

With a dramatic sigh, he finally closes his eyes. He doesn't know it, as soon as I saw the special space he made for me, I called his dad and begged him to help me update the old stable. I eagerly drag Logan all the way down the hall and out the back door. "We're going outside?" He voices his concern.

I only giggle and guide him forward until he's right in front of the door that I open so he can see inside as soon as he opens his eyes.

"Okay," I say, my nerves are audible. "Open your eyes."

Opening one eye at a time, he's silent as he takes it all in. A brand-new workbench for him to work on and whatever else he wants. A tall tool cabinet on the other wall. The broken window has been replaced, and his dad assured me all the floorboards are reinforced and everything is safe. Logan turns to me, a look of confusion on his face. "What is it? Did you find another letter?"

"You said the other day that your tools didn't have a home anymore since your dad retired and sold his warehouse. I know you have your home office, but I wanted you to have another space, just for you, but also here. With me."

His eyes pace side to side like he's trying to memorize my face. He's always slow to speak, if he even speaks at all. The longer he stays silent, I read his mind loud and clear.

"You hate it." Half-panicking, I pull his arm back toward the hotel, ready to forget this happened.

"No. I love it." He shakes his head slowly, his voice rough as he blurts out, "And... I love *you*."

My breath catches somewhere between my lungs and my lips. My whole body goes stiff as I wait for him to take it back. Sure, he's said he's falling in love. That's quite different from actually using the L word. We'd never said that before. It was clearly a slip.

His eyes don't waver, and he says it again louder this time. "I love you."

With my heart cracking wide open, I don't open my mouth to speak. Not that he would allow that now anyway, because his hand drops to my waist, and he literally sweeps me into a kiss. His free hand finds my neck and he holds it there like I'm the most precious thing, fragile even. My hands rise to his chest, curling into the fabric of his shirt as he kisses me deeper.

"I love you," he says again against my lips as he pulls away. "I don't care where you're from or what you do next. I'm tired of holding it in."

My smile spreads wide against his. "I love you too."

Both his hands drop to my waist, and he wraps them around me like he'll never let go. I gaze up at him looking at me, and I'm too breathless to even sigh. If this was an impossible decision before, it's getting easier. I can no longer imagine leaving Logan. My heart is here with him.

A week later, I stand quietly in the doorway of my now-empty apartment. I couldn't bring myself to sell it, but it is a drain on my income, and a space I'm not using. I found a renter, which wasn't hard with the dream location. I'm a little teary-eyed as I love this place. It's a symbol of so many wins for me. I'd passed the last box to the mover a moment ago, and they are headed on their way to the hotel.

All that's left for me to do is to let this place go.

I blow out an even breath as I turn, scanning what was my home. This was my first stable home after my mom passed. The first place I'd lived in for more than a few months. Where I worked all-nighters and dreamed all my dreams. I would never have imagined things to go the way they did. I'm hardly even sad. Oddly, it doesn't feel like home as it used to, especially with my stuff gone. It feels like empty walls.

My eyes land on the only thing left on the walls. The black heart I had drawn. Permanent marker wasn't such a good idea. I can't wash it off, even though I tried with many types of soap. It seems to echo now about the person I used to be. I'd drawn it after a breakup when I was feeling sad and missing my mom, and the guy I was dating said, "I wasn't loveable."

I know what he meant. He was trying. He was doing all the things and saying all the things, but I had kept my heart closed to him. At the time I thought I was broken. I wanted to be normal and be in love. No matter how hard I told myself he was a great guy, my heart didn't listen.

Of course, I was crushed to hear him say that. In protest, I ate a pint of ice cream and drew on my wall that symbol of my brokenness.

My feet move forward until my fingers hover just above it.

I cried a ton that night. I wrote a huge journal entry, and I swore I didn't *need* anyone. That I would be so successful I wouldn't even want anyone. Now I'm blinking back tears, not because of that guy. I honestly haven't thought of him in years. I'm crying because I had been so wrong. Sure, I didn't *need* anyone, but life is so much fuller with someone. My fingers trace the outline of the heart, and I whisper, "It's okay. You didn't know it yet, but you can love. You needed to find the right person."

I blink down the tears, letting them fall. Inhaling a deep breath in, I hold it before letting it out slowly, like I was letting all my past hurt go. And my apartment. And my younger self. The walls around my heart. My blackness.

Finally, when I turn back to the exit, I'm ready to go.

Surprise but no surprise, snow is falling when I finally pull into the hotel parking lot. Warm light glows from the windows, welcoming me back to the place that now feels like home. And there, on the front porch, bundled in his coat, is

Logan. He opens the door to my car before I even reach for the handle.

"Hey," he says, his easy smile greeting me. "You're home."

I step out of the car, shut the door as I move to the side, and lean into his embrace. When my arms slide around his waist, I get an instant whiff of the scent I've memorized. It's cedar or oak or whatever wood he's been working with. I bury my face into his chest, inhaling his aroma.

"How did it go?" he asks, quietly, like he's totally fine if I don't want to talk about it.

"Not as hard as I had originally thought." I look straight ahead as I tack on, "I'm still going to start my own brokerage, but I'm excited to be based mostly out of here—at least for right now. It was weird, the whole time I was there, it felt like I was away from home."

"Interesting." His lips graze the top of my forehead, and he whispers, "Something else that's also interesting is that it's your turn again for a surprise."

"No." I pull back. I'm way too emotionally tapped out to handle a surprise—good or bad. "It's not my turn. You've done enough for me."

"It's your turn to trust me again." He snatches my hand, leading me inside the hotel, past the hallway, and up the front staircase to the second-floor room I've been sleeping in. It's actually one of the smallest rooms, but I love it the most because it has a nice view of the lake. He opens the door, and

I keep my eyes on him until he motions forward. "I hope it's okay I broke into your room."

Above my bed is a hand-painted gold heart, trailing up in a gentle curve on the wall above my head where I sleep. The brushstrokes are soft, edged in metallic leaf that catches the light. I cut my focus to him as I'm so completely stunned.

He's watching me closely as he speaks, "You never really mentioned too much about what that black heart above your bed meant, but I wanted you to have a new one. A better one. One that's more reflective of the heart you have"

"You didn't have to—"

"I *wanted* to." His voice is low, the way I love it the most. "I want you to have something that proves you're not the same woman who drew those hearts. You're the woman who is starting over. Who is still chasing her dreams and who is worthy of all her hopes and desires."

I don't know how he does it. He takes all my words from my mouth again and again. I thought I was speechless the day he surprised me with the outside deck. This is something so much more sensitive. He really did see me and still sees me. He clearly wasn't kidding about that level two thing, either, because all I want to do is kiss him.

"Thank you." The words are barely out of my lips as I wrap my hands around his neck and pull him down to me. My hands tangle into the back of his hair, and my lips melt into the kiss that feels like it's been held inside of me for years.

He embraces me tighter, breaking the kiss for a moment to whisper, "I'm in this with you." He kisses me again and then whispers against my lips, "Every step of the way."

He doesn't even need to say it, because everything about him tells me he is. "I know you are."

Taking my hand, he folds it into his, and he looks down at me with the most loving expression. "So, I know it's your first official night here, and you're more than likely exhausted. I'll let you settle in, but I was going to mention that my mom wants me to invite you for dinner tomorrow to meet you."

"Oh." I smooth the front of my sweater, even though there's nothing wrong with it. "Are you sure this is a good idea?" I ask, trying not to sound as panicked as I feel.

Logan lifts an eyebrow and flashes that soothing smile of his. "Lo. It's dinner. You are going to need to eat anyway."

"You say that now, but I've seen *Meet the Parents*. Things spiral fast."

He chuckles and puts his hands on my waist again, tugging me closer. "Okay, first of all, you already know my dad, and he likes you."

"Well, he had to like me because we were working together."

He kisses the top of my head. "Semantics. He'll be fine. Plus, my mom is sweet, and my sisters are both going to be there. They're great for the most part. One is older than me, and one is younger. Both are a little chatty, but equally nice."

"That's exactly what someone with terrifying sisters would say," I murmur.

He chuckles against my hair. "You're going to have to meet them eventually, because you're going to be part of my life. Really, it doesn't matter if they like you or not, because I love you."

I exhale slowly, as I close my eyes and replay his words. He always knows the perfect thing to say, and it's not a line either. He truly means what he says. "If you insist, I will go, but you have to let me know what I can bring because I won't show up empty-handed."

"I'll call Mom in the morning and find out, but I know she will insist you don't need to bring a thing."

"Deal."

"It's not a deal yet until we kiss on it."

He doesn't have to ask me twice, and I lean in and press my lips to his, gently at first. He tightens his grip around my waist, tugging me closer, and I forget entirely what I was nervous about. My thoughts are replaced with a single, buzzing certainty—*this* is my favorite version of reassurance. Just as things get deliciously hazy, the door flies open with a bang, and we both freeze.

Pinsch Charming barrels into the room like he owns the place—which, to be fair, he kind of does—and hops onto my bed with zero chill.

Logan groans, "Dude. Seriously? We're going to have to talk about some boundaries."

Ignoring Logan, Pinsch turns once around, making a full circle in the center of my bed, and then flops down. I blink down at him, wide-eyed. "I think he's trying to assert his dominance."

"Well, he can try," Logan mutters, but I can tell he's joking because his smile is crooked and full of nothing but fondness for that dog. "But, technically, I saw you first."

Pinsch snorts, completely unbothered, and kicks out his paws, stretching out.

Logan checks the time on his phone and sighs. "I should go. I've got to start a new job in the morning, and I'm still all by myself. Plus, if I stay any longer..." His gaze drifts back to my lips. "I'm not going to want to leave."

I pretend to pout. "That would be tragic."

He leans in, brushing a quick kiss against my lips. "Just a little goodbye—"

But before I can even respond, he slides one arm around my waist, the other hand cradling the back of my neck. The goodbye kiss deepens in a fast heartbeat. I curl into him, already forgetting what day it is, what time it is, what *anything* is, except the way he's kissing me.

And then—*achoo!*

A sharp, unmistakable, disgusted little dog sneeze from the nearby bed.

We both jolt and look over.

Pinsch, wide-eyed and vaguely offended, sneezes again.

Logan groans and rests his forehead against mine. "I swear, he's trying to get rid of me already."

I laugh, breathless. "I don't think he's trying to get rid of you completely, but he's definitely keeping his eyes on you."

Logan presses a kiss to my forehead, lingering for a second longer than he needs to. "I'll pick you up at six tomorrow, okay? Dress comfy. Mom's making roast." He steps back slowly, like it physically pains him to leave.

"Logan?" I hadn't planned on calling him back, but it was a knee-jerk reflex. He pauses with one hand on the doorknob, and I finish my sentence, "I'm glad I'm meeting your family."

His smile softens. "Me too."

Then he's gone, and the room feels warmer and colder all at once. Pinsch snorts, and I turn my focus to him. "Don't be trying to run him off," I add a dreamy sigh before I say, "I love this one..."

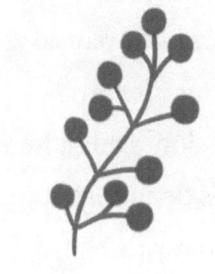

Thirty-Three

Logan

Penelope stands in front of me as I place one hand on her hip, making sure she doesn't run, and I reach my other hand around her shoulder to knock. "You already know my dad," I whisper. "You know he loves you. It's going to be easy."

She gives me a strained look, her eyes bulging with nerves. "Who said I'm nervous?"

"You've been tugging on the edge of your ponytail since I picked you up."

She mutters something indecipherable, but a smile tips on the corners of her lips, making her look more adorable than ever. Every day I look at her and ask myself how I got so lucky. I'm waiting to wake up from this dream, but it never happens.

It keeps getting better and better. The door swings open, and my mom pops her head around the edge. She's wearing a flour-dusted apron around her waist, and a bright smile.

"Come in," Mom says, ushering us both at once. "Penelope, I've heard so much about you. Not only from Logan but from Jerry. And I stalked the hotel's Christmas Ball photos, just so you know, Logan's already showed them all to me—"

"Mom." I can't help but cut in, because I thought she agreed to be cool. She's already blubbering, which will likely make Penelope more anxious. I get she's excited because she can tell how happy I am, but she's acting like I've never had a friend before.

She tips her head toward me, straightening her lips like she's physically sealing any more words, and she opens the door wider.

"Nice to meet you." Penelope offers the bouquet of flowers she brought to my mom. "Logan insisted you didn't need me to bring any food, so I hope you like flowers.

My mom quietly takes them, looking at me and then to Penelope, "Yes, I love them. Thank you."

Cringing on the inside, I lead Penelope farther inside. My sisters, Faith and Grace, are already seated at the table, smirking away while they sip out of their coffee cups.

We aren't even close to being late, but they look at me with strained smiles. "What's up with you?" I ask.

Before they can reply, Dad appears from the hallway with something in his hands, calling out, "Just in time."

"Did you eat it all?" I peel off my coat, hanging it on the nearby coatrack and then help Penelope out of her long winter coat. I suck back a hard inhale when I see the dress she's wearing. One of my favorites, a navy one that matches her eyes and hugs her hips perfectly.

"No, I didn't eat it all." Dad shakes his head, his voice a little more shy than normal. He extends the thing he's holding to Penelope. "I finished your present."

Penelope gives me a side-eye before she holds her hand out, retrieving the gift. "You didn't have to get me anything." Her voice is small while she turns the gift over in her hands to examine it. It's a small wooden box with two entwined hearts carved into the lid.

"It's not just a box," he says with kind eyes. I watch him closely. He never told me he was going to give Penelope a gift, or anyone for that matter. It's not a holiday. He clears his throat, like he's about to make a speech, and says, "I wanted to give you this as a reminder that there are two hearts involved in this thing you're doing with Logan. I know he's given you his heart, and I hope you'll take good care of it."

I didn't think I could cringe any harder with the way Mom had answered that door, but now I'm grinding my teeth. Penelope blinks, looks at the box, glances at me, and returns her attention to Dad. "Uh, thank you." Her thumbs seem to nervously attach to the hearts, tracing the outlines perfectly. I doubt she even knows she's doing it.

"Ah, that's very sweet of you, Dad." My cheeks flame, and I usher Penelope closer to the kitchen and quickly change the subject before he starts interrogating her, "Say, have you met everyone? I don't think you've met my sisters."

We walk toward the table, joining my sisters. "So," Grace's eyes bounce between me and Penelope. "How many embarrassing stories can we get through before the food's ready?"

"None, I hope," I mutter, but throw out a chuckle for good measure. "I can always take her for a walk outside if things get out of hand."

"Let's see..." Faith hums as she thinks, and I resist the urge to roll my eyes. These two are acting like this is my first girlfriend. "How about the time Mom asked you to pack your lunch for school, and you were too lazy to look for your lunch box, so you put your peanut butter and jelly sandwich in your back pocket—"

"Please," I cut her off. "I was, literally, like seven years old."

"Doesn't matter what age you were," Grace says, "Your pants still got stained."

Faith laughs, bless her. I'm going to ignore what's happening because I have twice as many embarrassing stories about her. Dad walks over, standing the straightest I've seen him stand since he hurt his back, and he plops down on his usual chair at the head of the table. He claps a heavy palm on the wooden table and looks me in the eye. "So, the hotel is done. What jobsite are you working at now?"

I clear my throat, shifting slightly. I figured this conversation was coming, and I knew he wouldn't mince words. I was hoping we could hold off until after we ate, and it was just the two of us. "Actually." I pause to scratch the back of my neck, and then spit everything out in one breath, "I've been doing some work in a different direction lately. I didn't take a construction job."

His eyebrows hike, but I don't give him the chance to interject, or I'll lose my nerve. "I got a call from the library. They heard about the love letter exhibit and remembered seeing me there. They asked if I could help restore some old books they had."

Dad's eyebrows slowly knit together while the rest of his body remains stoic. "Wait, you're working on books?" They aren't the meanest words he's ever said, but they land hard and right in my gut. Penelope's smile immediately flickers with unease. I wish Dad had waited to bring this up, but I'm not backing down now.

"It's preservation work," I defend myself, pulling my shoulders back. "Yeah, it's not the heavy lifting we're used to, but with your retirement, I felt it was time to take the business a step in another direction. I won't stop doing construction, as that pays my bills, but at least while this work is here, I'm going to take it."

There's a heavy beat of silence. Penelope reaches for her water glass. Since no one is saying anything, all the eyes follow her as she takes several sips. She has to be feeling this tension, and I hate this for her. Sweat slaps on my brow.

Mom strides closer to the table with her chin high. "Well, dinner's ready. Let's eat before the roast starts mooing." Polite chuckles ripple through the table, and plates start circulating. It doesn't take anything more for the conversation to switch to compliments about the meal, and questions about my mom's recipes. It's pleasant and comfortable for the most part. I didn't have any expectations about the conversation Dad and I had, but one thing is for sure, the heaviness in my gut lifts. It's a relief to have it out in the open, even if Dad doesn't understand yet. Some things take time.

After a while of zoning out, I tune back in to the conversation and find myself staring at Penelope. I knew I had fallen in love with her, and I'd fully surrender to all those feelings, loving every moment, stolen glances, and touches, but seeing her sit at my parents' table, casually sipping coffee while she chats roast seasoning with my mom puts me in a chokehold I'll never get out of.

Before I know it, dinner is over, and everyone heads to the living room to continue the conversation. For the shortest moment, it's only us. She looks over at me, smiling her brilliant smile, and I press a kiss to her temple. "Told you they'd love you."

"What a relief." She exhales a heavy breath. Her eyes sparkle happiness out of the core, making her more radiant than ever. It's not even her beauty that makes my breath grow weak. It's knowing she fits right in with my family, so much so my dad even recognized what she means to me, making her that gift.

"Well," I say with my breath quivering more than I would prefer. "Now that my people love you, there's really only one thing left to do..."

Thirty-Four

Penelope

Back at the hotel that night my feet drag down the hall to let Pinsch inside. I usually wait to let him inside until the last guest has disappeared into their room for the night. I'd hate for his presence to upset anyone. I have long since given up on the idea of calling animal control to get him. He clearly has claimed this place as his home just as much as I have. "Hey, buddy," I call, and he eagerly runs toward the back door, wagging his tail as he takes the treat I offer him. "Are you ready for bed?" I ask, but he already knows the routine, taking off up the back staircase toward my room.

As soon as I enter my room, my gaze goes to my golden heart, and my lips bend up into the largest smile. All I can think about is how lucky I am.

Lucky but tired.

Today has been a long day, with so many emotions. I'm glad to have that dinner over, and at least, in my opinion, it went okay. I can't wait to crawl into bed with Pinsch and go to sleep. Slowing the urgency in my steps as I approach my bed, I spot something on my pillow, and completely halt on my heel.

My heart revs.

The wooden box Jerry gave me is sitting on my pillow.

I distinctly recall leaving it downstairs on the back counter behind the front desk. "Did you do this?" I toss a glance at Pinsch, who doesn't seem to notice the box as he takes his place in front of the window, curling into his blanket.

My lips whoosh to the side as I pad back to the door, open it, and check down the hall both ways. No one is there. I'm unafraid though, because I know it's Logan—his knack for finding ways to surprise me is finally not surprising. When he dropped me off at the front door, he must have sneaked around to the back door and grabbed the box while I was in the bathroom washing up. Tipping my head, I recall he was acting a little strange. For the first time he was too tired to stay for a while, when he typically stays as long as possible. I usually have to push him out the door to get him to leave.

Curious, I sit on the edge of my bed and open the box. Like the boxes we'd found: this one has a note inside. It wasn't there earlier at Jerry's. My heart flutters before I even read the first word.

Penelope,

Dad's box inspired me to continue this tradition. I'm not as good with words as I am with fixing things, so I'll keep it short.

I love you.

I want you here.

In my arms.

Forever.

That's all. Logan

He's right. That's about the shortest love letter I've ever read, but it's touching. I clutch it close to my heart as my pulse races. How did he even do this without me finding him? I gently set the letter on my bed and retrieve my phone from the night stand, where I confirm it's almost midnight. That doesn't stop me from texting him because he has to be awake. If I know him, he's more than likely still hiding somewhere in the hotel.

Me: I found your letter. I love you too. Can you come over?

The reply comes almost instantly.

Logan: I'm outside waiting on the roof deck.

That's all it takes. With my heart thudding against my chest, I jump up and slip out of the room, walking briskly on

the tips of my toes to be as quiet as I can. By the time I reach
the fire escape, Logan opens the window, inviting me out to
our favorite spot where the fire's already going. He's silent,
which doesn't surprise me. He gives me a half-crooked grin,
and grabs my waist, drawing me into a kiss. For a moment the
world disappears.

My hand wraps around him, while his warm lips press
against mine. When he pulls me away mid-kiss, I tip my head
back, ready to see what's wrong.

His brows are straight, and his lips are even when he rasps,
"Marry me."

I blink. Then blink again. I didn't see this coming at all.
We've never talked about marriage. There's so much blinking
happening, Logan almost goes blurry.

He goes on, "Sorry, I didn't get a ring. I didn't plan this,
even though it's all I've thought about. I saw that box tonight.
I wish so badly I could have snuck a ring inside. I had
half-talked myself into doing it another night when I had
more time to make it perfect, but I had this burning in my
chest. I knew if I didn't do it tonight, I'd never sleep," he ram-
bles, not in a disorganized way. It feels sincere and possibly
rehearsed. "I want you," he says so quietly I have to lean in.
"Forever."

Okay, I could do with about seventy-five-percent blinking.
That's all that my body is capable of doing at the moment.
He stares at me with wide eyes, waiting. I blink.

And again.

His palm cups my face, and he stares into my eyes so deeply it creates a heat current that flows straight to my heart, finally unfreezing me enough to whisper, "Yes."

"Yes?" He quirks a brow, challenging me.

"Yes, I'll marry you."

His breath is one-part chuckle, one-part sigh, and he pulls me closer to him, pausing to gaze into my eyes as he hovers his lips close to mine, teasing a kiss. "Now," he whispers, bringing his lips so close to mine, they graze each other. "Level three is complete."

"I didn't know I passed level two." I blink as a smile grows on my lips.

"You passed." He nods, while leaning in like he's going to steal a kiss. "You definitely passed. I might have been too distracted by the kissing to say anything..."

Fighting the urge to playfully roll my eyes, I tip my head back and wait for his lips to meet mine. His smile presses against mine, and just like that, Logan, the sweet man I hired to fix that hotel, somehow managed to fix my heart too.

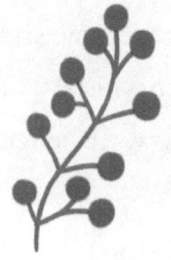

Epilogue

Sometime that Fall

The hotel garden glows in the golden light from the summer evening sunset. Strings of lights I diligently wrapped around each tree flicker like an extension of the stars in the sky. Penelope's favorite outdoor lanterns—the ones that hold the fake candles—sway gently in the breeze.

Leading Penelope under the floral archway, our eyes never leave one another's as we make our way to our wedding reception. I'm still in my shirt, although I've long since rolled up the sleeves and forgotten the jacket somewhere between the limo and the church.

Her white gown is simple, with light fabric that flows with the breeze. Though her hair has fallen slightly from the hours of taking photos and greeting guests, the loose tendrils curling along her neck make her that much more breathtaking.

We are met by about a dozen of our closest family and friends, applauding on their feet. I twirl Penelope with one hand above her head and the other steady on her waist as we make our way to the center of the garden for our first dance. Everyone waits on the side as I draw her in close and wrap both of my arms around her, something I've been waiting to do all day. The band switches from our entrance music to our favorite song. We never had a song, but over the last few months, we both admitted we loved the song "Home." It mirrors the vibes of our own story. "Are you ready for this Mrs. Legend?" I ask, my voice low.

"Always."

I slide my feet in a slow circle, guiding her around. Somewhere in the distance someone clinks a glass. It's a slow tapping at first. More taps eventually chime in, and it's about to get out of hand. I drop my gaze to Penelope. "I think they want us to kiss."

"Well, they are our guests, so we should make them happy."

I lower my face. There's always an invisible current from my lips to hers. When our lips meet, a spark fires through my body. Something comes over me, where I can't help but dip her low and deeply. It wasn't meant to be a performance. I can't help myself, but our guests love it and cheer for us.

Then—a weird sound.

Like a bell.

We freeze mid-kiss.

"What was that?" she whispers against my lips.

"Maybe the band?" I murmur, already tugging her gently back into a kiss.

But it happened again—clearer this time.

Not a chime. Something distant, and it's not coming from the band. We break apart, and without saying a word we look up.

A star.

One that pulses and shines brighter than anything else in the sky.

Her lips part. "Do you see that star?"

I nod slowly, but I'm still scanning the sky. "Yeah, but stars don't make that sound. It has to be a drone or something."

I stare up, trying to make out the outline of a plane but it's so bright. Penelope puts her head on my shoulder and sighs. "Do you ever think that maybe this whole place was waiting for us to be together?"

With my heart hammering in my chest, I look down and touch her cheek, still flushed from kissing. "I don't know about that, but I know my heart was waiting for you because I haven't ever been this happy."

She doesn't move as I lean down to kiss her, slowly. A feeling creeps into my chest that maybe *someone from another time* had given us their blessing.

Bonus Epilogue
One Year Later

The late summer sun slants through the tall windows of the east wing as I heave and tug away at the antique dresser I'm desperate to clean behind. I passed my test and received my broker's license, and since I moved into Logan's little house, I converted my old bedroom into the official location for my new brokerage, appropriately named The Legend House. "Okay," I huff out, as sweat pours off my brow. "That's good. I can fit between it and the wall now."

Logan releases his end with a teasing groan. "Shoot, I was hoping you'd get to take this down the stairs."

"Ha! Not in this lifetime." I laugh and slide over, as I get ready to wipe the wall, but something catches my attention.

A chunk of plaster where the dresser had rested has crumbled away.

"What?" I whisper as my heartrate immediately kicks up. "Did we bust the—"

Logan's already sliding in next to me, running his fingers along the wall. "I think it's a surface level scratch—wait..." His fingers disappear into the wall and reappear with *a wooden box*. "Did you hide that there?"

"I did not." My words are measured as I study his face for any inclination that he set me up. I raise my eyebrows. "Did you?"

"No." He moves slowly, more than likely as stunned as I am.

My hands tremble as I had given up on finding more letters. I hold my stomach with one hand as I back away from the wall, allowing him to come out too, and I urge, "Open it."

Like all the other boxes, a folded sheet of paper rests inside. Logan takes a moment to look at me. We smile at each other, knowingly. He carefully unfolds the paper, and we both lean in.

To My Beloved,

When you read this, I will be on my way to the island—the one we always said we'd disappear to. I'm not going to write the name here in case someone else finds this letter.

You know what this means.

I'll wait for you there.

You must never tell anyone, not even my family.

They would never forgive me, but I can't live without you. And I won't live a lie. It's also going to kill me to lose them, but it's the way it must be.

I'll never return, or my father will destroy me.

If I may ask a favor of you though. You can return once a year, perhaps at Christmas. You can bring everyone gifts, but most importantly, will you collect the stories of my family and then bring them back to me as a gift?

That will be my way of having them, even when I cannot see them.

And in exchange, I will give you everything.

A.D.

My hand flies to my mouth, and my jaw hangs down. "Are you kidding me? They actually made it!"

Logan's quiet as he reverently folds the letter the it was, tucking it back into the box. "It sounds like they did, but she gave up her whole family and everything she knew for him."

"And all she asked for was their stories." My chest is so tight, I'm only able to whisper. "That's the most devastating yet beautiful thing I've ever heard."

"What if he never found her?"

"Oh, don't say that." My hand covers my heart. The mere thought of that causes my heart to constrict. "I'm going to believe he made it to that island, and he visited every year to collect her stories, just as the letter says."

"Yeah, I think I like that idea." He's quiet for a moment as his gaze shifts back to the hole in the wall and then to me. "You can hold on to this until I have time to add it to the exhibit." Logan hands me the box but gives me a side-eye and a playful smile. "Do you ever think we should add something into the walls now that it's our home?"

Tipping my head to the side, I ask, "Like what?"

He raises a shoulder in a slow shrug, while shifting his gaze again to the hole in the wall. "We can leave anything we want. It's our story. A copy of our vows or the letter I wrote you."

"I can never stand to part with my letter, but I could make a photocopy."

"That sounds perfect." Logan smirks as he takes his hand into mine. "If you want to get everything together, I will put it inside before I fix this hole."

Rising to the tips of my toes, I press a kiss to his lips, knowing we are now the ones who get to live the real-life love story inside these walls. I couldn't be happier to carry on the traditions.

And so the tradition continued.

Yet unbeknownst to us, somewhere tucked high in the attic rafters, behind a beam no one had touched in years, another letter now flutters in the quiet.

Unread.

Unseen.

Waiting.

Because some love stories are meant to be discovered.

Are meant to live on forever.

Are legendary...

Also by J.P. Sterling

<u>Christmas Shenanigans (All Standalone)</u>

Mingle All the Way

Tis the Season to Get Married

Let's Not and Sleigh We Did

Hark! The Hot Santa Sings

<u>The Coffee Loft Series (All Standalones)</u>

Pardon My French Press

No More Mr. Chia Guy

Truely, Madly, Steeply Brew

<u>Sweet Hockey RomCom (All Standalones)</u>

The Pucker-Up Pact

Shot Through the Heart

All I Need is my Glove

Till Sudden Death Do Us Part

<u>Sweet Hockey RomCom Adjacent (Standalone)</u>

Driving Miss Crazy

<u>Timeless Christmas Tails (All Standalone)</u>

Have Yourself a Legendary Christmas

A Modern Fairy Tale Series (All Standalones)

Royally Rugged

Bosses and Billionaires Series (All Standalones)

Maid for my Billionaire Boss

Upcycling My Rig-Pig Boss

Kissed by My Billionaire Boss

Marooned with My Celebrity Boss

A Heart that Dances Series

Dancing on Broken Ankles

The Stars We See

A Heart that Dances

A Heart that Loves

Water and Stone Duet

Ruby in the Water

Lily in the Stone

About J.P. Sterling

J.P. Sterling grew up watching old reruns of Lucille Ball and Mary Tyler Moore and fell in love with wholesome entertainment and slapstick comedy. She loves leaning into the over-the-top humor and full circle moments, especially if it means the underdog gets to shine.

Aside from writing, she's also a wife, homeschooling mom, a holistic dietitian, a former college professor, and lover of all-things dark chocolate.

*No swears. Just kisses. No Blasphemies. *

Let's get social!

Hey, you amazing reader! You are invited to join my private reader group for all-things clean books and friends. Enter the

group here: https://www.facebook.com/groups/15008507
64081965

Other places to follow me:

Instagram: https://www.instagram.com/stories/authorjp
sterling/

Facebook: https://www.facebook.com/jpsterlingauthor/

Amazon: https://www.amazon.com/stores/author/B01
N9TJXJN/about